The Whereabouts of Eneas McNulty

SEBASTIAN BARRY was born in Dublin in 1955 and read Latin and English at Trinity College, Dublin. He began to write after university in 1977 and has published three collections of poems and three prose books, including the novel *The Engine of Owl-Light* (1986). He has written for the theatre since 1986, and his best-known play is *The Steward of Christendom* (1995), which has won numerous awards, most recently the Christopher Ewart-Biggs Literary Prize and the Ireland Funds' Literary Award. This is his first novel in ten years. He lives in Wicklow with his wife and three children.

ALSO BY SEBASTIAN BARRY

PLAYS

Boss Grady's Boys

Prayers of Sherkin

White Woman Street

The Only True History of Lizzie Finn

The Steward of Christendom

SHORT NOVELS

Macker's Garden

Time out of Mind and *Strappado Square*

NOVEL

The Engine of Owl-Light

POEMS

The Water-Colourist

The Rhetorical Town

Fanny Hawke Goes to the Mainland Forever

CHILDREN'S

Elsewhere

SEBASTIAN BARRY

*The Whereabouts of
Eneas McNulty*

PICADOR

First published 1998 by Picador

This edition published 1999 by Picador
an imprint of Macmillan Publishers Ltd
25 Eccleston Place, London SW1W 9NF
and Basingstoke

Associated companies throughout the world

ISBN 0 330 35196 6

1 3 5 7 9 8 6 4 2

A CIP catalogue record for this book is available from
the British Library.

Typeset by SetSystems Ltd, Saffron Walden, Essex
Printed and bound in Great Britain by
Mackays of Chatham plc, Chatham, Kent

TO RITA CONNOLLY

'And whosoever was not found written in the book of life was cast into the lake of fire'

Revelation, Ch. 20: v. 15

PART ONE

I

IN THE MIDDLE OF the lonesome town, at the back of John Street, in the third house from the end, there is a little room. For this small bracket in the long paragraph of the street's history, it belongs to Eneas McNulty. All about him the century has just begun, a century some of which he will endure, but none of which will belong to him. There are all the broken continents of the earth, there is the town park named after Father Moran, with its forlorn roses – all equal to Eneas at five, and nothing his own, but that temporary little room. The dark linoleum curls at the edge where it meets the dark wall. There is a pewter jug on the bedside table that likes to hoard the sun and moon on its curve. There is a tall skinny wardrobe with an ancient hatbox on top, dusty, with or without a hat, he does not know. A room perfectly attuned to him, perfectly tempered, with the long spinning of time perfect and patterned in the bright windowframe, the sleeping of sunlight on the dirty leaves of the maple, the wars of the sparrows and the blue tits for the net of suet his mother ties in the tree, the angry rain that puts its narrow fingers in through the putty, the powerful sudden seaside snow that never sits, the lurch of the dark and the utter merriment of mornings.

At twilight his father stands beside him at the window, a low man in his black clothes and his white skin pale and

3

damp like a dandelion under a stone. He is showing Eneas the ruins of the Lungey House at the end of the yard, an old jumble of walls and gaps, with brickwork about the empty windows, the rest granite and bluer shale.

'Never forget the people that went in and out of that place in their time,' says Tom his father, 'because, Eneas, they were your own people, and wore the better clothes and were respected. They had plentiful carriages and were respected. People with your own face' – and his father's neat fingertips touch the top of his head – 'that sent butter down the river and out into the wide ocean to Spain and Portugal where cows are scarce.'

Their own circumstances are pinched, that's the truth. Tom rises with the lark if there ever were a lark in John Street and off he goes with a dapper air to the lunatic asylum to stitch suits for the madmen. That is his father's work. And his mother too once entered there each day, to be a seamstress to the distressed women. And that was how they met, over their needles and thread, and Eneas is the fruit of their union. A sort of child thrown together out of oddments, lanky, only later to find good muscles pile on his bones, but weak at five.

He does not believe so much in the old butter exporters but he believes in the black rooks, *craws* his mother says they are but he does not think she is right, that call the Lungey House their home and screech and bawl like winged babes in the old sycamores above the Presbyterian graves. An old sycamore is a lovely thing with the bark gone to elephants, as ruckled and rough as elephants. He believes in the gangs of wallflowers that take over each summer, and on a rare day in the wild kids that go along the walltops heading for the orchard of the minister. He believes in those children and some day they will call to him and he will follow. Some day he will be famous for his friendships or so he believes. No treasure in life beyond pals, his father decrees. He will be heroic and carry the round red apples off into the town in his best gansey, that his grandma Mrs Byrne created – *created*, says his mother – out of an exhausted shawl, and the people of Sligo will admire him for it, the boys of Sligo anyhow.

He sees the wild boys go by the house too, at the front, his own thin and narrow house on John Street and he longs, he longs to open the door and fight them and win his place among them, but he is lanky and weak as yet. The day of strength has not yet come. But it will. He likes the soft face of the leader boy that is called Jonno. He hears the other boys calling Jonno's name in the dusk of the autumn when the apples are ripe and the minister not guarding his possession. He longs to call out Jonno's name through the dusk and be one among many, with torn ganseys and trousers too big, all hand-me-downs from their brothers.

Those days will dawn he devoutly believes and he practises his fighting in the back parlour with the dog Tam. He wrestles with Tam beside the autumn fire and his mother laughs and urges him on. She lifts her black skirts and dances suddenly on the hearth, throwing back her little head, and dances, and Tam goes spark crazy and jumps almost over her head. And the lamb stew boils on the stove with a slightly evil air, mutton really, and Tam is hoarse from barking now, and Eneas is not truly the victor yet.

His mother is a dixie, a lovely dancer, she bangs her shoes on the big black stone of the hearth, where the Spanish gold is buried snugly. The Spanish ran around Ireland in a filthy storm in lovely ships and fetched up among McNultys who ate them, his mother says. The hearth, that is where she tells him that story and all the stories, and dances for him. She is as daft as the dog, he knows. She put dresses on the lunatic women. And the old dames half dead in the beds, lying doggo for decades and decades, in turn, in thanks, in sisterhood, put little seams of daftness into her, little cross-stitches and patterns. She sat under the early windowlight stitching in her youth, in the asylum, before his father stole her away. Isn't she dour too, a deal of the time, dour as a fallen loaf in a cold oven, a disappointed loaf? But when the spirit strikes her, fires through her, when some surge of delight infects her, up go the skirts and out the short legs and there is dancing to beat the band.

Tom is often gone for days over to Bundoran or such places with his little orchestra and he plays for the holiday folk and the townspeople letting off steam after the long weeks of work. He plays waltzes, polkas and foxtrots and lately he has been giving them a touch of the new music, the ragtime and the like, that the Negramen of famed America play, because there is a call for it, a call. His father gets in the music in exciting batches, it comes from New York and Galveston, passing the Azores through the light-filled summer storms, the music purposefully silent in the little folded books, waiting for landfall on the Garravogue, waiting for Tom McNulty. But he has the older music too, and the Irish, so you might get a touch of Carolan, Strauss and New Orleans' finest in the one night in the lobby say of the Grand at Bundoran. He goes off winter evenings with his piccolo, his violin, his wooden flutes and oftentimes his cello, and he is not heard of till Monday. He might come in Monday itself early, five or six, long before the milkman's cart, and have a few mugs of strong tea, and then be gone up to the asylum as right as rain as if he had spent Saturday and Sunday in his doss.

'And how is it, Pappy, that you're not weary?' Eneas asks him, the pair of them sitting together at the scrubbed kitchen table, the loud clock hurrying on above the stove. Eneas's own eyes are heavy as bullets. He looks in astonishment at his father, with the brightened face and the drumming hand beside the mug, and the neat feet tapping the floor beneath, his smiles cracking his face like a rip in a cloth. And Eneas rose from his tight sheets because he can never resist the lure of his father's noises below him, but he is nevertheless pole-axed with tiredness.

'Life, Eneas, life keeps me awake – don't it you? Here, boy, let me play you a tune I was given last night, by Tom Mangan of Enniscrone...' And he's reaching again for the tin whistle.

Eneas likes that father of his. He has a rake of friends. There is fellas calling for him all hours. Fellas that want to give him that jig out of North Sligo maybe, for a Yank come home that wants to hear it the one more time. Or now and then a wedding arrangement is made on the doorstep, and Eneas's father Tom will play you through the streets of Sligo, from your house to the church and back again, if you have but twelve bob and three shots of Scotch. His great ambition is to have his dancing hall in the fabulous glooms of Strandhill.

Doesn't he rent a garden over in Finisklin, just under Midleton's hazel woods that used to be coppiced, but have been left to chance now with the coming in of foreign timber? There's more muck comes up the Garravogue in ships than goes down in the dredgers, his father avers. His garden is the mighty spot. It was a big square of wild grasses and meadow-rue and heart's-ease, eyebright and strawberry clovers till Tom went in there with his spades and his plans done out on rasher paper and dug the whole thing. And it isn't long while you're digging till it's dug though you might think it would take an age, just looking at it first, the peaceful neglect of the place with the sombre old walls and the locked iron door that used to lead into Midleton's. He put seventeen cartloads of dung into the black soil the first year till he had his compost going off the vegetable peels and the leavings of tea. Eneas played the while on the little space of grass that was left for his sole use, and his father dug till nightfall and the sprinkle of Sligo stars came out above their heads. The minute, the second he ates a bit of clay he is heartily smacked for it – so he keeps to the patch of grass after that playing with a handy weeding trowel and maybe truth to tell giving the isolated sniff despite himself. Over the seasons ensuing his father sets in a mighty system of paths with sacks of cinders bought from the laundry, from fuel that had done the convent's water heaters. He rakes them out and his son Eneas trots along the paths gratefully, not in any way eating the alluring cinders. In go the hollyhocks and the peonies and the hebes and the blue hydrangeas, in splendid great rows, and the sweet pea along Midleton's wall and he has a few young pear trees in a warm and windless corner. One spring at last after much asking a fella comes up from the lake with big flat stones worn by the lapping of waves and there are five steps down from the pears in the passing of an afternoon. That is a great day for the garden.

At night he is brought back to the little back bedroom with the dark blue linoleum through the nuns' field gone dark with a pitch darkness that no child could like, hand in hand they go, gaining the little house at last, and enjoying the spot of supper in the lamplit parlour at first, and then away up to bed like a ghost, his mother after scrubbing at his nails fiercely, as tired and contented as humankind may be.

These are the ancient days when his father plays the piccolo and his mother dances for him and he sits on the hearthstone smiling crazily at them, smiling, smiling, his face opened by that smile, such an honest happy smile, cracking his face like a miniature of his father's, generous, amazed. When in truth the world is simple with pleasure, and precise, and he hears the boys calling Jonno in the dusk and thinks of the apples going off in the ganseys as the light fails in the arms of the sycamores.

2

THEY BOTH HAVE a cargo of brown parcels – small but enough to fetter their hands – and it begins to rain. The rain comes in over Sligo deviously, searching them out in the sunken street. It is funny how quickly even such a light rain manages to cover the paper with its drops till there are precious few dry gaps. So the two go cantering along the sidewalk, his mother surprisingly agile, but maybe not so considering her dances, they are both in clothes quite black, running, and it is the Easter, and they are after having a gander at the big candle in the cathedral, and into the Café Cairo with them both, from the sublime to the ridiculous his mother gasps, for the shelter. Usually they would not go into such a place, out of respect for the expense of bought tea – a mere pot of it for ninepence, gracious. But his mother is too – too ashamed maybe to shelter without purchasing anything, so they tuck themselves into a table. They have to build a veritable wall with the parcels.

'Look at the style of us,' his mother whispers. 'And us with a half-pound bag of best Fast Clipper tea.'

And the server, a mere girl of sixteen in an apron stiff as a nun's hat, comes up to them lazily with a neat book and pencil stub and he stares up at her, at her ruby lips and her eyes loose with lights and the queer impression she gives that she believes that she will live and look so for ever.

'Tea for the two of us, dear,' his mother says innocently.

'Is that it?' says the server severely, as if millionaires like her are offended by such tiny orders, and Eneas relaxes because she talks just the same as himself, with the grey pebbles of the Sligo slingshot talk.

'We were gone past the Abbey and there was two wildcats in it,' he says to her. But the server scribbles on her book and clips away on her hard, hard shoes. There is a star on the arch of each strap. Her stockings are coal-black, she looks like two young trees in her stockings. His mother smiles at him in her odour of panic.

There are two ladies at a near table and they are staring at his mother he notices. Staring like there was no sin in staring, so he gives his mother a private signal and his mother gracefully swivels her head and meets their pesky eyes. The ladies are heaped up into huge hats and their coat collars are worse than wings. They might be insects. At any rate they are still whispering away like bees. Now his mother's face has two plaques of red where her cheeks were. The red is seeping down her neck, into her collar with the blue stitching following the up and down of the lace. Eneas is staring at her too now, because of the fiery colour. If a flame were to lick out of her skin he would not express his surprise.

The tea comes down and his mother and himself take it in the blue cups, furtively. He has five sugars for the sake of the free bowl of it, despite his despair. The old hats across the way nod and tip at each other, the ragged feathers swept about minutely. It is not so long before his mother and himself can bear it no longer and up they rises and away with them. Happily the rain has let up. He thinks of the wildcats in the ruined yards of the Abbey. He wishes he were a wildcat, sheltering under the heavy leaves of the laurel, looking out in fearless alarm as wildcats do.

*

'Pappy, how is it that the Mam goes puce in the Café Cairo and we're getting stares?' he says, under the shelter of the cloudy moon in John Street.

'I don't know rightly, Eneas,' says Tom. 'Were you getting stares?'

'We were, Pappy, stares like staring was no sin, Pappy.'

His father is looking at him quietly. He has the old bedtime book on his lap, the one he likes to read, the one his own father used read to him in the old days. He saved the book for his own children.

'On the other hand, Pappy,' says Eneas, 'we passed the Abbey and there were these two cats in the bushes.'

'Cats?'

'Wild ones, I would say, Pappy, desperadoes.'

'No doubt!'

'And we were after seeing the Easter candle in the Cathedral too, and had a great gape at it, the two of us. We were happy. And then down comes the rain and we ducked into the Café Cairo and then we got the stares.'

'Don't mind it,' says his father.

'A star on each shoe, she had,' he says.

'Who, boy?'

'The poor wee girl giving us out the tea.'

'She never.'

'She did. Mam said she was just the sort of girl you'd see hanging out of a fella up the steps of the picture house Fridays.'

'Who'd believe it, a star on each shoe.'

His father closes over the old book and folds his hands across the ancient cardboard and lets his eyes run out the window to rest maybe on the moonlit catastrophe of the Lungey House.

Eneas is almost gone over into sleep, gone over like a rose goes over into decrepitude, no one sees just when. He has almost left his father's side for the monstrous side of sleep itself.

'Some people have trouble that they never themselves did cause. Some people have a queer start in the world because those that have them in the first place don't know what they're at. Mams and Pappys are not the same, parish by parish. Some fall at the first fence, and little mites are left to fend for themselves. It's a story old as mountains, your Mam's own story. But, she's a queen. She is. Who is it that talks under the stones, only slugs and weevils. I should know, the gardener! Never mind, child, what you hear, the whispers of a little town, the little whispers of Sligo. Some words have no tune for themselves,' says Tom with the expertise of the musician behind his words, in the undeniable gloom. And mostly his own words are a delicious, lulling tune to his sinking son, benignant and eternal.

*

Three calamities befall him then, calamities that to his Mam and Pappy are contrariwise wonders and like to days of carnival and funfair. His three siblings pop into view, one after the other, with barely a decent interval between, Jack, Young Tom, and Teasy, the mite of a girl. And they are fine creatures in their way and indeed Jack sports a head of hair as red as a dog's and in the beginning of these new times Eneas is much struck by the little length of boy in his lacy cloths and the crushed face like an Injun.

But it's not long before Eneas is driven from his little kingdom, an exiled being, shorn of his mighty privileges. Five, three and two are their ages when Eneas comes into the double-numbered realm of ten, and a realm of scant attention and privacy it is. No more the Sahara of Strandhill with his Mam alone in the summer, no more Buck Rogers and the Dark Queen going about Sligo, marauding secretly from premises to premises. And what can he say about his siblings, except that they are devious, loved and needy for things at all times of day. There is no sacrosanct hour, the sun goes down on every day leaving each as cluttered and provisional as the last. Maybe his father too takes fright because there is less of the Pappy now, he is gone out to Finisklin on his own to dig out the remnant flowers of summer, and put in the contracted sacks of manure, alone, pristine, confused. And Eneas is not taken as before in the old glory days because his Pappy is not a man to be accused of favouritism. He likes to shun them all equally, though pleasantly.

Difficult for Eneas, these peopled years, the house buckling and banging under the weight of lives, John Street racketing to the fierce hands and feet, formerly so quiet, composed, intent. His serious nature is jolted out of its tracks, his small engine of interest and joy must jar along the wretched stones. He looks at his mother, he regards her, passing in her dark clothes, not a dancer any more, not a conspirator, but a kind of slave truly to four or five mouths, herself ever more silent, tetchy, windblown. The family blows through the sacred house like a bad wind and at every

14

door there is an interloper, interloping about the place. So he imagines. If she is not scraping shit off Teasy's nappies, she is trying to keep cuts on Jack together with her bare hand. Jack is a fierce one for the accidents. You couldn't let him out with a ball of wool till he'd cut himself with it.

His rescuers are those pleasing and mighty kids that are the living death for the poor Presbyterian rector in his handsome house. A handsome house may boast a handsome orchard, but an orchard draws wild kids to it as bees to lavender, as hopes to the prisoner, and Eneas is an expert on the ways of those robbers long before he ever talks to one of them, because he can see them go nimbly along the glass-strewn wall, he can see them disappear down into the green bowel of the trees in the heavy musk of autumn, he can see the tips of branches moving as they pluck the fruit, as if dogs were moving through corn. Oh, they are the rabbits, the dogs, the very wildlife of the orchard, they are heroes and desperadoes and robbers and kings.

One evening, watching from his dark window, he spies the tormented rector returning to his house unknown to the stealthy robbers already within the trees. He spies the heavy door closing and a little while later the same door opening and the rector creeping from it like a very kid himself and going like a beetle along the base of his mottled wall. There is a little gate and for this gate no doubt the clergyman possesses a mighty key.

Eneas on an impulse without word or thought flies from his perch and out on to John Street and up the Lungey and hard left like a demon into the old cathedral lane, where the rector's house is built into the boundary wall. He is a blue flame passing up the lane thick with the wet scent of mosses and the dirty shadows of the sycamores in the pitch cathedral copses. It is his joy to run so, to stop even at the hem of the rector and to cry out his famous warning to the robber Jonno and his crew within. And the robbers come up on the wall, they appear there, like winged boys, like cherubs, and they are all of them laughing like the mad, and flapping their jackets like birds and Eneas even in the dusk can see a long piercing cut appear on the leg of the leader Jonno as a shard of glass uncharacteristically catches him as he lets himself fall to the deep lane. And forever he is falling there, Jonno, boy of lightning, falling. And the rector, with his poor Protestant blind eyes Eneas has heard it mentioned, gropes into the vicinity for to capture at least some member of the gang, and takes a great hoult of the hair on Eneas's head and grips there like a monster in a nightmare. And Jonno burgeons up and lets go a precise and perfect kick into the legs of the rector and an oath, polite but enormous, gushes out of him, and Eneas feels the loose growing-in bit of his gansey pulled, and the great velocity of Jonno's strength hauls him back down the lane, spirits him back down, and the rest of the mob shouting and screaming like veritable Africans. And this is his proper and perhaps fateful meeting with the captain of his boyhood, Jonno Lynch.

*

Maybe it is normal and everyday the manner of their going about, but truth to tell Jonno Lynch is an upright man. He is a bucko. He doesn't walk along the streets but marches, to his own hidden fife and drum. When dangers blow against him, as when the glass gashes his leg, there is a wonderful enjoyment in him of these disasters. He is a soldier through and through.

And he enlists Eneas simply and heartily into the small

spinning thing that is the gang's warfare and mischief. They spiral about, the gang of them, after school, boxing the fox of any orchard in their ken. There's a mighty plan to construct a flying machine out of sheets filched from the Convent laundry that only comes unstuck on the superior battle capabilities of Sister Dolorosa, the nun from Mullingar. Always afterwards Jonno Lynch and Eneas gaze up at the wooded hills beyond the town and know in their souls that those would have harboured somewhere the site of their amazing flying achievement, the wonder and the news item of all the continents, but for the arms of Sister Dolorosa, six foot in span if they are a yard. It is the golden age of friendship, when to leave the gates of the school is to run in a fever to Mrs Foley's two foul rooms in Kitchen Lane, where Jonno is fostered, and to embrace with always requited fervour the challenges of the evening, whether it is to remove the brasses moulded in Wales from the mayor's carriage and attach them to the back of the dung collector's cart, or only to fire at each other with catapults, using the dark blue seeds of the ivy beloved of the wood pigeons. And in this frenzy Eneas dances and is eternally pleased.

*

And it is some recompense for the loss of the older kingdom, where his Mam and his Pappy were enthroned. And maybe there is always a little secret yard, mossy and ill-frequented, where he is morose and unforgiving about the matter, where the character of himself is wont to moon about and say hard things about parents and life itself in general, yes. For a boy cannot be expected quite to survive the lovely rainbow and the blissful shower all streaked and freaked with sunlight that is the lot of the single child amid resplendent parents.

Maybe in dark moods he thinks Jonno Lynch for all his majesty is not the skirts lifted and the wild clacking dances of his mother's former self, or the confidences at the exhausted breakfasts of his Pappy. Ah but, as the siblings come bawling out of babyhood and into the calmer country where children amaze their gaping fathers and mothers, perhaps he is reconciled a little to the terrible interlopers. And if Teasy seems eternally the baby, what harm? And in his position as elder brother he finds the elixir of superiority and a class of fearlessness, an adventurousness that they can never possess but which they infinitely admire in him. And if he has been wrenched a little from the breasts of his Mam and his Pappy he has also been released into the nether world, the interesting hell of Jonno Lynch's heart, where Mrs Foley's hideous manners are forever itemized, her teeth as loose as oyster shells, her arse as big as Ben Bulben, her striking hand as hard as a seagull's head. On the other hand there are times he thinks that if a *pleasant* accident were to befall his siblings, if they were instantly crushed by rocks, or quickly drowned by a biblical sort of flood, he might regain his true happiness.

3

OH, IT IS SUMMER. He is sitting in the high grass that infests the back field of the Convent where his little brother Young Tom and his sister Teasy learn their letters and their sums and gather to their minds the old stories of Little Jack Horner and the other Jack, of the Beanstalk. His middle brother, also Jack of course, though all of seven years old, is still too far off and young to make a companion for Eneas. And he feels this, the lonesomeness that five years have constructed between himself and Jack. Because he likes Jack now but Jack is bold with the Mam, and Eneas will shout at Jack. This puts the mufflers on Jack, and Eneas cannot get a word out of him because of the instances of shouting. He would prefer in the general run of things for him and Jack to be companions and rob the minister's orchard but he has lost Jack by the shouting.

Also Jack shines at his schoolwork and he has been nominated brilliant by the schoolmasters and this never happened to Eneas. Well, he knows he is no fool himself, but you cannot compete with the brilliant. The brilliant are hauled up into a realm without mysteries, and scribble better and count better than such as Eneas. Even Young Tom is admired for his scholarship and God knows he is only four. If his sister were not a complete baby she too would he supposes be raised beyond his country of average knowledge and average comprehension.

His suspicion is that he has been given his father's brains and they have got hold of the Mam's. He ate a feed of sheep's brains the once, and as he ate he knew sorrowfully that his father's brain and his own brain were such as he toyed with on his fork. He never ate such a sorrowful meal before nor since.

There is the war now beyond and a few of the men of Sligo have departed and many more are saying they will go. There is a great feeling in the town that they must send soldiers to the war, and aside from that it is in the line of genuine employment. The docks are still a mighty enterprise, but people are saying the docks are doomed and the grass will grow between the old bollards yet and it is the devil's own job to keep the channels clear. Some are saying that there is a new terrible drift of sea-sand come down from Coney Island and thereabouts, that the autumn tides have gouged the channel by the Rosses ever deeper and pushed a frightful tonnage of sand and silt and God knows up into the docks. Men have seen salmon in shallows of the Garravogue where formerly there were deeps, and they are dredging but some hold that dredging is a fool's errand in that no matter where you dump the sand, as far out into the sea as you like, the tides will carry it back for you in due course. But there is a tremendous trade in butter from all the western farms. There is still butter going down the Garravogue and excellent things coming up it. Now the men, the few that are most willing, are getting into the trains for Dublin and shipping out to England and beyond. You can sense the press of men behind them, the truer flood of men, held in just as yet by the ramparts of the wishes of their wives. But all in all the war is there and the men of Sligo cannot resist for long, nor ever could, whether Africa or Turkey or long ago in France herself. There is a frightful, some would say a peculiar love among the men of Sligo for the land of France, it is an old feeling that has survived. Eneas himself has strong views for France. He thinks her pleasing rivers and fragrant meads must be solemnly, solemnly protected. And he has half a notion that he might up and depart in the fullness of time, and do his bit, as the papers put it. Why wouldn't he? Isn't Sligo such a little place and mightn't there be realms beyond it of great interest and high tone aspects, as wonderful as the magic lantern show or the mighty flicks themselves, those galloping and well kitted-out cowboys? And that damp yard of his bitterness echoes with agreement. He feels betimes a sort of rage to go, temporary, but fierce and shocking while it blows. Trouble is, everything is imagined, a picture painted with hints and horrors and news items. But, by God, he might chance it, should he live to see sixteen. Comfortably enough, that is some time off.

Well he is sitting in the high grass at the back of the Convent for the moment, with Tuppenny Jane, and indeed it is warlike enough for him the while. The grasses are rich in meadowsweet and big yellow flares of ragwort, it is a sight. There is a thrumming of crickets to beat the band. How the world gets itself into such a state of heat, he does not know. Jane is no more than thirteen herself. Sometimes she acts thirteen and has a go at being with such as himself. But the world knows that Tuppenny Jane has been down the lanes often with some of the family men of the town. It is given out by some as a fact and, humorously, as the gospel truth, that the young priest, a man from the very cream of

Castleblaney, gave her one for herself in the depths of winter, the time he was so down in his spirits and on the sauce and not long before he hung himself on one of the oaks in Dempsey's dairy fields. He has heard it said that the men go for her because she cannot take to herself or in herself babbies yet, and as she is loose she is preferred as a place of refuge by the family men. In the meantime the priest has died for her and in that respect she is like France to Eneas, remote but important, vague but fatal. It is tricky for him to picture the priest with her. Maybe it was something else drove him to the oak branch. Maybe it was the sweets of Tuppenny Jane. Yes, Jane herself hinted as much with a lovely little handful of golden and sparkling hints that she likes to entertain with.

She has a nose too big for beauty it is often said, and Eneas fears her. One night with Jonno Lynch he lay beside her in the ruined summerhouse in one of the old gardens in Finisklin, not his father's, for safety. Jonno kissed her and put his hands in under her skirts and felt at her clammy crotch in a set of big school knickers. You might as well have tried to find the entrance in an Arab's tent, Jonno avowed afterwards, a notorious difficulty in desert life. He got that out of a book – or *buke*, was his better word. Despite his erudition, she kept squirming Jonno's hands away. Eneas put his own hand in for the heck of it and in the veritable tangle of Jonno's fingers thought he felt something. He was truly surprised and all he could think of was that something unlikely had happened, unlikely but desirable, like seeing a rabbit in the door of its burrow and the creature for a change not running in immediately, not fearing his approach.

Oh, he cherished that moment. He felt something like a blow on the back of the head. Some great hand of Destiny, like they'd be saying in the flicks, clutched the column of his spine and yanked at it. For a year he had been dreaming of such a matter. He had tried to picture the tropical harbour of long leaves and hot storms that he imagined a woman's sex might be. Suddenly he docked there, briefly.

Now he sits with her in the high grass, alone, without Jonno, because Jonno is off cutting turf on Mrs Foley's patch of bog the far side of Knocknarea, that her bloody uncle left her, for the specific torturing of Jonno Lynch, but no matter, a man bows to his fate as best he can, and it is one of those dry and polleny June evenings with a rake of sunlight still to come. His heart is new halfpennies, all the more so as he imagines poor Jonno labouring. Not that he would fear the labour himself, he might like it, but Jonno is ever the town boy. He looks at her mousy hair and the nose and the breasts in her gansey that seem to shout of their own accord somehow, and now and then casts a glance at her skinny legs, and prays for courage. He wonders hard to himself why he is so overcome with fright and silence and uselessness and a sense of his own youth in her presence.

'Do you remember that old time at all,' he says, 'with Jonno and meself in the summerhouse, do you?'

'I do,' she says, 'and I do because I was mad that night to go and pee and nather of you boys would let me, it was cruel.'

'Did you have a need to?' he says, choking with sympathy, it being a particular curse on himself, a weak bladder and no courage either to declare it in many a pressing moment but a moment often crowded with other people.

'Why,' he says, 'I never knew, the whole time.'

'Boys never do know anything, boys are too busy with their roving hands.'

There is truth in this. Then he thinks to himself maybe she is a noble sort of a person after all, if he could reform her. He might, and if he knew where to start he would.

'Jane,' he says, 'where do you stand with hollyhocks?'

'How do you mean, hollyhocks?' she says.

'Hollyhocks, do you care for them?'

'What are they like?' she says, reasonably.

'Flowers, you know, my father grows them mightily there in his garden under Midleton's and I would be now proud and happy to give you a bunch maybe going home if you liked, Jane.'

'My mother wouldn't stand for me bringing flowers into the house,' she says. Quite noble in her demean.

'Why?' he says.

'Because she married an American.'

He is puzzled now, greatly.

'What's that?' he says.

'She married an American my father, you know, and she will not allow herself pleasures now since he left us and not two pennies to rub together.'

He laughs. Two pennies for Tuppenny Jane.

'What's humorous?' she says, very sharp.

'Nothing,' he says, laughing, secure, comfortable.

'You're cack-cacking there at me,' she says, 'and your own mother not better than me, in the upshot, really. I won't say I'm a good one. But she's no different.'

He is silenced.

'You see,' she says, 'the long gawping mouth on you

now. You don't laugh so loud when it's your own ould Mam is the topic and the figure of raillery.'

'How is she?'

And he wants dearly, fearlessly, and indeed hopelessly, to hit her. He has no courage to feel her damp knickers again because Jonno is not there, Jonno of the apple-booty, but by the good Christ, by the dark statue of Christ in the Cathedral eyeless in the glooms, he thinks he might find the courage now to strike her, the doll, the doll.

'Your own mother,' she says, lying back in the grasses with a great relaxation and contentment, 'that was raised by another and never had a real certificate, never had a document with her name on it in her born days, the brat of some ould piece of dacency, my ma says, that didn't want the whore's melt, and threw her down to the muck!'

He stands there and strikes his own breast, strikes it again and again, for want of striking her. He has the height but that chest is skinny as her legs and it hurts him to beat there, but he needs the hurt.

'You dog,' he says, 'you low dog on all fours, you poor fighting pup with your tail bitten off by a tinker at birth.'

This is an obscure insult, and has no force even to him.

'Go on,' she says, raising her dress, and she is pristine, her linens are sparkling, the evening sun shows how dandy and scrubbed she is, what a jewel she is for cleanliness, like the breast of a cat, 'I won't ask you for tuppence, I knew your ould joke to yourself there, aren't we the same, the one and the same, me and your ma, go on, put that little snaily thing of yours in there that has you dizzy in the bed, nights, from steering it, and we'll be happy. There's nothing to happiness only generosity. That's a lesson more than you'll ever learn, you boyo, you poor skinny bucko, look at you, burning like the toast!'

And off he goes right enough, stumbling, burning, fit to burn. And he thinks of the ould ones staring at his Mam in the Café Cairo, and by God he'll go off to war now if there's terrible secrets to be endured, he will. Why couldn't his father have told him, the good man that he is? Hasn't he told him the why and the what of many a thing, why must he hear mysteries from Tuppenny Jane? By God!

*

His mother cuts the thick-crusted bread with her usual artistry – which is to say, she saws lightly back and forth, putting no pressure on the loaf, creating perfect slices. If his father Tom got his hands on that loaf it would be askew in a trice, in the sewing of a wren's mitten. Jack and Young Tom mill about. Eneas watches his Mam as is his present custom. Watches and rarely speaks. He cannot gain any proper sense of her shame in his heart. He knows he must. It is the key to everything. The world seems agitated by her condition of shame right enough. He thinks he must be unsuited to the world, if he cannot understand the strictures applied to his mother. Every Saturday in the month she goes down to Athlone on mysterious business, but will never say what. There she is, quietly cutting, quietly laying each piece on the blue and white enamel plate. He could be a-dream for all he really knows. His father sits over in the corner polishing a flute with the accustomed rag and at the same time searching in the morning paper for good japes. When he finds a jape he turns about and reads it to them, bouncing himself with glee. Maybe he likes them all better these days, now everyone is up on their pins, more or less. Although soon he will up himself and wander out, into the unimaginable splendours of a Sligo night.

Is she not still an artist among mothers, cutting that bread? He has heard Micky Moore, a boy reared up in the deepest and poorest part of the docks, who is not understood in the better shops in Sligo itself his mouth is so full of black words, called an artist on horseback, because he won fourteen races in a summer, including two at the Phoenix Park in front of the Viceroy, in the capital. An artist. His mother is an artist with the breadknife. He is estranged from her a little maybe but, he admires her. He loves her.

He sits through school all day, under the vast wall-map of the leviathan world, crisp Latin and the muddle of mathematics forming weather clouds over his head, trying to extricate the kernel of the matter. He knows that on the floor above in the higher class Jonno Lynch his bosom pal is conning hard for his certificate. Jonno is going serious on the world and because Jonno is but an orphan and has to live with Mrs Foley, the terror of all orphans, he is intent on escape into the world of shillings and employments. By God, he is. And no doubt rightly. Meanwhile in the lesser class, Eneas puzzles out his own ancestry. The master Mr Jackson is a person so wise much of his teaching pours over the shaved or narrowly cut heads of his pupils. When Eneas first came into the class Mr Jackson showed some interest in the name Eneas, pointing out it was taken from the Roman story about a long-suffering and wandering sea-captain. But Eneas was only called Eneas after some old great-grandfather of his father's, maybe even the mighty butter-exporter himself. And the discussion was ended suddenly by one of the boys offering the information that in Cork the name is pronounced *anus*.

Mr Jackson talks without much pausing always, and it is, Eneas supposes, to place a bulwark against the waiting tide of filth that passes among schoolboys for knowledge. He tells them extraordinary things and he likes to give them samples from your man Homer, in a funny little pip-squeak voice. In fact, his favourite talk is of the old Greeks, and their dooms and their wars, and how the Gods were forever decreeing the fates of the mortals, and girls were turned into trees, and the like. And from what Eneas hears him say, the fellas in Rome later on weren't that much better fixed, nor indeed that other Eneas fella. But he can't try and catch these curious trout of information now, he has other legends to puzzle out. Legends of Sligo. The master tries to swamp his head with decent information from what he magnificently calls the Classical Eras of the World, but the terrier of his mother's origins sees him off every time. It means something for himself, this business of his mother, and he senses what it might mean hovering close by, but elusive and foggy. The death or the life of him, he cannot say. Just out of reach, just out of reach. The heads of the boys about him nod in the slow fever of the afternoon. The elms full of fresh leaves, all inflated and shining after the buckets of thick rain, wash about gently below the windows. Thank God the weather has brightness. The hard world mills about in the dark streets of the town. And is all the world of Sligo abreast of his mysterious Mam? The jokes of the butcher boys and the draper's assistants are against him!

That night his little room seems dangerous to him. The Lungey House swelters in the June night, accusatory, high-

28

faluting. Shame is a sort of silence, slightly whistling, slightly humming. And he thinks of the young priest from Castleblaney that hanged himself. There in the silent bed he thinks of him. He sees the grasses all sere and the yellow wind invading the lost fields. What a sough in the deep branches there is as the Castleblaney priest climbs to his early and possibly ignoble death, with the length of mooring rope stolen, it transpires, from the prow of a gillie's salmon-boat. He has tasted the very honey of Tuppenny Jane's damp crotch, eternally, generously damp and sweet and deep in the starched petal of her knickers. Higher he climbs and places the rope about his Castleblaney neck. He sits on the rough branch. What's he thinking, what's he thinking? He gives a little kick away, all that learning and aspiration rushing towards oblivion, in such a manner as Eneas often imagined doing while tree climbing, scaring the daylights out of his legs, paralysing himself aloft. Away he tips, the priest in his relic-like clothes, his dog collar under the collar of rope, his polished shoes, his fine linen, his handsome belt. The rope snaps tight, his neck-bone is banged sideways in a way it cannot endure. The tongue protrudes slowly as it fills with blood and the face goes black as sins. The maw of hell roars like an opened kiln. The once saintly bowels loosen into the excellent trousers, purchased, Eneas believes, in the particular shop in Marlborough Street in Dublin. Eneas sweats in the cosy bed. Shame is not sweet, shame is not like Tuppenny Jane's crotch! Through and through he is shot with the arrows of shame. He understands it. It is a filthy pain, an attack, an affront to lonesomeness. His little room is transformed into a chamber of shame. The priest dangles. By God, he will go to the war, Eneas, as soon as he is let, if his fine pride in himself is to be eroded.

The images subside and the moon hastens over sleeping Sligo into the shapely hills of Ben Bulben and Knocknarea. Perhaps he ought to say, his mother is a woman of mystery. Well, it is not satisfactory, but still. Shame flees away. He feels for her. It is curious. Perhaps Tuppenny Jane has been his liberator of sorts. He has a sudden sensation of freedom, a surge of it, like a bump in his heart, a lump in his throat. The love for his mother and his distance from her is a sort of freedom. It is liberty. Anything is possible with such liberty, he knows. Love, and distance. He loves her, he loves her. Perhaps he is to be a grown man soon, after all – old in the bed, at fourteen.

*

The next year Jonno Lynch launches himself into the informal suit of a messenger boy, full of whistles and wads of orders stuck in his important pockets. He must escape and he doesn't care much whose heart he has to break to do it. He is employed by the auctioneer, O'Dowd, and some of the boys left in the school maintain that many of Jonno Lynch's errands are peculiar and little linked to land deals and such. Indeed Eneas sees him shooting up back streets on his silver bicycle and the worst that is said about him is that he is the Mercury to all the dark men in the town, the big men, the boyos, the lads on the make and the lads all murky and serious with ideals and plots. It is all a mish-mash of men and Jonno is the living spoon stirring it all about. So it is said, and Eneas would like to ask Jonno, but Jonno has become like his own bicycle, his Dawes premier machine, fleet and solemn and silent on the tar of Sligo. And Eneas's heart is heavy and two prize-fighters of doubt and hurt are bashing away in there. He can conquer the horror of his mother's mystery, but never the loss of Jonno, he thinks.

So the following year after that it behoves Eneas to look hard about him for some spot to plant his sense of affronted liberty, or some avenue to preserve it. Jack only grows in his scholarly achievements, now Young Tom has shown a happy aptitude for the instruments beloved of his father, the bulbous cello, the reedy piccolo, and Teasy is a miasma of pious notions. Jonno is but the nickel shadow. No help to Eneas.

He goes in to his Mam and Pappy's room one night, a little tornado, a Texas twister, of youth and confusion. It is a place he has not gone often in the last years, though once he was the prince of their pillow, the saint of their window-sill, looking out, the two faces pressed to his each side, with space for nothing between them. He goes in and stands there and spots the surprise in his Mam's face, as she lifts her head from peering into her big scrapbook, where she sticks all manner of stray items and illuminations, without rhyme or reason, he would venture to say. And his father, with his hands behind his head as nimble as a bather, though the hair is white as dandelion milk, lowers his hands and pulls the embroidered coverlet over his bony breast, maybe without thinking. That same white breast where once Eneas lay loose as a jellyfish, hours without end.

'I'm thinking,' he says, 'I'm thinking, Mam, of going out there to the war they have in France.'

'What war?' says his Pappy, ever the man up on current news. It is the first time Eneas has thought, for a second, a second, that his Pappy is a bit of a fool, a bit of a colossal fool.

'The one they're at over in France, this last while.'

'Jesus, that's for English boys, Eneas,' says his Pappy, kindly.

'No,' says Eneas. 'There's rakes of Sligomen gone out.'

'Now, but not boys,' says his mother. 'Not boys.'

'I tell you,' says Eneas, 'they'll have boys of sixteen if you present yourself. In some manner or fashion. The navy might take me. Look at all the boys in sea stories. But I'd like dearly to go.'

'What about your great friend Jonno, that's made good now in the land trade?'

'Never mind that,' says Eneas, hard instead of tearful, he's bone-weary now of crying in the nights because of Jonno and his bicycle. 'I'd rather go fighting.'

'Why?' says his Pappy. 'Why go so far? I never knew you to be footloose, Eneas. Sligo's a good place. A dandy.'

'It wouldn't be for ever, Pappy. Wars don't go on for ever.'

'I don't think I'd like you fighting in a foreigner's war,' says his Mam. 'Nor any war, where my own first-born boy might be murdered.'

'What's foreign? If there's Irishmen in it?'

'Still, boy,' says his mother. 'I couldn't see the use of it. No, but the lack of use. The waste.'

'It mightn't suit you once you're there, Eneas, and the army's fierce hard to get out of,' says Old Tom.

'It's like prison,' says his Mam, 'so it is.'

'When school's done with, well, I'd like to,' says Eneas.

'Well,' says his father, as if a-dream, as if singing the words secretly within, 'think it over well.'

'And I will, Pappy,' he says, the stars jostling for room in the windowpanes. The two of them in the bed like one of them tombs in the Protestant church, where he and Jonno once crept, to fright their mortal souls, and steal what they could of missals, full of the devil's words – the Knight and his Lady.

4

As the boat comes up the river at Galveston his soul is sixteen summers old. And yet he knows this Galveston. Oh, like many a port he has noticed it possesses unexpectedly the qualities and signs of the port of home, though it is not. A queer romance enshrouds it. He will be at home among docks and shipping. The nearest to the war he could get was the British Merchant Navy and now here he is in Texas! Texas is hotter than the Tropical Plant House in Belfast, where he signed himself up for this French war. In Texas!

It was better, and more discreet with the politics going about those days, to cross from wily Connaught into the indifferent and more English-minded counties, for to take the King's shilling in Belfast. Or for to become an honest Jack Tar anyhow. And in the upshot the makeshift counter in the Plant House appealed to him, as if, though the decision was surely made, it was made lightly, even humorously. Because it was a queer thing for the recruiting captain of the British Merchant Navy, aping all the custom and ceremony of the navy proper, because of the times of shortage that were in it, to be set in his dapper white uniform against the gigantic fronds and flourishes of some lost South American world, adrift in a stormy, red-bricked Belfast. But with the local trouble a-flare in Dublin, with your man Pearse and the rest all shot and the public everywhere it was said in ferment about it, it was best, his Mam decreed, for a sixteen-year-old boy to make his compact with the British Merchant Navy in the privacy and ease of the Protestant counties, which indeed were more neighbour to Sligo by the atlas than Dublin herself. And though both had a thimble of politics between them, Eneas's Pappy deemed it wise also.

They are fetching machine parts in Galveston and he understands in his heart that he may still serve the King and save France from this vantage point. He may still gaze over France in his bunk-imprisoned dreams and bless her sacred vineyards and walk with the endangered French monks through the groves of threatened – what other blasted thing do they grow in France, peaches, apricots, bananas? Galveston is buried in its summer doldrums, the very river thick as treacle, oiling along between the wharves, past the shrimp boats and the toiling goods trains. The boats of America are never brightly painted, but to him as he leans as sailors must upon the rail they are informal as the men he likes, the quick men, the joking men, sorrowful, who cry after a few beers and drag out the mementoes of home lugubriously. There are fine times to be had in the absolute bleakness of the evenings playing cards for English pennies and weeping after the sights and girls of home. He is not a-feared of those men as he thought he might be, indeed as his mother said he would be. He has all his cloths of muscles now on the eternal frame of his bones. They are men bawdier than bawds, quieter sometimes than corncrakes when the scything men are near, lonesomer than broken farmland, happier oftentimes than dogs, crueller betimes than Spartans. But they are men that know home, and every port in their

35

company is home. It is a mystery dear to him, a mystery he thanks his stars for. That a handful of men can jimmy up a semblance of home, or nearly. And maybe it is because they are oftentimes so far from the warmth of wives and the enthusiasms of children that their hearts are in so great a fever always to make a world, if only a lean-to of a world that a boat is, nailed and angled to the dark emotions of the sea. His youth makes him a willing builder, adding his ha'p'orth of nails to the structure, placing something of his parents into the speckled wood, a tincture of his Pappy especially, so remarkable in the company of other people, tuneful and liked. He thinks it is not such a bad thing to be adrift on the limitless ocean, a creature itself so vast, so intimately gripping the hard earth herself, it cannot be seen entire, even in extraordinary dreams. Perhaps he has a talent for sailoring, he suspects he might, and it gives him great heart at his tasks, whether sluicing out the jakes or whatever he is assigned on the roster of muck duties, as they are rightly termed. Perhaps if he had been robbed off the quays and press-ganged as some of the old sailoring men were in the distant days of their youth, he might resent the bockety world of the boat. But as he has chosen to come out upon the sea, it suits him, if not down to the ground at least to the last timber of his vessel. He knows that if a man chooses to go, he may freely in the next breath choose to return home, wherever true home lies. And this is his liberty, his home reachable behind him, and all the different versions of home in the ports of the world, and the peculiar but adequate home in the person of the boat. He really does think the world is various and immense, and curiously homely. Happy thoughts, no doubt, happy illusions, on the great circus and stage of the sea, with the drug of youth in his blood. And he knows now many an important star, and he has seen the canopies of the Northern Lights, falling in light more blue than shells from the domains where no God abides. Many a moment his formerly bleak heart sings privately in the dark of the thrumming boat. The old sailors laugh at him for calling the ship a boat but everything was a boat in Sligo that sat upon the waters.

*

'Where is that West they talk about?' he asks.

He is relaxed in the welcome gloom of a bar in Galveston, Texas, tucked in amid the huge decorated warehouses, where a British sailor may rest easy and drink unmolested. The bar is called Gabe's and he was given the name on his ticket of shore leave because he is of course youthful and an easy thing therefore for a Galveston man to rob. But he hasn't got but the four dollars in his britches anyhow, so they may roll him if they wish he reckons, though on second reckoning four dollars would buy a high old time in Galveston. Indeed he was told of a certain avenue, named for some dark reason Avenue $1\frac{1}{2}$, as if it had no need of the extravagance of a full number, where all the fine loose girls had their quarters, among the general mass of Negramen and women.

'Where is that West?'

It is a question offered generally to the simple collection of men about him, dressed in clothes that were new a decade since, in hats of the same vintage, large, lop-sided, attitudinal. They have felt bound to mention in the manner of human persons everywhere on the homely earth the sameness of the weather in South Texas, provided always you allow for the tornado and typhoon at the back of everybody's mind, but the freshening effect nonetheless of the gratifying sea. Shrimpers, waders, engineers, knockabouts, carters, boozers . . .

'Where is that West, the West I hear often mentioned?' asks Eneas.

And it is generally then agreed among the gentlemen present that you will have to go a long way beyond Ohio these times to find that selfsame West. Ohio is so loaded under farmers it cannot be sanctioned with the term West. No doubt it was always East by the map, but wilderness, open plain, made West of everywhere beyond New England one time. Was Iowa West? This is discussed fervently enough.

'No, friend. You would not be West till you saw South Dakota. Till you crossed the Plate River itself. And that's a fact.'

'How would you know that,' says a weasely-looking man in a restitched sack for a set of trews, that has been shovelling shrimp all day to judge by the filthy pink stain up to his oxters, 'you, that never saw a cow or a prairie or nothing like that, all your born days?'

'I read the *Galveston Echo*,' says the challenged man. 'And,' he says, 'there never was, nor ever will be, a call for a shrimp-boat captain in South Dakota, so why would I go?'

This is the definitive information. Eneas is reduced now to taking the fresh chilly beer into his gullet. He wonders how they get it so cold in these frightful climes. Broken Heart is the name of it. Broken Heart beer. He likes it. He feels a great liking generally lifting himself on to the terrain of these men, he would like to be an American. It is a matter of hailing himself as such, he supposes, in his own mind. But he could scarcely expect his own captain to relish him going off now to be an American Eneas. Still, he is sixteen, he is strong, he harbours no ties to anything above the ties of his childhood place, which sometimes he thinks might be overcome, and ought to be, all things considered. Nothing moors him only his feeling for this and that, of course his love for his Mam and Pappy is an ingredient there, and his enthusiasm for the proper dealing in friendship and so forth. The first effects of the beer are a ravaging hopefulness that dances through his brain. How easy, conquerable, perfectly interesting, engrossing, even ennobling, the bloody old earth is! He would not offend these drinking men for the world with a faulty remark. He plans every inch of what he says to them, as any man ought who wishes to be among friends and liked, and is hooded above his own words, watchful, as much as he can, easy though he is among them. He understands the force, the fooling, the arrogance and the victory of that very clock behind the Negraman tending bar, ticking away their lives and chances.

'I heard there was a war in your part of the world,' says the pleasant weasel man. 'Our friend here is not the only poor fool reads the *Galveston Echo* with his dinner.'

'There is,' says Eneas. 'There is a big war back there in France, across the sea.'

'I read as much. The President himself has concerned himself with your war, so you have no need to fear.'

'Why has the boy no need to fear?' says the regular *Echo* reader, with the added expertise on the Plate River, wherever it was. 'No president I ever heard of could lessen the fears of a young man like him. A young man, drinking Broken Heart. Or any other young man.'

'There are men dying all across the fields of France,' says Eneas suddenly, startling the arguers. The few men listening

39

at the bar look at Eneas. Funny how some men talk and some men listen.

'That's just what I'm reading,' says the weasel, distantly, as if he too suffered the terrible nostalgia for France that Eneas does, though neither truly has set foot upon her soil.

'Like lambs,' says Eneas.

'Yes. Like lambs they die,' says the weasel. 'And before you object to what I'm saying,' he says to his friend, 'I went to war in my day, and wore that blue cloth upon my back,' and he turns again to Eneas, 'when I was young like you.'

'I don't object,' says the other man, sincerely.

Long into that night Eneas talks with the lonesome men. He fills them in on the great facts of France. How the fields of France used swell in the summer with the drunken fragrance of the vines. The men are dizzy with knowledge, they love this young man of knowledge. The beer makes him more than happy. Its chill instigates in him an unknown sense of distance and at last he senses the bitter, wholesome, liberating, lonesome idea that being an American must be. He hears now about the fine families of Texas that are still struggling with the Redman in the furthest West, in the morning fog and evening suffering of the desert. He hears about the big-boned women that such families feature. He is astounded again and again by the facts of Texas. They try to tell him how big this Texas is but it's not within his grasp. He knows the blown lovely Azores, out there in the centre of the sea, but a land that they tell him is as big as the sea, he cannot grasp it. The pagan Redman out there in the West fighting the fine families excites him. He gulps at the beer. If he were aboard ship now, the topic of mothers would have been raised, as it always was when there was

40

drinking, and he would be doubtless weeping. Here his mother seems too skinny and small to have much fire for him beside the Texan matriarchs. And she would not thrive in Texas, she could not be an American. Jonno might make an American, but not his Pappy or his Mam. There is something, what can he call it, an edge of murderousness that is new to him, in these peaceful companions. They are at repose in the bar and at the edges he senses the ghosts of death and hardship. What would his father do, all small with his piccolo in the cruel kingdoms of the Redman? They would eat him. They would stir the soup with the piccolo. He is thankful he has got tall and strong himself in the upshot. He gives thanks to the good God that he has got tall and strong. Why, here at the foot of America, where he is drinking, the Negraman humming the while with the struck lights of the drinking glasses at his looming back, and where a filthy sea leaks out into the sombre Bay of Mexico, and Jamaica is beyond, he is astonished at everything. Everything seems suddenly an accident, maybe even a conspiracy, his mother's parentage, the glorious foolishness of his father, the brilliance of his brother Jack, Young Tom's musical gifts, his sister Teasy's weird piety. The things that have driven him away to be the saviour of France, to be a soldier of sorts for France, for those extraordinary vine-yards, seem things now to make him laugh. America dwarfs him! He is laughing out loud, drunk as a tequila maggot. He is banging the bar joyously. It is unbearably humorous. He is a British sailor. It is death to say the words, he is tortured by the humour of it. He notices the weasel is so wickedly intoxicated now that his face has fallen forward from the forehead to the chin and he's dribbling like one of his father's lunatics. Simple facts under the bright pall of drink are wild and strange to him. A British sailor. A Christian. Now he laughs the loudest. A Christian!

*

The captain makes Galveston the centre of their journeys so Galveston becomes as familiar to him as a district of Ireland. He comes to understand all the natures of the sea creatures captured by the famous fishermen of Galveston, in their boats rusty but glamorous, and the scientific gradations of shrimps, their sizes and their characters. This is the talk of Galveston, along the water. The handsome brick wharfhouses stand cooly in the fiery middays. He cannot but have admiration for the citizens of Galveston, he cannot help it, some of the older sailors find grievous fault with matters and detest the sodden heat, but Eneas with his youthful heart rejoices in the clamour of talk and business of remote concerns, and when he is perforce crawling up the coast to attend to the captain's ambitions in Bermuda, or crossing the strange ruckled shallows of the Bay of Mexico to have truck and trade with the small Mexicans, he misses the simplicities and carefree sights of Galveston, and thinks of himself walking there, and greeting the shrimpers and, in the curious avenues, the easy sorts of people holding court on collapsing stoops.

*

He is dreaming of Avenue 1½. Two nights distant from America. The sea again below. This time they are heading back for England. Bull Mottram the master gunner – they are carrying two guns into the filthy storms of mid-Atlantic in honour of the far-off war – well, Bull Mottram has regaled the tribe of the poop with a tale of Avenue 1½ that was mostly about a whore's drawers, a whore's conversation, and a whore's treachery. It is not the whore that Eneas dreams of, but the Avenue itself, in its chambers of heat, the Negramen parading and calling. Negramen came out of Africa to Galveston nigh on three hundred years ago, big fancy princes of men he is informed, with gold on their arms and high ways, soon battered out of them. Or they came in like dead men, side by side in gigantic rows, stuffed in like herring, or the playing bones of herring in the very herring of a ship. And he knows his own uncle went from Sligo in a ship not so unlike that kind, or his father's uncle it was maybe, in the days of hunger, and became a trooper in the Union Army, and wrote home many's the time to say so, but precious little damn tin in the letters, according to Eneas's mother. He wonders now in the giant pitch and toss of the new Atlantic whether he might have been best advised to go out there into wide America and find his great-uncle and upbraid him on that matter – or better, join him in his Indian or kindred adventures? Somewhere out there Trooper McNulty bears a face like his but older. Good luck to him! Good luck to the old fellow! He does not suppose in his heart that that man would be seen again ever on Sinbad's Yellow Shore, that's to say, Sligo herself.

There is a deal in America that reminds him not so much of home itself, but the dreams and the stories of home. Yes, it was a drastically interesting place, falling away though it might be behind him. To think of the Negramen coming in, all those long centuries past, only to have their gold taken, and now their many generations living the life of Reilly or not as the case may be on Avenue 1½. He could have lived easily there himself, peacefully, strolling down to the fly-blown store in the cool refuge of the time between sunlight and dark when the insects' murderous thrumming dies away, and the piercing violin music of the night crickets begins. *Hey ho, Charlie*, and *How's it goin', Emmanuel*, for all them Negramen got their names out of the Bible, and best of all out of that Old Testament. And if they cannot find a name they like in the Old Testament, to all appearances, they will go forward to the Book of Revelation, that the second St John wrote in fever on an island. In a pitch-dark cave on an island in the pure realms of Greece, like an Irish poet of the old times. Some of the sailors that have seen bad times and know the streets of big city ports only too well and know the doss houses and the soup kitchens, well, they have that book off by heart, from all the blessed times that crazy preachers sang it out to them that was waiting for a drop of soup. The great thing is not to get taken from the book of life, not to get your damned name taken out for sin and wickedness, of a kind that sailors outbest all other trades at, it must be allowed. Well, it is a tricky world for a sailor, all told. Preachers delight to read frightening things to poor hungry sailors down on their heels and on their luck.

It is a drastically interesting country, America is, and you are lucky to get away without regret, loss of tin, or the Spanish clap. So he is sad enough in the bowel of his boat dreaming of Avenue 1½, but at the same time kind of glad to have passed up the whores. Everyone lets Bull Mottram know he is in for a right cruel dose as a sad memento of good times had on Avenue 1½.

*

He has earned his own brass for a year and more now and the war is over and he feels the inclination of a pigeon to go home, to his proper home. It is farewell to Bull Mottram and all his fellows. He has been but a poor hand at the letter writing. Now in the night oftentimes he surrenders to the feeling that he has slipped the clothes of romance, of the Romantic Life at sea. The sea has gone grey for him and deep in himself there is a sea-change. There's a tenderness in him, a softened thing about his heart like an old cloak, which makes him helpless before thoughts of his mother. It is as if she's signalling to him over the wastes of England as he languishes in Southampton among the serviceable ships. Or he hears and attends to her unhappiness by some unknown but human arrangement of Morse or telegraph. The poles carry the hurt singing of the wires across the war-deserted Midlands, across Worcester and points west, that have fewer young men now to bring honour to their boundaries. England has fallen into victory. The wideboys smiling at the shop doors and barely a job of work even for them. The best lie under his beloved fields of France he supposes. In honour of France there's no one to bring honour to lonesome England.

His father is sacrosanct again in the inner heart of Eneas. He does not know how. He was peering too closely at his father and now he has stepped back and it's his old childish eyes that look upon Tom McNulty. Unhappiness infects the victory and even the dogs of Southampton slink about the harbour. The coin of joy is soon spent. It is a glorious thing he supposes to fight France's war in Texas with the lonesome Negramen. No! He has a contempt for himself, for his smiling, his ould talking and his youth! There's someone

else or new habiting him who is grievous critical of that boy
setting off to sea as if the world being his oyster he could
really go like that, untrammelled, and with no price at length
to pay. He yearns to hear a tune from his father's hoard of
tunes, to comment on it and to be easy with the slight man.
He fears he will never be. And he fears the new man both
critical of the fading boy he was and by the same token alas
only too soft to face the truth of the world. For he believes
he sees some of that truth – the iron waves, the iron waves
rearing up.

He is not so grateful for the fear.

*

At the very edge of the huge port there are the huge gates.
He will be a sailor no more and after he passes through with
a nod to the gatekeeper Nangle – one of the host of Sligomen
that have spread out upon the wide world, to hold gates,
sweep dark English streets, muck out the stables of New-
market and Chester – after he passes through, that will be
that and he may consider himself a man unwelcome to such
as Nangle. No more will the gates of ports open for him, no
more will he pass through to the ships. Nor read the proud
names and the names disgraced, know the flags of con-
venience and which ships are carrying the Chinese poppy
or the Russian spirits. Once it was cognacs out of far France
coming into the coves of the west of Ireland, coming into
places without roads whose people would greet you with a
stone in their fist held in readiness behind their backs. Now
it's other contraband in all the ports of the earth.

He feels a sadness to be tendering up his kit. Farewell to
blue cloth and the starchy hat. Farewell to the lofty captain
and his infallible orders. Farewell to the king, the queen and

46

the knave and the numbers two to ten, played fiercely under the singing timbers. In addition to Eneas Bull Mottram has taken a fancy to another life. The two walk for the last time along the private stones. There is a sudden and unpleasant hint that, in this new adventure and with this new freedom, they are, he and Bill, ordinary strangers to each other.

'It's foolish maybe to give away a year at sea,' says Eneas. 'Maybe, Bull, it's flighty. Every trade deserves a lifetime I've heard it said.'

'But you're going,' says Bull.

'Seems so.'

'There's an old saw you'll also hear said below to the effect,' says Bull, as they reach Nangle's fearsome gates, and see the moil of more regular and even earthly traffic beyond, the gross shires and their mucky drivers, the smarter commercial vans and such, 'if a boy don't see himself shipwrecked before the age of seventeen then he may lay up his plans to make a life at sea.'

'Is that so, Bull? And were you yourself in that predicament?'

'I was, man, I was. In Madagascar many years ago I stood upon a sandbar of some half a mile in length with thirty other men and waited for rescue those five long weeks. We put up shelters and ate what we'd held back from the pilfering of the bloody storm. And we lived every moment in terror of storm on such a useless spit of land, and terror of thirst, and terror of being eaten by your mates. But I lived through and seven men lived through with me and it hardens your guts for the trade afterwards. I tried my hand at riding with cattle in Argentina for some years then, for the fear the sea had caused me, but in the upshot I was content to take a berth again and be a poor sailor.'

'I expect that sort of high adventure makes the difference right enough,' says Eneas, gloomily. It was another apparent fragment of gospel truth to torment him.

'Don't take it hard, man,' says Bull. 'The life at sea is an old life and men won't go for it much longer the way they have it fixed for them. You'll see now men will want their comfort after a war. See if they don't. Even myself, that knows hardship like a street girl, won't mind some ease.'

'What will you go for?' says Eneas, passing at last through the gates into the earthly noise.

'I imagine I'll pass down on the train to the Isle of Dogs and see what they say down there where I have pals, in London. Sailors and such are well understood there, if you want to know.'

Then Bull Mottram the master gunner retired takes a hand of Eneas in one of his own hard hands and gives it a firm and hearty shake. There is nothing else to say but Bull Mottram says it anyway, for the sake of friendship.

'Good luck to you, man,' he says. 'Take care now and so long. I have to go across the road there to the port doctor for I must ask him to attend to the waterworks promptly. Every visit to the jakes is a little hell. So long, brother.'

There is nothing for it but to relinquish Bull and go on into the milling town. Where is his confidence in the daily beauty of the world, not meaning outstanding beauty such as is expounded on the question of paradise, but the simple beauties that he has ever relished in things? The vans and shire-horses seem cruelly to advance, their custodians leaning greedily and smilelessly into the whipping wind. He looks back and sees old Bull go from light into the shadow of the doctor's door. Bull, spick and span, but for those fatal waterworks. Oh, freshly, stubbornly, he laughs in the street.

His heart lightens. He has the world before him after all. The sorrow of leaving is yes also the joy of going forth or borders each upon each.

And he hastens home to Sligo, with all the speed and trust of the swallow seeking the first fringes of summer. There is a wildness in him to see his Pappy and his Mam, and maybe even a lesser wildness to view his siblings. And there's a rip in his head where Jonno Lynch's friendship once was, and he'd like to patch it. So, away home with himself he goes.

5

MAYBE HE IS WRONG to have come back, he doesn't know. The men that were soldiers have come home too – to a brief spit of celebration and a wide, deep sea of idleness. Great friendships and even sorrows dissolve in the meagre eternity of daily life. Veterans still in their twenties gum up the alleyways of Sligo and their eyes sometimes are as blank as their days. And it's no better in England herself where the very heroes of Passchendaele and the Somme have survived to become the mighty fools of England with only time on their hands and something in their bleak hearts as devious as a cancer. Eneas sees all this clear enough. It's written all about, in the measly faces of wives as they bargain for single rashers, for awful cuts of meat, for blackening wings of spinach. Maybe Eneas feels a thousand years of life have passed in himself, mysteriously. Fellas his own age look older and bleaker than him though, without the darkness of weather that he has on his face. He can't find a niche in the world of Sligo to slot himself back into – not just a niche for living in, but a niche of time itself. The sea has put a different clock into him. He's always got the wrong time in Sligo.

And the war finishing was only the signal to the hidden men of Ireland to brew their own war, and sometimes in the ironic song of Ireland those selfsame cornerboys so recently out of the King's uniform leak away into the secret corners of the town to drill and become another kind of soldier – dark, uniformless, quick-striking like the patient heron by the spratty stream, men to menace and harm, if they can, the huge confetti of troops scattered over the island in the old wedding of death. Troops of course composed of ordinary Irishmen. Their recent brothers in the ruined fields of France. And other men that kept their hands clean of the European war are inclined to get blood on the selfsame hands in a war for the old prize of freedom for Ireland.

And Eneas knows that Jonno Lynch is one such, because two weeks home in Sligo he passes Jonno Lynch in Main Street and gets no nod or word. Now Jonno Lynch is the man he most wanted to see, because having knocked about the world he has a notion that he might be a fitting friend for him again, the two of them, one the sailor and the other the man of – business affairs, could he say? They could pick up now where they left off at school, and be going about, and have the odd quiet drink here and there like gents, and be dandy, be easy and open-hearted. Why not? And he has gone round to Mrs Foster's hovel but by heavens she is dead of an embolism in the back of her knee and all her charges scattered into Roscommon and further. And across the town in O'Dowd's premises he gets short shrift from the lassie on the counter, who will tender no information and take no messages. So it is left to chance, the smallness of the town and the will of God to bring Jonno Lynch along Main Street in a very, well, surprising blue suit, with a thread of quite striking green running down it, the latest fashion Eneas guesses of New York or suchlike. And he crosses the cart-cluttered street easy as a jackdaw, and tries to intercept his bosom pal, but his bosom pal presses on past him like he was only another stranger to negotiate on the thoroughfare.

'Jonno,' he says, 'it's me, Eneas, back from sea. Don't you know me?'

But nary a nod does he get, nor even a curse or a dark look, and Eneas is greatly puzzled. And he drifts home with a sober tread and sits in against the free wall of the little kitchen and talks to his Mam about other things, the piety of Teasy and the scholarship to the big secondary school that Jack has his sights on.

'And when Teasy is right for it, I have her promised to an order in Bexhill-on-Sea, in England. By the good graces, we'll have a nun in this pagan family at last. Father Moynihan is in and out of here all the time, taking tea and talking up a storm of religion to her, delighted with her. Delighted with us all.'

'She's only seven or eight yet, Mam,' he says.

'That's right. High time to be turning in the right direction. Look at yourself, gone out sailoring at the age of sixteen.'

And his brother Jack comes in laden with the books of a wise scholar and slams them on the rickety table and gives Eneas a grimacing look.

'I met Jonno Lynch on the school road,' says Jack, 'and he says to lay off him.'

'How do you mean?' says their Mam, outraged.

'Lay off him. Don't be trying to talk to him in the street.'

'He was passing by and said it or what?' says Eneas.

'No, he came special. Came over the roundy wall special to tell me. To give me the message. And to stay well away from O'Dowd's place, he says. In particular. He says are you the greatest eejit in the world or what?'

'Don't speak to your poor brother like that, John McNulty,' says the Mam of peace. 'You're only a whelp. Have sense.'

'Well, Mam, he may be older than me, but, Jimmy Mack, is he wiser?'

'What nonsense is Jonno Lynch speaking?' says the Mam.

'Not so much, nonsense,' says Jack, just a little smugly. 'Anyway, Jonno Lynch told me to tell you.'

And his brother Jack, who is old enough now to comment on the practices of Sligo, seemingly, because he is as bright as daylight, tells him this is because Eneas has been going about in ships as if he were an Englishman and busying himself during an English war. How can Jack have a grasp of these things? A low-looking red-headed lad as green as a cabbage? Is he even twelve years of age, the same scrap of wisdom?

Oh, the British Merchant Navy, the British. You'd want to rise early to be up with them, the heroes of Ireland. Deep thinkers. The blessed British Merchant Navy! Poor sailors, afraid of sea, afraid of land. In rusty traders and toiling oceanic tubs. Desperadoes of salt dreams and wind as tall as heaven. Even that is enough for silence and suspicion, is it?

Still and all it's a sort of sorrow to him that Jonno Lynch will not greet the old going-about companion of his boyhood. What's left of his boy's heart is wrung by it. It's a little thing maybe, a nod or a word flung across Main Street, or even to heel up, the two of them, like two cabbage carts against the wall of Plimpton's or even God knows head into the Café Cairo for a citron lemonade and swap all the ould recent histories. But it's recent histories indeed are the damnable problem. Jack, younger though he may be, has a better grasp of these affairs. He says bright boys and wide boys and bitter-hearted older men with tribes of brats and hard wives too are milling about up on the Showgrounds of a Sunday night and under their floorboards are real guns and in their souls the foul pith of rebellion. So Jack says. Jack's reading Tennyson noon to night. He's a wonder.

*

But there's worse to come in all manner of things. A long year passes, a long round of weather and eating his mother's grub. Eneas roams the town asking everywhere and anywhere for a job and finds oh, kindness here and there, but mostly indifferent no's and even aggression. And gradually Eneas understands that the little rebellion that took place just recent in Dublin and other points, with barely a flare-up in Sligo, barely a flash of fire on the hill, has done nonetheless great altering in the hearts and minds of the townspeople. And if it isn't that, it's the worsening state of money matters cited, and true enough men are being let go everywhere in the country, not just Sligo, and wise people are pulling in their feet so the elephant of poverty won't crush them. Even the Protestant businesses won't touch him, which he tries in the last resort. Not that they would have been likely to employ him in the first place, inclined as they were, and rightly, to see to their own. Yet, having sailed about for the sake of France, though a little uselessly, is he not a hero of sorts? A servant of the King? A trustworthy man? No. He wonders what fear it is or weather that has changed everything so. It is that to-do in Dublin and its aftermath no doubt. And maybe he gets a grasp now of why Jonno Lynch calls him an eejit. There's a lot of slip and tug and pulling of tidal waters that he can't make out the pattern of. Not for want of banging his head against all the new stone walls of Sligo.

Even his Pappy is beyond helping him and seemingly has no connection or debt due in the town that would jimmy up a job for him. Oh, this is all a tremendous shock for Eneas, to be this buffeted figure. His quiet nature is all blown about, all windy and ragged.

The carefree mood as he bade farewell to Bull Mottram is no more. Now the days are heavy and bare and dangerous to him. Maybe he exaggerates the rejection of the townspeople, maybe everyone now has their troubles, but, his blood withers, his heart shrinks, his step on the rainy granite of the pavement shortens. And he feels afraid just as he used to as a little boy, half in the hands of sleep, the visages of old demons leering and looming at him.

But in the end it's his Pappy after all that has the remedy. Old Tom has been working the last while in the asylum, to the exclusion of his band work. He'd rather be raising the rafters in the hotel in Bundoran where formerly he excited the visitors. It's been an atrocious summer for holidaying and little call has there been for music. But, a lad belonging to the under-surgeon in the asylum has just gone into the peelers, only back himself from Flanders. He's a silent boy and a ruined one maybe by the ferocity of that war, but the peelers take him readily enough.

Eneas looks at it all with simple eyes and having no desire to loiter the rest of his days, joins at the hint of his Pappy the Royal Irish Constabulary. He's not the complete eejit as Jonno may believe, he's not the last innocent on earth. He knows why there are places in the peelers when there are places nowhere else. The RIC is composed no doubt of lost men, ordinary fellas from the back farms of Ireland, fools and flotsam and youngsters without an ounce of sense or understanding. And the legends of the RIC are all evictions, murders and the like, though many an Irish family was reared on those wages, and many a peeler was a straightforward decent man. Still, the word Royal is there before all, and they carry arms, and the top men are all out-and-out Castle men. But no matter. He can't live a life to please Jonno Lynch, much as his heart is grateful for the adventures of his youth. Or he would lead a life to please Jonno Lynch if Jonno still had a grá for him, a friendly love for him. But he does not, clearly. And a fella must work, must toil in the dry vale of the world.

*

A fresh recruit by the wisdom and mercy of headquarters in the Phoenix Park is never let serve in his own town and especially so in the new world of guerrilla war and reprisal, for a policeman is a target now, like one of those wooden ducks in the fairground going round and round on the wooden hill. Every recruited man is suspected by both sides of informing, one way or another, and a man is rendered greater innocence by being posted to an unfamiliar town. So Eneas finds himself in Athlone with the bright peaked cap and the shining boots and the black suit. For a brace of months he is drilled and perfected in the barracks square. Out at six they are in their greatcoats, the peaks on the caps as black as blackbirds' feathers, and rain or shine the boots making the crippled cobbles ring, and they wheel and stamp and take the orders as the one animal. A hundred boys in similar coats, and the fresh reds of the dawn cluttering up the lower gaps between the buildings. The name for a raw boy is a shoofly, and each man aims to be a constable, but the name among the historical-minded people of the town is the peelers, the polis. At end of training each man gets his gun and bullets. All about the barracks the countryside is boiling with sedition and treachery and hatred according to the sergeant, William Doyle of Leitrim, of Leitrim in these latter years, but an Athlone boy in times gone by, so he will tell you. As such a useful man to herd his men about the dangerous districts.

And indeed ferocious events are afoot in the sacred web of fields and rainy towns. It isn't just murders and such or killings, you couldn't call them that. Wherever an RIC man uses a gun and wounds or kills in a skirmish, some man in his uniform is taken and God help him in the dark hedges and isolated farms. Such a man might be gutted with a big knife and his entrails fed to the homely pig in front of him, and the last leaks of life drained out of him then slowly and silently with terrible swipes.

Next thing the RIC is augmented, as the official word goes, with an Auxiliary Force and now the merry dance gets wilder back and forth. For these are men as strange and driven as the Irish heroes themselves. They're quaffing long bottles of beer and whisky at every juncture and resting-spot, and visiting themselves upon guilty and innocent alike with the fierce passion and separateness of lions. Perhaps this isn't an easy matter for recruits like Eneas, jostled in the very police barracks by these haunted faces.

They have come back most of them from the other war and what haunts them now is the blood and torn matter of those lost, bewildering days. Many of the Auxiliaries are decorated boys, boys that ran out into no-man's-land and took positions that only bodiless gods could have, and rescued men from the teeth of slaughter and saw sights worse than the drearest nightmares. And they have come back altered for ever and in a way more marked by atrocity than honoured by medals. They are half nightmare themselves, in their uniforms patched together from army and RIC stores, some of them handsome and elegant men, with shining accents, some terrible dark boys from the worst back-alleys of England, but all with the blank light of death and drear unimportance of being alive in their eyes. As ancient as old stories. And every auxiliary has the strength of four ordinary men you would think, as if death and fearlessness were an elixir.

And they are visited upon the countryside lethally and notoriously. Reprisals are daily sorrows, daily sad persons are found in ditches of a morning and no matter what allegiance was in their hearts at any daybreak. Because they are broken, bloody, vanished hearts now, auxiliary and guerrilla alike. Eneas's principal duty is the finding and motoring of these remnants back to the coroner's premises in Athlone town.

The king of the Auxiliaries is the man called the Reprisal Man and Eneas knows him by no other name. It's said generally that he comes from the dark north of England and killed seven Germans in a bomb hole somewhere in the muddy wastes of the Somme. He's a person as big and real as one of the cowboys in the flicks – Athlone has its passionate cinema too. How he does it nobody can tell on his poor wages but the man is never but spick and span and the crease straight and ridged in the old trews from stores. A hero in other places no doubt, but a tongue of pure avenging fire in the backroads of the lands about the town.

This is a fella never to be seen with and if the rule of thumb among the recruits and indeed the RIC men in general is to stay clear of the Auxiliaries, or the Tans as they are called by the people, an article of faith is to avoid the Reprisal Man like the devil himself. To be spotted in the company of such as he either in hours of duty or relaxing in the bars of the town would be noted on some black-list of marked men.

Even the sergeant Doyle stays away from him and Doyle is a policeman of the old school, loyal as a child to the kings and queens of England, Scotland and Ireland and the princes of Wales also. His father was a simple cabinkeeper in Leitrim after losing the huxter's shop in Athlone when the sergeant was only a scrap. His grandfather died, it was said, during the hunger of the forties in the old century, killed by a mob for feeding Indian grain meant for paupers to his fattening pig. This isn't information that Eneas gets from the sergeant, but the sort of thing you'll get whispered to you by the older men less useful than the sergeant, less promoted.

Well, the whole business is mightily complicated one way and another and Eneas in his heart cannot say that he enjoys the policing he is set to do. He had had in mind the more usual duties of the RIC, in days more peaceful, when he joined, and never had the ambition to be a carter of corpses or a young fella atop a cart weeping from bewilderment. No man fool or sage could get used to the scenes of murder, because they are ever changing and unnatural. Indeed older men long years in the force have taken their own lives in answer to the crushing horror of the times, and rakes of others in the country generally are said to be housed now in the county homes and the asylums. They were unfit for such sights. Eneas tries many a stratagem to water down what he sees, to satisfy his heart that it is a passing matter, but truth to tell each dead soul afflicts him. The trouble and sorrow of being a peeler is a revelation to him.

Doyle is the man who tries to keep his men true and indeed safe. No constable walks alone now through the streets of Athlone, and many a homespun speech issues forth from Doyle's lips on the topics of duty and order and loyalty and God. God is the chief superintendent, right enough, or even a commissioner.

Bit by bit Eneas understands that a fella by the name of Mick Collins is the big man behind the wild lads willing to kill for the lovely trout of freedom. No decent description of him exists in police files, but a field of stories growing fast with brambles and tares attaches to the name. And yet the name rises immaculate and bright as a sovereign from the mire of events that muddy all normal men. It's a mystery. Eneas could call Collins the enemy except in his private mind he does not. If he had a picture of him maybe he could. He sees the Reprisal Man every so often stomping through the wooden corridors of the barracks or passing up the street in a Crossley tender like a savage prince, and it seems to Eneas that that same Reprisal Man is more his enemy than the invisible Mick Collins. But both are men of blood no doubt. Eneas's head rackets with warring notions. He's adrift on the shallow sea of his homeland.

At first he tries to get home to his Mam and Pappy every furlough but the cat's cradle of Sligo talk is against him. His Pappy is stopped in the street and talked to by O'Dowd, the auctioneer, one of Collins's men it may be, but a proper bowsie, according to Old Tom McNulty. Yes, a proper bowsie, a scam merchant and the son of a boxty cooker from over Strandhill way, an unkempt boiler of a fella that used mash up spuds for the trippers and their kids hungry after the salt sea and the wild playing. So it is a mighty affront for Old Tom to be stopped by the son of O'Dowd the boxty man and at the same time the words he says to Old Tom are precise and calm.

'Let your son keep out of Sligo, man, if he wants to keep his ability to walk.'

There's no misunderstanding that song and Eneas keeps to barracks when other men are able to catch motor-buses or trains or go on the long walk and lift-cadging home to towns and rural places, and no word said against them, as yet. But Eneas knows that the stint at sea is held against him also, the stint at sea and maybe also his old friendship with Jonno Lynch, which might be a useful thing to a policeman bent on gathering intelligence. Eneas is not bent on anything except daily life but O'Dowd's imagination and the imaginations of a score of worried men in Sligo are afire with conspiracy and secrecy.

At any rate something occurs that puts such straight-forward matters in the halfpenny place. There's a right old hooley of a series of tit-for-tat jobs between the Roscommon rebels and the Tans, with the RIC mixed in somewhere too. And the doings of the rebels are further tangled by betrayals in their own number as the curious war grows in months like a terrible child, and certain quaint advantages are to be got out of the situation. Sometimes now Eneas carts back creatures done in by their own comrades, mightily done in. And fellas say now that it's like the old famine days when some of the worst cruelty was visited on the poor of Ireland by them that were slightly less poor, and Doyle's ould grandfather is darkly cited. When a strong farmer was content to see his rentless neighbour driven off to fever, death or America, if he could only get a hoult of the vacated farm, and attach it to his own. If this is not the bedevilment of Irish historical goings-on, Eneas doesn't know what is, or so he says plainly to his companions, though indeed the matter is not quite so clear as that in his head.

Well, he's going up the town one night in Athlone with Sergeant Doyle himself as a companion, and they've been idly drinking in the old Great Western Hotel where the proprietor is above politics and beneath neutrality. It has become a policeman and soldier's drinking spot but no matter, the two are well watered now but not drunk as such and climbing the little hill past the curious pewter of the black river and the mossy walls of the Cathedral. And there's a little stone-covered alleyway there that would bring you up conveniently to the sacristy if you were a priest, and there are two dark men in the gap there that get a good hold on Doyle and a penknife to his throat. And Eneas hangs back from jumping at the men or trying to get his gun out of his cut-down holster because he piercingly sees how honed and steel the knife is, as thin as the leg of a sandpiper.

'Come in, you bugger, out of the light,' says one of the men, 'or I'll tear out the gullet of your sergeant.'

So Eneas steps in carefully, into the holy dark, where priests and priests' messengers have often darted, and Doyle says not a word, for fear of inciting a regretful move. These are clearly some of the bould men themselves, some of the heroes of Athlone, the dark men of freedom. Some of Jonno Lynch's crowd, or the Athlone branch anyhow. They have an air about them fretful and desperate, not like policemen or soldiers but like hunters, fellas that go out after hares with big long streels of dogs in the blessed autumns. Townies with guns – nothing worse, nothing more danger-ous to the peace of the countryside. And Eneas is silent, as indeed his training recommends. For an attacker is like a snake that strikes at movement, at history, at words.

'We're taking you for the job done on Stephen Jackson,' says the same man, 'just so you know why we're doing this to you.'

And Eneas knows who Jackson is or was and so does Doyle, because Eneas took Jackson to the coroner's icy room with bullets of the Reprisal Man in his cold head.

'I don't know nothing about that,' says Doyle in his Leitrim accent.

'Ah, you do, and you did,' says the man.

'It's the feckin Tans you want,' says Doyle, simply.

'Jaysus, that'll be the day, the day we get him, the long bollocks that he is. The Reprisal Man, in all his glory. That'll be the day of history, the time we get that shite. But he's no easy sparrow like yourselves. We'll get him too some day, some day. In the meantime, your ticket's come good, Doyle, and we know you're mixed up in it.'

'I hadn't got a finger in it,' says Doyle. 'I never even met the man.'

'Arra,' says the murdering man, 'isn't that a big fib. Ha? Didn't you go to school with the fella, up with the brothers in Mount Temple? Aren't you on the old register there, and anyway, don't I know you knew him, because he told me himself, with his dying breath. Said he'd know your skin on a board. After the Reprisal Man put bullets in his face at point-blank range and the poor bastard came running down Cook Street with his life leaking from his ears, blind from blood and pain, and into my arms like a boy, oh yes, and the last thing he said was it must have been yourself put his name in the Big Man's way, because you were pals in the school on the hill with the Brothers.'

And Eneas looks at Doyle to see if this could be accurate, at least about the schooling together, and he can see from Doyle's simple face that there's no lie in it.

'We've been waiting for you to make something of your old associations, you hooer's melt, ye. And didn't your grandfather make his money in the hungry days, you poor witless cunt, ye?'

'That's just an ould story, men,' says Doyle. Now Eneas smells a strange smell, a smell he's smelt once or twice only, and it's the stink of fear that rises from a man when he's in mortal dread.

'You had a hand in it as sure as cowshite, and if you didn't, aren't you peeler enough for our intentions?'

And Doyle hangs now in the man's arms, as if every grain of energy's gone out of him. And his face acquires a complete deep look of stupidity and gracelessness. Eneas himself stares like a calf. No course of action presents itself. A few people even going home late in their raincoats pass up the street but he doesn't feel inspired to call out to them, with the thin knife sparking at Doyle's scraggled throat. The four of them know something is going to happen, they are united at least in that certainty. It could be the flicks or a dark penny dreadful, the way the four of them know all that. And their different histories, their different childhoods, their different ages and faces and hopes even, their different souls sullied up by different matters, all seem to tend towards the same event, this cold and shadowy event in the little granite slipway of the cathedral priests.

'Say goodnight, Doyle,' says the speaking man, and never a word from the other. 'May God forgive me.'

And he takes a snug gun from his coat of darkness and places it up against the bullocky face of Doyle no doubt just as the Reprisal Man did with Stephen Jackson, Doyle's childhood companion in the roistering schoolyard, and he prints the O of the little barrel against the right cheekbone and fires into the suddenly flashing face. And places the gun a second time into the left cheekbone, or where it might well be if the blood and splinters and scraps of flesh were cleaned off, and fires again and Eneas looks into the face of the killer and it has the set effort in it of a person struggling for precision in a world of vagueness and doubt, struggling with a physical task in a world of Godless souls and wormy hearts.

'Will I do this poor bastard too?' says the trembling killer to his friend, turning the little gun on Eneas.

'One's enough for the night,' says the other man. 'One's enough. The whole town will be stirring now. That's McNulty, the Sligoman. Let Sligo look after him, if they want. I'm not killing a simpleton like that. Look at the gawmy stare of him. Look at the stare of him.'

So he looks at Eneas for a second, the killer man, as if having been bidden to do so, he is honour-bound to do it, to fulfil every article of talk and action. For the freedom of Ireland and the Republic so earnestly wished for.

'Oh, let's feckin run for it,' says the assassin, weary as a donkey.

Then off indeed, truthful and exact, they run like they are kids hooering out of an orchard and the apples bubbling from their ganseys and banging on the metalled roads. And

Eneas is left there standing indeed like a gom, like a remnant, like an oddment. Couldn't they have shot him too, for the look of things? For courtesy even? He thinks that and in another corner of his head he knows it is a daft thought. He feels a tremendous love as long as an English mile for the poor corpse in the lane. He knew him but slightly, yet all the purposes of that ordinary life, the tobacco, the papers, the idle talk, the dreams of promotion that never came true, afflict Eneas in the darkness. He wants to kneel down and embrace the dead man, soothe him, do something to send him up safe and sound to his Maker. But he stirs not a muscle. He finds he is frozen by terror. And Doyle is at his feet, simple as a song, all ruined and wrecked like Humpty Dumpty. Doyle is at his stupid feet, his bloody feet familiar and square, cased brightly in their police-issue boots.

*

Not even Eneas's superiors believe he knows nothing about it when the Reprisal Man duly removes the killers of Doyle from the hastening world of Athlone. Mere days after, yes, they're found, out by the distillery, perfunctorily destroyed. It's assumed Eneas has given, given gladly, to the Reprisal Man descriptions and the like, and when he denies it simply, they know he is exercising a clever caution and concealment. But he is not. The Reprisal Man has been able to ferret out his rabbits without him, ferret them out with the drear force of his broken mind. And no great task perhaps.

At any rate he is honourably discharged from his duties. It is not considered wise in the worsening days to leave him to the see-saw of reprisals. His turn would come round as surely as the sun. It is, he is told, the opinion of District Inspector O'Callaghan up in barracks that though the RIC is short of men, desperately, they are not short of corpses, and Constable McNulty is shortly to be such if he lingers. But it's also whispered around the barracks Chinese-fashion that the Republicans have issued a death-threat against Eneas McNulty on account of the foul words of betrayal he has spoken to the Tans, and he languishes now on the black-list that they all know exists. A black-list growing as long as the Shannon. And when the whisper reaches Eneas it is mightily embellished and includes possible modes of execution if he remains in the force. His balls tied about his head like two roots of garlic and his tongue torn out and fed to pigs. And so whether it is horse-trading or honest concern for his safety that has prompted the District Inspector he cannot say. Another recruit who has never been his pal tells him that even if all the fools of Ireland are in the peelers, as the saying goes, some fools are more fool than other fools. Some fools are beyond the pale.

At any rate the handsome uniform is perforce handed back, and he returns, raw as a scrape, to Sligo.

*

He sits fast in his Pappy's house, not daring to go out in the daylight, expecting even so the sky to fall on his head through the dark blue slates. In his dreams all manner of talk flows swiftly, swiftly, like the intent waters of the Garravogue, mutters and threats, clear as the bells of death. He senses the fright of his brilliant brother Jack, just preparing himself for his own assault on the world and in need of no scandalous brother, and he knows his Mam understands only too well the ticket of terror flying in the wind, but they don't speak about it. They've taken silence to themselves like an adopted dog. Because it's all manner

67

of talk, any manner of talk, might be the knife now. Luck in silence or at any rate a sort of murk and darkness. Only his Pappy is content to blunder about in words.

'It's a bad sort of time to have your head up, you know, in any class of a political manner,' says his father, the two of them standing as of old by the back window, looking out over the eternal ruins of the Lungey House. How different it is now, Old Tom older, and Eneas a ruined twenty-year-old.

'The worst of it is,' says his Pappy, laying a hand in familiar fashion on the broad back of his son, a back indeed all strength and youth, hard as a saddle. 'The worst of it is, I blame myself.'

'Why so, Pappy?' says Eneas, surprised.

'Didn't I steer you into the polis, with my talk of the under-surgeon's son? Christ, and the same boy killed last month in Donegal, a stone tied to his leg and drowned in an estuary. Arra, child, I done you a bad turn that time, that I spoke of the peelers.'

'Ah, Pappy, I don't think so. A policeman's there to take the villain out of the village. Trouble is, these times, a good citizen is a rare one. Or I don't know, maybe that's nonsense. But, Pappy, I feel it as a terrible thing to be hiding in my own town, from my own people, and what remedy will there be for it?'

His father stands fast by him in the dwindling light. Not a sound is there. Certainly no wild boys go sneaking to box the minister's fox.

'Maybe I should be just going away. Going away quietly with myself somewhere.'

His father says nothing at all for a long bit.

'Trouble is,' says his Pappy, 'a man goes away like that and maybe he never comes back to his people.'

'Better than to be killed here, Pappy.'

'Trouble is, a man could go away, and the buggers would go after him.'

'You don't think they would, Pappy?'

'I was reading, there was a fella got in Brisbane for something like this, now he was a fella that did something bad, or so it was believed, and he probably did at that, not like yourself' – and he touches the back of his child's head gently, hardly noticing himself do it, and stroking the bristles of the short back and sides – 'and he was followed out to Australia, and that's a long way.'

'You can't go further, I believe, Pappy.'

'If you abide near us, sure, maybe that will content them. If you tuck yourself in near us. You're only a young fella. Maybe they'll content themselves with frightening us all. I don't know. Maybe, sure, jaysus, the British Army in all its glory will deal with them. The Tans are a queer wild lot. Maybe they'll settle their hash.'

'Jesus, it's not a good business, when you have to wish a thing like that.'

'The matter of sons is above politics. Maybe you'll see that one day, if you have your own. I hope so. I do.'

He can feel the odd thrumming of his father beside him, his heartbeat it must be, the same feeling as holding a wild bird in your hand, the ache and the muscle of it to be away free again. He has put his father under a strain certainly, and the old man is quiet and easy about it, but Eneas can sense that strain, that thrumming, that beating of the heart. Jesus, he's sorry for the old man. He's sorry for all the old fathers of foolish sons. Having to dip their heads in matters too foreign, too deep, too curious – too murderous. Truth is he doesn't know what to do, any more than his Pappy knows.

'A black-list,' says his father, musingly, half a-dream. 'A funny way to describe something. On the black-list. Funny, that.

'Aye.'

'You know, Eneas,' says his father. 'Well, you see me always going about, up to the asylum, to measure the poor fellas there, or over in better days with the orchestra to, well, to play for the people in Bundoran and the like, and you probably think, there he goes, Old Tom, my Pappy, there he goes, and maybe you don't think much else about it.'

'Well, I do, Pappy.'

'Aye, well, it's good for a young man to know certain things, and I often think of my own father, and the habit of silence he had, and why not, he worked like a slave all his days. And I suppose poor low people we've always been, and I used to be gassing to you here about the damn Lungey House, and all that codswallop . . .'

'Ah, sure, well.'

'Aye, well, we are poor people, and God knows when there was hunger we felt it, and when there was cold we felt it, and we were never people above cold or hunger. No. But, child, though I learnt silence off of my father—'

And Old Tom stops there. Fact of the matter is, he's weeping. Or something's come up in his throat, more likely, a stopper that is the stopper on a father's feeling for his son, generally. To a degree it's worse than being shot by patriots, being shot by his father's obvious love.

*

So he must resolve on something. A person can tire of being that mortal leaf twisting and shrugging on the galloping river. The scorch on his heart where Jonno Lynch snubbed him on Main Street doesn't suggest to him that there might be a gap in the hedge where Jonno stands. There must be someone he can march out to beard, even if all the secrecy and terror of the days says otherwise. He fixes on a plan of sorts. He doesn't know if anyone has succeeded, before execution, in being taken off a black-list, but then the history of Sligo is not the history of great escapes. They are more doomed and fixed in their courses, the men of Sligo, it seems to him, than those bewildered and doomed Greeks of old that the master used to relish.

Sunday bright early he hies to the Cathedral for the mass that all the big people of the town attend. For it is considered slothful and perhaps even evil to go to the later masses, unless a person is old, sickly or poor. The poor lads and lassies from the asylum are carted down for the evening mass, and no one goes to that who can help it, unless you are a travelling merchant or the like and would rather get late mass than rot in hell.

Eneas is not a perfect mass-goer and rarely would he be out his door in the old days for the eight o'clock, though when he was a mere boy amid his siblings, his mother naturally herded them all out and around the ancient walls and up the mosaic steps of the Cathedral. And Old Tom is an immaculate mass-goer always and is respected for it in the town, considering the immense weariness that might be on a band-leader on a Sunday morning. Not everyone understands the deep spring of life in Old Tom McNulty as Eneas does.

And though he lies as if abed that morning and allows

Jack and Young Tom and Teasy to spill out into the little street, Teasy with a clutch of missals to beat the band and a mantilla of black lace on her poor head like a Christmas pudding boiling under muslin in the pot, he spruces himself as best he can before the small yellowing mirror on the landing, slicking his hair down with Jack's hair-grease and fetching one of his father's work ties from the leaning cupboard. It is a good tie for a man, with a design of swallows, and it's very blue altogether, which Eneas obscurely thinks might be a help to him, why he could not say. Clothes maketh the man, as a tailor like his Pappy never tires of saying. And maybe his father is the worst tailor on earth like people say, furnishing jackets and trousers so tight for the lunatics that their arms are hitched up as they go, and the life is squeezed out of their poor bollocks. Maybe that is so, but in other respects he is a kingly man, a very Greek of a man.

In the Cathedral he takes a dark seat over by the side chapel of the Virgin of Modena, and lurks there, trying to spy his target. He soon spots his family because his brother Jack's hair flames out amid the mantillas and dark heads of ordinary Sligo people. Suddenly, sitting there like a thief, he realizes what a trench of distance his trouble has created between his shadowed form and their line of heads easy and open among the townspeople. As he is in a crowd, he wonders how many of them are against him or against his kind, how many would be indifferent to or ignorant of the whole matter and how many would be for him. For the latter he despairs.

But keeps his eyes roaming over the multitude, and when he spots at last Jonno Lynch, he knows his quarry cannot be far away, and sure enough, there's Mr O'Dowd in the dapperest coat in Sligo, a treasure of a coat, sleek and brushed and tailored to perfection. It wasn't his father cut that coat, certainly.

The great crowd spills out into the fresh and speckled sunshine. The sycamores once so sacred to Jonno Lynch blow about a little in the sea-breeze. No doubt the minds of the people are full of the canon's sermon, about the evils of gold in the modern world, or merely the sense of their own cleanliness, both spiritual and in the matter of their shirts and blouses. Pounds of starch unite the crowd, and for a moment in his distress Eneas can think only of the clothes hung on the people, as if hearts and souls were in the materials and not in the bodies they hide from view. It is a rackety thought and no help to him as he tries to move through the mass of talking and laughing citizens. He sees O'Dowd now talking to the canon on the steps of the cathedral and he is abashed in his task by the sight but what can he do? He must pursue what feels now more and more like a stupid notion, feeble and even dangerous. But he'll be a Greek in this now if it kills him, and when O'Dowd finally detaches himself from the little red mouth and chinless round face of the canon and descends the concrete steps with a smile of some grandeur on him, Eneas stands in his way. And Eneas has never seen O'Dowd up close, indeed has only glimpsed him passing in his Ford motorcar, and he is surprised by how young the man is, maybe not more than ten years older than himself. But he has a fierce balding head, which he is just covering now with an excellent hat, angling it expertly against the flow of sun and fashion. Eneas stands in his way as best he can, because O'Dowd is not inclined to look anywhere except further out over the heads, perhaps to his waiting car. And it occurs to Eneas, being trained in those matters, that there might be some D men about in their plainclothes so obvious to the world. Certainly there must be RIC men posted about quietly, because it would be part of their duties to guard a mass crowd. In Enniscrone only the last week two men were arrested by the Tans coming out of mass, which caused the most tremendous furore in the district. Not so much because the two men were undoubtedly murderers of a patriotic bent, but because shopkeepers' wives were present and one at least fainted in terror of those large rusty-looking guns the Tans carried. At any rate, Tans, RIC, rebels, it was all the one to Eneas now, and he raises his right hand gently to impede O'Dowd.

'What's the whatsa?' says O'Dowd, pleasantly, maybe not knowing Eneas's face, as if Eneas were just another of the young men of Sligo with their heads sleeked like film-stars.

'Mr O'Dowd, I'd like a word with you, if you had a minute.'

'Sure, son,' he says, 'step over under the trees a little.'

And Eneas, following O'Dowd's bright shoes across to the grubby trees, is astonished by his success. Also, yes, he is even sicker at heart now because he realizes that O'Dowd has totally mistaken him for a decent man, a man with some decent request, a true man of Sligo. When they reach the dappled desert under the sycamores, and O'Dowd turns to him grandly, Eneas's mind is turning over like a terrible engine. There are trapped animals in there, birds, lions, elephants, a zoo of panic and fear. This is so much harder than he imagined, him cool and measured, and O'Dowd at best silent and nodding. But the vast friendliness of the man is destroying him.

'I don't think you know me,' says Eneas, obliteratedly.

'Well, who are you, then?' says O'Dowd, laughing a slight laugh.

'McNulty is my name,' says Eneas, 'Eneas McNulty, that was a friend of Jonno Lynch's.'

'You're a friend of Jonno's?'

'Well, I was, I was. Indeed I was, formerly.'

'OK. So what is it you want of me?'

Oh Jesus, this is bad, the pleasantness of the man. The ordinary chat and pleasantness of him. The fresh face and the fine clothes. Eneas senses his father's tie on his breast, like a blue blight, absurdly. And he's stoppering up himself now, like his father the night before, but with different causes.

'I was hoping,' he says, 'no, I am hoping to say something to you, about my time in the RIC.'

'What?' says O'Dowd, entirely differently.

'My time in the RIC, do you see?'

'Your time in the RIC, do I see?' And it's terrifying how O'Dowd almost sings the words.

'Look it,' says Eneas. He can see only dimly what he wants O'Dowd to look at. But he presses on. 'When I was in the RIC in Athlone there was two men killed by the Tans and it was said I was the man fingered them and so I was supposed to have been placed on a black-list by, by, you know, the, eh, insurrectionists, and the fact was, or is, or was that, I didn't, you know, say a word about them, I mean, I knew nothing about them anyway, it was the Reprisal Man got them by his own intelligence network, do you see?'

O'Dowd looks at him. He might be looking at ragworm in a fisherman's fold of bait. He's very quiet for a good ten seconds. Very quiet. Thinking, sort of secure, immaculate, not like Eneas, filthy now to himself, like the scum of time and birds on the sycamores.

'What's that to do with me?' says O'Dowd. And now Eneas wonders why O'Dowd lingers. There's something about it, the way he lingers, intent.

'I don't know,' says Eneas, stupid, stupid in his own ears. Of course he knows, for the love of Christ.

'No, no, because, I'd like to know,' says O'Dowd. 'I'd like to know why you've come to me, I mean, I am concerned to know why.'

The politeness is awful. Yes, and the concern is awful. He realizes why O'Dowd lingers. Because of this concern. Eneas is suddenly in another realm altogether, the realm of O'Dowd's safety, or O'Dowd's sense of his own safety. And by God he is more lost there than he was in his own danger. O'Dowd leans in. Eneas can smell something like a woman's scent off trim, he doesn't know what it could be.

'I am concerned to know,' he repeats. 'Did Jonno Lynch for instance say something about me to you?'

'No,' says Eneas, forceful as he can. Christ, now it's Jonno Lynch's safety he's floundering in. Too many safeties! 'No, Jonno Lynch won't even speak to me since I was, what did they do to me, there's a word for it, discharged me – no, I don't know why I came to you. I had an idea.'

'Aye, what idea? That's my question to you, young fella.'

'I had an idea that I could say to you that, I, that someone in Sligo could have a go and see if I mightn't be taken off the, the black-list, so that I could stay in Sligo as an ordinary man and get a job and just live among my people, you know.'

'I couldn't give an ass's shite about that,' says O'Dowd ferociously. 'That's not what I'm asking, you little bollocks. Do you know what I do in Sligo? I buy and sell land. I buy and sell land. What do I do?'

It's like the master years ago, what seems like years ago. *Amo, amas, amat.* Repeat after me. I love, you love, he, she or it loves.

'You buy and sell land,' says Eneas obediently.

'That's what I'm anxious for you to know.'

'Right,' says Eneas.

'Got it?'

'Yes.'

'Don't come ever fucking near me again. Got it?'

'Yes.'

*

The next night after the helpful dark has fallen on the town someone knocks on the door of his Mam's house. He's sitting almost toe to toe with his Mam on the old dancing hearth. He knows well there is no gold buried there. He has a powerful sense that he has made everything much worse. He would like to broach the subject with his Mam but he is afraid now to say anything more to anyone. He is afraid of the concerns of other people that he might awake like the spaniel raising birds willy-nilly on the bog. He could not say exactly how he is. But there is a shape of fear in him that is just a size too big for his brain, he can feel it trying to burst out there. His blood feels ill, and he can neither taste food or relish it. All night he saw his childish night-mares, just as potent as when he was four, the twisted hags leering and looming at him. And mixed in there, traversing his dreams, was poor Doyle with his foolish cheeks all burst

77

by bullets and his foolish words strewn on the ground of the lane like pennies. He sits in his iron box of fear. Even so near to the hem of his mother's big dress he is sweating, unwell, alarmed, banging about from thought to thought.

She goes down the little length of the hall and lets in the visitor. He supposes it might be a gentleman come like of old to get the run of a tune off his Pappy or the like. Or sure, Jesus, a murderer to put bullets into his Mam and himself, like you read every day in the paper.

The last man he expects is Jonno Lynch, stepping into the parlour with the slight spring fire ticking away in the grate.

'Jonno,' he says, leaping up.

'Howaya,' says Jonno, clearly under the restraint of the Mam's presence.

'Would you ever leave us alone, Mam, dear,' he says, 'in these special circumstances. I wouldn't put you out of your own parlour.'

'Ah sure, yes,' says his Mam simply, and closes the black-stained door after her.

The two friends of boyhood face each other across Mrs McNulty's famished pattern of a rug. Jonno is almost as well turned out as O'Dowd, he's very shipshape and tight with clothes. Jonno Lynch seems to be interested in the paltry rug, because he stares at it mercilessly.

'Are you trying to get me killed?' he says.

'No, Jonno.'

'Do you know where I was all evening?'

'No.'

'I was up the back of the town and I was being interrogated.'

It does strike Eneas that he is a very clean man for an interrogated one, but maybe the rebels do things differently.

'Do you have any idea, Eneas, of my position in Sligo?'

'Your position?'

'Yeh. Don't make it sound like something else. While you've been in the British navy and going about as an RIC constable, you know, gadding about, gadding about, I've been working hard to make something of myself, you know. You know best of any man in Sligo where I come from. I never had no Mam and Pappy like you. I was whipped every night of my life by the old bitch in Kitchen Lane. Now, I've done something about all that. I've worked at it. And I believe in certain things. And one of those things, the biggest of them, is the freedom that's coming to Ireland. Every sign is, Eneas, this will be the last year of war, and next year we'll see something big, something good, yeh, and I'll be part of that.'

'That's good, Jonno.'

'Yeh, that's good. Right, now you're concentrating. I can see you are with your big sweaty face there. Now, I was sitting the back of the town with some of the lads, you know, and I was wondering why they were so, well, what can I say, how can I describe it, so quiet, I think is the word I'm looking for. And then another man comes in, a divisional officer, a very high-up man, and he talks to me, talks to me, and I don't know what's going on, and I give my answers, and then your name is mentioned.'

'My name?'

'Yeh. Your man McNulty, the black-listed man, he says. And he says you were just yesterday, in the bright open spaces of the cathedral, talking to a certain man, and you

79

were saying all manner of peculiar things, and the connection between you and that man was yours truly. And the man asked you about this, and you were saying something about your feckin ould days in the RIC and so on. So I'm being questioned now all evening by this officer and I don't know for sure at certain points if I'm going to be shot or not, the way they look at me. And then it eases up, and the thing appears to be settled and I'm thinking, I'm going to go over to Eneas McNulty's house and knock his head off.'

Eneas is exhausted. He can hardly speak to his erstwhile friend.

'I told him you had completely broken with me.'

'Yeh, so they said eventually. Which luckily is what I said to them. Which luckily happened to be the truth.'

Eneas sits down. 'Jesus,' he says.

'You don't know where you are, do you?' says Jonno.

'No, and I'm getting fed up with it.'

'I bet.'

Eneas sinks his head and even allows his hands to come up and cover his face. He wouldn't normally want to show his despair to Jonno Lynch of all people but he's too tired now. He doesn't believe he could walk to the door. He supposes that when they kill him it will be with great force and pain. He wonders could he feel pain now, in his dead limbs?

'You've one chance at this, Eneas.'

'What?' says Eneas.

'They'll take your name off the black-list if you do two things.'

'What?'

'First thing is, you'll have to tell them everything you

80

know about the RIC and especially that fella down in Athlone that heads up the Tans.'

'I don't know much about him.'

'Maybe. He's a clever bastard by all accounts. But you could get near him.'

'How do you mean?'

Jonno sits now in his Mam's chair and leans off the edge of it, his dapper little arse on the hard wood.

'Eneas, don't you get it? There's going to be independence in Ireland. You know what that means to a fecker like you? No force on earth could protect you after that. God himself will put a curse on you as a traitor and a betrayer of your brothers.'

'Of my brothers? Jack and Tom?'

'No, fuck you, you gammy cunt, your brothers in the nation. Me, you stupid cunt. There's this freedom coming, and by God, Eneas, you have to see how it will be for you.'

'This is kind of you, Jonno, but, I did what I did, and I was trying to make my way just like you, and I don't see what you're saying to me. I mean, I don't mind being shot, not really. Lots of men have been shot. It's not being part of the world, mind. It's, well, it's yourself walking by me in the street, and the whole mess of it. I don't know what's going on half the time.'

'Right, well, I'll tell you. I'll tell you, Eneas, so you know. Yeh, right, OK, I set some store by you. I remember all the going about that we did. You were always a brave bastard. I never had a complaint about you. OK, all those years in Kitchen Lane, right, I'll tell you, you deserve it, you kept me going, boyo, you did, you were in my heart always, the friend, and there's nothing really better than that, you know,

81

you can kiss all the girls you like at the back of the Gaiety, but the friend of youth is the business, that's the one there that's important.'

'Right,' says Eneas. After a moment then, 'I agree.'

'So, see what we got here. They talk to me, I reassure them. Because Eneas, you don't seem to realize what's going on here. This is war, Eneas, we're in the middle of a war. Do you think all I do is go about and run errands for, for your man? No, sir, I'm, and I take a risk saying this to you, but, I'm a soldier, Eneas, a real soldier with proper papers, and one of Collins's trusted men, now, I don't mean he knows me or anything, I'm not an officer as such, but, I will be, or I will be if you don't go around mentioning my name, you know. No, no, but listen, Eneas, this is a grand thing, this is like Cuchullain and the like, you know, and Ferdia, and fighting, and Ireland, and freedom. It's me who'll be the hero of all that, you know, I don't mean especially. It's like when we robbed the orchards, or tried to build the flying machine, remember, we were going to take it up the hills or out to Strandhill and climb the grass dune and wait for a good wind in off the sea, remember all those plans, and going up to the town engineer's house and asking him about it, and he says, "Drains, boys, drains is all I knows," you remember, fuck's sake.'

'Jonno. What are you saying?'

'What I'm saying is, you can get your name off the black-list, it can be you and me going round again like the old days, and it isn't a bad thing you have to do, it's a grand thing, it's a noble thing, and noble things are being done everywhere now on the island to try and be sure of this freedom, and to keep the party clean, and to act the whiteman.'

'What? What is it?' And now Eneas's head miraculously clears. He's calm, he's easy. It's like he's done the thing Jonno is suggesting and he's Jonno's pal and a hero of Ireland and everything is hunky-dory as the fella said.

'You have to go and get in close to the Reprisal Man, I'm not saying in the open, but get in close to him some way when it's just you and him, and you have to kill him.'

Eneas's answer is right at the front of his head. He doesn't even consider it for a second. Maybe he knew this is what was going to be asked of him, maybe somehow he knew.

'I couldn't do that,' he says.

'Why not?'

'I couldn't.'

'It would be for Ireland. It would be for yourself.'

But Eneas just sees Doyle as Jonno speaks. He sees Doyle saying those last words, and the little snubby gun against his cheek, and then the other cheek, and the blood and uselessness of it.

'Did you ever see a man killed?' he says.

'Eneas, you have got to do this thing.'

'I seen it. I don't mean I seen bodies. I mean, I seen a man killed just beside me, executed, you know, by the fellas you were talking about there.'

'And?'

'Look, maybe it would be a good thing, the way you think about it. Maybe the freedom of Ireland and all that is right and proper. But, killing a man is a very, particular thing, a particular thing, it is, Jonno, and I couldn't do it. Even if I was able to get near a man like that, which is not likely, because he's a brilliant man, he's like the devil himself for brilliance, and sure he'd take the whistle out of my throat before I could do anything to him, but that's not it, that's not what I'm saying to you. I appreciate what you're saying, and what you said there about our going about, but, freedom or no freedom, I can't see that I will ever want to bring death to a man, not that I ever did, but, when you carry a gun, you could be using it.'

Jonno sits back in the old chair. He doesn't say anything, but wipes his dry brow with his handkerchief. Jonno with a handkerchief, that's a sight. Jonno looks at him. All his face is different. The passion, the simple force, are gone.

'Pity,' is all he says.

Jonno gets up and plucks his tie out a little from his gansey, so it sits up on it like a tongue.

'So what do you say now?' says Eneas.

'You're dead,' says Jonno, and goes into the hall and away, not slamming the door even.

'Well, why don't you kill me now?' says Eneas, risen to his feet, shouting like a madman. Like a madman up in the asylum. Oh, give him a suit to hitch his arms! 'Why don't you! Why don't you!'

6

BUT THEY DON'T COME to kill him immediately, help-fully, and he doesn't know why. He sits like an owl in the house and hears footsteps everywhere, but they are not the footsteps of real men. Weeks and weeks go by, and the leak of summer comes in under the door.

Slowly he salvages the daylight hours, going out one morning at six to walk along the river with the fishermen's beloved flies blowing in perilous clouds along the bog-pewter of the Garravogue, going out another to the lip of the public streets, like a ghost of himself, peering at the early-morning children crossing the town to their school beyond the bridge at Finisklin.

What angel keeps him alive he does not know. Nor devil either. One morning equally early he climbs Knocknarea, carrying a stone from the foot of the mountain as is the proper custom and adding it to Maeve's Cairn at the top. He looks around at the country that is his world and is not his world. He wonders how it is for the old dead queen in her pile of rocks and for the small tombs of her warriors that lie near her. He seems himself to be closer to their kingdom than his own. He can't seem to get himself to sit in his own time. Drifting, drifting. There's Coney Island below and the slow walk of the tide across the broad strand. Well, he is tearless. There's Captain Midleton's broken cove, where he still troubles the ruined house with his roars, there's Rosses Point all pristine and exact, the shape of a bittern in the cold sea, and Strandhill where his own Pappy dreams of playing to regular dancers in a wind-bitten hall. And stony Eneas is, looking at it all, stony and separate. And afeared. A cold iron rod has been lowered into him, and he finds himself stiff and awkward with it. To the left and right of him is terror and terror. Even there at the top of the mountain as far from the world as he can go, there's no aspirin for his fear.

And he goes about in the nights and the fringes of the days and eats no more than a sickly baby and is a very strange man. And he is in danger of gathering to himself, his Mam says, all the odd stories of the place, he'll be the man that scares the children through a hedge. He'll be the man that robs the bread off sills and breaks the harrow while it lies idle in a yard waiting for its season, he will be the curse and the bogeyman of the district. So she says. But what can he do about that, roaming round and round, and if there was a pencil under him what great useless circles he would make on the tricky map of Sligo and environs.

Nevertheless he is not murdered, and fill his days he must.

All the while he favours the more distant places, and one time he begs a perch for his bum on the early-morning van that goes out to Enniscrone with the papers.

And away out on the wild sea-marsh and grasses of Enniscrone he is able to spread wide his arms and have the sun sit along them as if they were the fierce white featherings of a seabird.

Sure enough he is seen and reported here and there. Some not knowing his trouble think he is simply mad, abroad so early and silent and never answering a nod or a greeting.

And they say that the son has caught madness off of the father's work. And maybe, he thinks, they are right.

*

He discovers districts of Sligo he never found even as a boy, odd beaches not used by bathers as a rule, isolated places. And out upon the strand that lies in a frozen arc beyond Finisklin one day towards midday he sees leaning in privacy against a rock a young woman in a blowing dress. White as a sail the dress is and the sea-wind has no bother taking it and tugging it and slapping it against her legs but she pays it no heed. She leans against the rock with its dried weeds and barnacles hanging on for dear life, and her head is turned back for to get the sun on her face. Her eyes are closed fast. And he knows she is pretty as a penny even in the distance and he stands against the dunes with their freckled grasses turned mightily one way and another by the combing wind and is stymied by the sight of her. The sand is powdered gold there where she is, all bucketed up against her feet. Her shoes are thrown off near her, little red summer shoes he thinks, and he has never thought of such a matter in his life. She is soft and hard and good against the rock.

He knows well he is a menace to her in his lonesome walk, and that if she sees him she'll be fearful of him and rightly. Because it is far and without people over here, it is not like Enniscrone where the summer children swing back and forth on the huge swingboats and swimmers venture everywhere on the sunny acres. This is not a spot that visitors seek out, but a different matter, golden and windy and left alone. The sunlight is laying fresh strands of gold in her hair, he can see them, he thinks they must be solid were he to touch them. And he would love dearly to touch them, put his body close to her, quietly, welcomed, healing. Yes, he would. But instead he turns about to head back behind the dunes and across the wet sand and weeds betrayed by the tide, as his Mam might say.

He sets his left foot down in the normal thoughtless process of his stride and lets a bellow out of him to shame an ass. He doesn't like to think of himself as a bellower, but the bellow rises and is out and gone before he can think about it. He lifts his foot from the sand and there's blood dropping out of the sole of it and when he puts his hand gingerly into the sand he pulls up a long shard of glass, dark green glass off of a lobster float maybe, though it would be a hard job and a long one to smash a lobster float, he knows, the glass is that thick. You could throw a lobster float down a gully on to a rock and it wouldn't break for you. You could be desperate for it to break, and it wouldn't. What is he on about, sure the blood is ruining the sand and if the sand was a carpet there'd be hell to pay to the housekeeper.

Now Christ in His mercy, his shouting has alerted the woman, and she is over by him now, fearless and mighty after all. He shows her his bloody foot and by the Good Lord, she tears off her sweater and her shirt, puts the sweater back on herself with a show of her breast that almost dries the flow of blood in his foot, because he feels the blood rushing to the back of his head. Now he is dizzy and rocketing, it may be the loss of blood, but he thinks not, truly. She binds, the dear girl, his foot with the lovely shirt or should it be blouse you'd say about such a thing, light and starched and pleasant with a printing of forget-me-nots on the collar, he notices.

'You don't want to put a thing like that on my old foot,' he says.

'It's nothing,' she says, 'just a rag. Two summers ago sure I bought that old thing.'

'Well, it's very good of you, mightily so, to trouble yourself.'

'Aren't you a wounded man, God help us? Come on and we'll see if we can't hobble back to the road.'

And she's strong at his side and more or less carries him hopping but poorly to the sea-wall and the tarred road and fetches a lift for him off of a car heading back into the town. She puts him in the car but doesn't get in herself.

'Thanks, Mr Murphy,' she says to the driver, and it doesn't surprise him that she knows him, she probably knows everybody, because of her beauty. And away he goes with her blouse about his foot and yet the drops of blood venturing out on to the sandy floor of Mr Murphy's Ford motorcar. But Mr Murphy is blithe enough and with her instructions no doubt ringing in his head drives Eneas to the public nurse, driving nimbly by clutch and brake, like a dancer, like a dancer. The roads and the town slide by, and Eneas is indifferent to his foot.

'You wouldn't know that girl's name, by any chance, would you?' he says.

'Vivienne,' says Mr Murphy, 'Roche's daughter, the stone-mason.'

'Roche's, over by the old bridge?'

'That's it.'

'Sideburns...'

'Aye...'

A little cup of silence gratefully drunk.

'You'll be contacting her again, I suppose,' says Mr Murphy pleasantly.

Eneas says nothing but his blood, so busy and disturbed of late, rushes into his ears.

'Just to thank her, of course,' says Mr Murphy mercifully.

'Yeh, yeh,' says Eneas. 'Surely.'

They're not far now from bandages and hooks. Mr Murphy stops the Ford and gets out to open the other door for Eneas.

'I'll go in and fetch the nurse for you,' says Mr Murphy, 'and we'll help you in together. You'd be too much for me on my own.'

But it was nothing to that girl against the rock, to that Vivienne Roche herself whose father cut the stone for the new bridge this side of Enniscrone. He knows that about her but little else. Roche the stonemason is a well-known figure about the town, a man with sideburns on him like a shire's blinkers. He keeps greyhounds and would be racing them all over the place, Dublin even, Harold's Cross even, the premier track. And he put in that bridge good, and a good solid bridge it is, from the day of finishing to the end of doom no doubt it will stand, a monument to Roche and his mighty sideburns. That's what he knows, because any fool knows Roche the stonemason. But nothing else. Except, she has a body warm as a stove. And eyes with little glints in them, little scraps of jewels like the stones out of engagement rings that people might have lost swimming on the strand when the cold water shrinks their fingers.

'All right,' says Eneas. 'Thank you.'

'All right,' says Mr Murphy.

'Tell us,' says Eneas, 'before you go. Where would I buy a decent blouse?'

'Well, I don't know like,' says Mr Murphy for all the world as if it was spuds he just said.

'Man to man,' says Eneas. 'Any ould blouse, if you don't know a good shop.'

'Would a fella try Greaney's, in Mill Lane?'

'I don't know. Would he?'

'He might.'

'I'll drop in there so.'

'Greaney's might do the trick.'

'Rightyo,' says Eneas.

'Ah sure, yes,' says Mr Murphy, pausing to make sure Eneas has no more to say, then turning softly from him.

*

He doesn't know if he is courting or wooing or what, he knows well he has not the freedom to court and woo. Certainly he knows it. Nevertheless he prospers in his purchasing of a blouse, presents it to her, brings her the next week up the steps between the dark green hedges of the Gaiety cinema, only half praying that he is not seen, the adventure of it bridging the great gap that fear has made in him, as if bridge-building was her talent too. And near the whispers of the little stream, by the old bridge, at the pillar of her father's gate, she gives him a mighty kiss. She takes his face in her hands like a farmer's wife lifting a swede in pride from the earth and plants her mouth on to his and in the same moment sucks the life out of him and forces the life into him. Or so he tries to settle the matter later, going home himself like a mechanical man, upright, young, but deeply shaken.

*

He is left alone in this fearful happiness all through the mid-winter. There is great fighting in the country now worse than ever but the new song is the hints of peace in every report, just as Jonno said. He wonders how Jonno has been such a prophet, but then Jonno resides in that world. He wonders also does Jonno ever wake sudden in the morning and feel for a second a doubt or a guilt for what he does? Or is he so certain and firm in his truths? Maybe so. O'Dowd is clearly the leader of the town and is sometimes seen going out in a car into the countryside like a general, with his captains about him. There is a military air over Sligo and the barracks is teeming with the real soldiers. Astonishing stories of the ongoing reprisals hurt or enthral the citizens, depending on their allegiances. O'Dowd is not so afraid of being known for what he is, maybe now he wants people to know, in preparation for the tremendous days of freedom just ahead. So Eneas thinks. Eneas is in a position to know because he receives a letter from O'Dowd, signed right enough only with one initial, but who else could it be? And clearly the writer had no fear of any agency in the current state of things to accuse him of the writing of it, or a fear indeed that Eneas had anyone to show it to, or would. It is a succinct, businesslike letter, that arrives normally in the King's post.

A chara,
It would be my opinion that the best for you would be at the present juncture to attend to the instructions of your former friend Mr Lynch. The nature of these instructions you understand, they having been communicated to you in the proper manner on a date of which you are well aware. In the interval since this instruction that came to you from the highest sources, it has pained us greatly to see no furtherance of the task or commitment to it, and we wish to absolve you from your

reluctance in the first instance and urge you by obligation of your position as a man living under sufferance of the council of Sligo, to immediately and without further delay carry out the order as posited to you in good faith and honesty by Mr Lynch. The man we speak of is an utmost enemy of the Irish people, as you are yourself in the dereliction of this task. An eye for an eye and a tooth for a tooth. Please to understand that we are very aware of your present conduct with an Irish woman to whom you have no right in your present cloud of disgrace. And we will take measures to rectify this situation and also in the event of your ignoring this order fulfil as heretofore promised the intent of your place on the list of enemies.

Signed, by order, O.

Eneas sketches in his head various replies to this letter, some of them long and pleading, and in moments of defiance, abrupt and dicey, such as, *No can do*, *yours M*. But he sends nothing because when he searches out a pencil and paper in his Mam's cluttered drawer, the image of O'Dowd rises up against him like one of those pagan schoolmasters at school who were the Deans of Discipline and could break the bones in a boy's hand with sixpences sewn into the leather strap. And though he is a man himself, there is something about O'Dowd that stymies him, that stops him in a queer mud, something in the square set of O'Dowd, the confidence and how he bears down on you like a priest. Fear is the best name for it. So he sends nothing because his hand will not write. In a strange way he does not want O'Dowd to view his poor writing-hand, and know that he is an ignoramus and a fool.

*

Time is diminishing of course for reprisals, because peace will necessitate peaceful manners. It's not just by this letter that Eneas suspects one last great round of killing, because the papers are full of such matters every day. Scores must be settled, and he supposes it is a measure of O'Dowd's hurry and even desperation that such a letter has been written. He senses some dreadful door being not so much closed against him as closed on top of him. All is dark and bad within. The worst of the letter is not the renewed threat of death but the mentioning in such a context of Viv. That is the true hand of power and doom, threatening to reach in and cancel the ground of his love.

7

HE IS STANDING THERE CRYING in his dancing-suit on the beach at Strandhill where his father has realized his grand ambition and established a little corrugated dance-hall beside the waves. And such moody waves they are famously, often so fierce and high that children are kept locked in the daytime cars as if the beach were plagued by hungry lions. Great winds have come in from the Atlantic that once he knew so well, all afternoon, and now the sea is poised in the ruins of its own ruckus. The sun throws long golden arms out each side like an Indian idol, making the richest path of gold in answer across the hurt waves that he has ever seen. He stands there crying in his dancing suit. Jonno's prophecy has come to pass. Freedom. The lights of the dance-hall touch out on to the wet tar where the big Fords and the baby Austins are gathered, with their head-lamps left on to help the arrivers on foot. The little breeze freshens under the skirts of the women in the half-dark and just rearranges the hairdos slightly, and the men have oil in their short hair and they think of themselves as being in America. They think of themselves as in America and the sun flounders a moment and blunders down, and a redness different to the first redness rises up and spreads about generally and even seems to tinge the very iron of the upper cloud and sits in black glimmers on the big curved mud-guards of the Fords.

Eneas hears the laughter over at the motorcars but he sees and thinks he understands something about the sun, and though it is dark or darker now, he cannot stay in Sligo if he is to live. Not because he has done things he regrets but because he has done things that they would not forgive him for, most of those men within, dancing with their girls. If they knew, and shortly he supposes everyone will know. O'Dowd will tell everyone, for now O'Dowd has the opportunity to say what he likes, and be what he wants to be. For this is the famous day of freedom, freedom for Ireland. Eneas has not much time left as a sort of guilty innocent in Sligo. The dancers are dancing so hard the narrow dance-hall is echoing like a drum. It's exhilarating in spite of everything! And he remembers the row his brother Young Tom put up when his mother wouldn't let him come out to the dance in the cars because he's still just too young. And Young Tom wild to get in among the girls and be up on the platform with his father, playing all the tunes his father has bestowed on him. But his mother is law enough to halt him where he is back in the house in John Street. Eneas wishes it was only the simple word of his mother that troubled his own ease. He wishes it was simple like that. And not the collective wish of all those young men within in his father's dance-hall with the folds of corrugated iron to beat the elements. Those men and their girls, excited no doubt by the news from London, and the great mass of them in the night of seeming victory overwhelmed by this untouchable, untastable, unknowable almost, sense of free-dom. For Collins has gone out in his fierce boots and wrested something from the arms of the British that they have held there so jealously for so long. Some are saying the phrase seven hundred years, and even if there are mutterings here and there in pockets about the shortcomings of this treaty, nevertheless on this night an elixir of freedom has invaded their hearts and they are united in a rushing, a tide, a sunset of freedom. Nothing has changed except the news, the grains of sand on the beach are the same, the moon that will establish herself after the disaster of the sun setting will be the same. Freedom is a grand drink for the young. Up in the dark town maybe, definitely, there are more vociferous mutterings, angry shouting, a sense of something far more invasive than freedom, of bitterness and hurt, betrayal – but here in the narrow realm of the young, Eneas understands well enough the jubilation and the wildness inside the hall. He knows from the manner in which the newly arrived greet each other under the lights of the portal that the excitement is general. He feels like a spy under the pall of night. Therefore he alone weeps. He can be neither happy nor bitter at the news. It is not news for him, he cannot walk across to the lights, the word freedom playing on his lips, and smile at his fellow countrymen and women. It is not to be. He knows it.

But he may weep. He is one of the fearing men. He supposes there must be others like him all over Ireland, the boys of the black-lists. Having seen the wickedness done and lived through it and seen men killed and one man murdered at his very side and lost his friend into the bargain he cannot stay in a place he can call home. He will ask Viv to come with him, if she likes. He must be wandering as a displaced man and wandering and never coming back and always maybe be telling strangers of his love for Sligo and never seeing Sligo again or taking her in his arms again, never seeing her gold and blooded suns again, never hearing the laughter of these dancers, that mean all of three bob each to his father and the girlfriend free in. He weeps tears and he supposes the salt sits in them from the blown tide.

He will go in to dance tonight all right, lost in the dark mêlée, but then he will pack his case and be a wanderer. His mother must make of it what she will, he cannot help it. Maybe his father will be knocked sideways for a bit, but a tuneful man like him cannot be lonesome long. Of course, he knows in the next breath this is not true, his father will be grieving, grieving. And these, the men and women of his own time, they will let him be for tonight because they are surprised by freedom and don't know what he is. He has lost the love of his fellow people and maybe he should term himself an outcast instead of a wanderer. A wanderer is a romantic thing like someone in a western picture at the Gaiety or the Savoy. A wanderer is someone you might like to be after watching a western and walking back down Wine Street with mysterious gunsmoke in your head or traipsing past the Priory depending on where the picture was showing. Jesus, but going up between the clipped hedges to the doors of the Gaiety was a thrilling pastime right enough on a Friday. It would be world enough for anybody, and some ordinary work between.

He knows there is a scattering of other souls like his own, shocked and fearful in their shoes, and he expects they are hiding in their homes and he would not have come out himself in his dancing clothes but that it is his own father's hall and Jack's car brought them, his own brother's car, and this has allowed him to stand here on the beach at the very threshold of heaven. A Ford motorcar is a magical thing in the night with the spraying lamps against the pitch road and the smell of metal and perfume under the clothy roof.

His sister Teasy spent the whole fortnight of the nego-
tiations on her knees in her bedroom, praying for Collins,
praying like that at the age of – twelve, was she, was she as
much as that? – and it had infuriated him but at the same
time fascinated him, such peculiar piety all mixed up with a
big man she had never met nor seen. It was not Jesus Christ
that Collins was by any means, a man with thousands of
murders to his account. Eneas knew the figures, he had
scanned them day by day and week by week in the station
in the old days of his employment. He had gone out as was
his duty to carry back bodies and try to work out the
manner of their deaths. He had carried a number of his own
companions, mostly country lads or small town lads like
himself, dead to the station house. Somehow for Teasy it
was all mixed up with the rotten pictures in the cathedral
and the gold on the altar and the sewing that had gone into
the priests' vestments at the back. He still believes he had
the right to work, to take a wage, to put himself against the
task, even policing. In his heart he believes he has shown
courage in his chosen trade. Part of him still hopes he was a
good policeman. And he knows he's a fool to think anything
of the sort. Oh, what use was it all in the upshot now that
this thing was achieved? No earthly use to him anyhow.
Certainly no use to the dead. Perhaps it could not be helped.
Perhaps his tears were for a reason he couldn't name.
Perhaps somewhere in his tears there was a pride, a defiance,
a love. But he has said these things to himself a thousand
times, over and over like the very moil and tumbrel of the
waves, pulled and shaken by the moon.

Viv is coming towards him in her blue dress, the one she
showed him in the Café Cairo that very afternoon. A
Chinesy pattern she called it, slipping it out of its flimsy

paper and showing him the delicate colour of it, the wings of bluebirds he thought hinted at, softly, and indeed he had been glad to tell her, to declare to her, it was lovely, and it was. Finan's gave it to her for twenty-three shillings if he remembers rightly, no bargain there. His mother is always severe about Finan's because they are a Jewish family and in her open opinion, call her a Christian if you liked, the Jews had crucified Christ Himself in the old days of the Romans, they were all in on it. Eneas had sailed with men that were English and Jewish, Portuguese and Jewish too, or met such men in the ports, that he perhaps romanticized because they were different, like Americans were different somehow. A Jewish man should never let himself be at ease among the blasted Christians, that was clear, or he would regret it, if the knife in his back gave him time. Finan's is the best shop in town and his mother finds the prices beyond her, and indeed the atmosphere in the shop itself, that is the impetus behind her old fiddle-playing. You do not get a bargain there but you get quality instead. The Midletons and all the other Protestants from the houses with names shop there avidly. Thornhill, Rathedmond, Merville, Ardmore, Forthill ... His mother detests them all, and all their ways. She thinks the Protestants have cloven feet. But if they have, they put lovely shoes over them, as a rule. Of course there are always the lost Protestants, the fallen ones with no money or land or vocabulary, to put a balance on it. No stranger sight.

Some of the excitement among the matrons of the town at Collins's achievement was due to the fact that it made them all now as good as the Protestants after a fashion. And you didn't even have to talk like them now. As a man that has sailed about a bit and seen other worlds and dearly felt the pull of America for instance he cannot share in such a view, leaving aside even the strictures of his recent occupation. No doubt he is a small man, but nevertheless there are vistas of foreign ports and sea-roads unknown to the stay-at-home, that stand to him, and at least give him *more* wrong ideas than others might have, blowing about in the noggin. But weren't they certain times, those sailing days, certain, romantic and far off.

Viv comes across to him in her Chinesy dress. She has a good inkling of what a good dress can do for her, and though all humans look the better for finery, she looks now like a blessed film-star, like your woman Lillian Gish all flame with white light crossing the dark screen. Viv crosses the bright screen created by his father's lights and the huge penumbras of the night grown black about them. Her shoes clack a little on the bleak surfacing of the promenade, with that same slight breeze in the blue dress.

He turns his head sadly and watches her approach with all the love of a condemned man. Because he must be a wanderer now he knows. He will ask her but he does not think that she will go. She's no dark person. She would not be suited to travelling poorly, living under a poor light. He has not questioned her liking for him, for fear of destroying the miracle with stupid questions. At any rate it's not explicable because he is a fool to himself of some sort, and she is really an admired individual in Sligo. He knows this because he has seen her walking in the streets at her ease, at her great and deserved ease.

It is overwhelming to him all the same to look at her as if for the last time. She has hard angles to her, softened by her shapeliness. Her shoulders especially are hard against him sometimes like something made of metal. Then all her breast is soft naturally enough, and her backside is delightfully soft. He admires her character, her breasts and her backside, immeasurably. He worships them. When she dances, the peculiar hardness and the peculiar softness are united, as she turns for the vivid dance.

'Eneas, darling,' she says, quiet enough, confident he is listening and watching. The high mound of drifted sand, that the spot has got its name from he supposes, rises behind them like a child's sketch of a mountain. The dark is blistered by the few holiday shacks dotted here and there, the lamps lit, the holidaying kids of the world abed.

'Eneas, darling, are you cold there?'

'No,' he says, 'Viv, dear, no, I am warm enough. Is your own stole enough to keep yourself warm down here by the waves?'

'Yes,' she says.

'I watched the sun going down,' he says, 'that's all. It was grand to see it. It's good, Strandhill, you know. Maybe not for rich people so much. I like to get out here, dance in the old fella's place . . .'

'I know,' she says, and takes an arm, crinkling the material, and stands by him, holding his thick arm with both her small hands. 'Ah, we've all played here as children and known each other and thrown sand at each other and feared the waves and I thought I'd miss all that terrible but truly, Eneas, it's lovely too to be grown and all and able to go to the dances.'

'Isn't it?' he says.

'Oh, if I ever left Sligo I would surely dream of Strandhill and the dance-hall, that old corrugated iron thing I suppose but on certain nights as glamorous as – what's the name of the place in America where they make the pictures?'

'California,' he says, like a song, Cal-i-forn-i-ay.

'Yes,' she says.

'Oh yes,' he says. 'Yes, sometimes – it is that.'

'And,' she says, 'Eneas, though I do love to hear you talk, kiss me, will you, Eneas, of your kindness?'

'Of my kindness?' he says, laughing, and he stoops his mouth to hers.

'It's a big night for Ireland,' she whispers, quickly.

'Apparently,' he says, quicker, and they kiss. They know each other's ways thoroughly and they kiss well. She's a cruel hand at forcing her tongue into his mouth slowly, cruel. He gets dizzy now answering her chatty kiss. They stop the kiss then and stand there forehead to forehead and by Christ, the Christ of Sligo, he would love to lie her in the nook of the sand decently but the dress, the dress. He doesn't want to destroy the dress. It is their emblem tonight, this night of freedom after seven hundred years of British – what's the word they like to use? – occupation, domination, something along those lines. Perhaps there is truth in it, a truth he has never considered. He can tell nothing from anything any more, there are no signs, no means to nose your way along the roads. Suddenly he tastes the fear in his gob like a leak of repeated food. Her dress of blue and freedom for Ireland. For himself, his prick is as stiff as a sea-stone. He wants her. It is all madness. And they have lain down together often, but he doesn't want to destroy her dress and indeed there is plenty of time, plenty of time, after the dance. Now he feels light-headed, inclined to laugh. And he would not like to place the bile of his fear into her swimming mouth. Fear they say has a smell, a stench. Her hair smells like roses and dogs, her father breeds greyhounds for the track at the edge of town, up the lake road, by the old bridge. Jesus Christ, they're young enough to have ten children if they wished, there'd be acres of years ahead if they were to marry. Acres, acres, time, plenty of it. My God, my God.

'Viv,' he says, halted of a sudden, sober, his boots solid in the blowing sand. 'I think all in all I have to leave Sligo.'

'Why so, love?'

'Truth is, they won't let me stay now. I can't see how they would.'

'Who, Eneas?'

'All these fellas that are happy now, that are in control now, as of this day, O'Dowd the auctioneer and the like, and others.'

'Why would they want you gone?'

'Because of my time in the peelers.'

'You did nothing wrong there.'

'I know it. But they'll make a simple story of nothing. It's a very dark matter. I'm kissing you here and wanting you as much as always and, I was going to ask you to come with me, but sure I know you couldn't do that.'

'Well – that would be a hard thing right enough.'

'Of course.'

His boots exist, and if there is such a thing as a feeling heart it's down in those boots now. He's astonished at himself, the racket of stupid despair in him now. The old cauldron of it. What did he expect her to say? How could she leave all the people she knows and that admire her and her father and his dogs and stones?

'I'll talk to my father about it,' she says then, and it's the first time she ever said a thing like that, something a child might say, a child's notion. And it's the force of the times that such an independent person of some magnificence should find herself saying such a thing.

'I tell you, girl, I never did anything wrong in the peelers, and if they say I did, please to know I didn't.'

Now he can't even speak, and she holds him snug against her, and she's crying, it's a long odd time and strange, and at last they go into the dance-hall together, passing from the deep inky lights of the shore into the fast lights and dresses and suits all a-mingle under the corrugated roof, and over them all blows a little flag, dancing to the dark tune of the night breeze, a fancy of his Pappy's, with 'Plaza' emblazoned proudly on it.

8

SHE SPEAKS TO HER FATHER and her father the stone-
mason doesn't think much of it. In fact he thinks it is the
worst thing he could ever imagine for his beloved daughter.
And when she tells Eneas he agrees in his very heart, even
though his feeling for her lies there like a nesting bird.

He talks to his own Mam about it and is surprised not so
much by what she says about Viv, but by the sudden
greyness of her face when he says he is going.

'Look,' she says, 'I'll pop on me hat and go down to
O'Dowd and sort it out with him. Do you not know that
he's a cousin of yours? His, what would it be, his father's
sister's husband's family were cousins to the Byrnes in some
fashion, I don't know. Anyway, I'll go down to him, yes,
and I'll broach the matter, and see what can't be done for
you, Eneas.'

'Mam, don't do that, don't get mixed up in it. He's a
strange man, a terrible man. He's done things, Mam, that
brings him a bit beyond being a cousin or whatnot. He's a
leaner, Mam, you know what I mean? He's talking to you
and you feel like something hard as a rock is pressing down
on you.'

'But, Eneas, that Viv Roche is a grand girl, a lovely girl,
perfect for you. Oh, Eneas, when I seen you going out with
a girl like that, taking her up to the Gaiety, Eneas, a princess,

oh, and lovely people. Not tradespeople at all, sure the father there is almost an engineer, a civil engineer, building fine bridges and the like for the town. When I saw you with her on your arm, I was content, I was happy as a mother. I couldn't ask for a finer daughter.'

'I know, Mam, only too well.'

'Aye, well, son, we'll see what happens, and sure, Christ, aren't these new times, peaceful times, and all the hope that there is in the country. The King of England himself has shaken Collins's hand and wished him and the country well. New times, son. Hold your hour now the minute.'

Well, he holds it. And the upshot of it is, his mother despite his word does make a sortie out to talk to O'Dowd, and O'Dowd is very polite and pleasant with her, disavowing all understanding of her visit. He assures her there is no danger to her son from his quarter, nor indeed from the new dispensation generally. That all slates are wiped clean, and he has never heard of any case of a man being black-listed or executed in Sligo. That her son is free to go about as he wishes, and when his mother mentions Viv Roche, O'Dowd says he has no opinion of the matter as he does not know the girl, but that her father is certainly a very fine Sligoman and a first-class greyhound breeder and a patriot, and he even goes so far as to say he wishes his cousin well. And Mrs McNulty comes away with a high opinion of Stephen O'Dowd.

But it's just poison to the blood of her son when she tells him. To disavow all knowledge of black-lists and executions is the crux, and though she is a hero to him in the matter he wishes she had not gone.

And heartily wishes it even more so the next day when he goes down to the house by the old bridge and tries to gain entry. For the house is closed against him. And Mr Roche steps out to him right enough and tells him some fellas have been in their dark coats and have talked to him seriously about history and right, and of how a man might prosper in Sligo and how a man might not. And poor Viv was approached, he says, on Main Street and told to keep away from traitors or she would have her hair cut very short for herself. And the man on Main Street had called her some terrible names and she was mightily upset about it and is inside in the house like a rag, a wrung-out rag. And her father with the softness in his voice quite vanished tells Eneas to be gone and to come that road no more.

*

Truth to tell the effect of this is worse on Eneas than a threat of death. To be separated from Viv for ever, even though he knows he must be separate from her and could have decided that himself even if he had been let alone, douses the flame of the old life in him. He is a new man and not so good a one, he believes. And no matter how much he goes about the strands and weeps and shivers and even curses his own God, he will not mend into the shape he was before. Sligo's feeling about him is now complete and clear, and he should be off immediately. But somehow he lingers. He's sort of killed anyway, already. Someone will come he supposes to do the task official-like. In the meantime he's like one of them foxes, crushed and battered by the wheel of a car somewhere out on a dark night road.

*

It's amusing to him almost that in the end they send Jonno, his own lost friend Jonno, of the apples, to sort him out. Of course, he is the obvious choice. Oddly enough too they have waited till the summer. They have been too busy killing each other to bother with him. The civil war that followed the so-called peace is eating Ireland. He has heard that Jonno is a most boisterous hero now, excitable, passionate, and dangerous. He understands that tincture, that suggestion of madness. He feels it himself in this course of his own private war. Craziness, indifference, weeping, euphoria. Endless. In all the months of hanging on, he has been amazed at his indifference to his own death or his own survival. He has been almost bizarrely at peace, if everyone else has not. And Sligo, the tinny life of the town, the swift kids in the streets, the toiling trucks, has seemed to him unchanged by this murderous freedom. It is as if somewhere, maybe on the outskirts, or in some secret town field, there is a bull-ring, where every day a man is slaughtered, or a number, and you can read about it in the *Sligo Champion* with your tea. You can read about it, but never see a body or hear a shot. And yet there are legions of the dead now, or at least a battalion. Surely, just the same as England, this useless war will take away all the good young men, or the hardiest, and leave only the astutest killers. Those that have stalked most expertly, murdered most adroitly, the very dancing men of murder.

Jonno comes to him in the little shed in the garden at Finisklin. Everyone knows he is there, he's not hiding exactly, but he does not wish to bring disaster on his family by staying in John Street. He does not wish to bring the spirit of the bull-ring to John Street, no, so he has set himself up with a truckle bed and a table, and though a certain wildness is creeping into the once immaculate garden, it's a pleasure to sit at the door of the shed in the summer sun and ruminate and drink tea and not mind. Even having no work does not torment him as once it might well have. Perhaps this time is a time between other times, there's a word for that, he struggles to find it, an official word he once saw used by his sergeant at the station. Interregnum – yes, yes, a beautiful word. A time between kingdoms does it mean? If so, it is apt.

When he sees the hollyhocks struggling up despite the rash of weeds and tall grass, he smiles to himself remembering Tuppenny Jane. Those times, not of innocence but of long ago, are marvels to him now, his amusements. Only the day before he has astonished himself by realizing he is only, by the clock, twenty-two years old. He feels like an ould fella. He feels like a fabled wanderer of old and he hasn't left the spot yet. He has not endured shipwreck maybe but maybe he has – the shipwreck of freedom so general and welcomed in the land.

Jonno comes to him. Jonno is more kempt now, more groomed, more allied to the pictures, more strange than Eneas remembers him – not more haunted as he would expect, but more buoyant, more up in the waves, more airy, more terrible. Spick and span like a new knife, even more than before. It is afternoon, soaked with a wet heat after the night rain, the grasses melting, and Eneas sees Jonno just the second he comes in the old wrought-iron gate and steps on to the cinder path. Not a weed has dared trespass upon those his father's cinders, certainly. The poor hollyhocks are having to keep their tresses above the fronds of rich, wild grass. There is a battle on between his father's handiwork and he supposes the reckless handiwork of God, a more savage gardener.

It could be miles instead of yards that Jonno has in front

of him, sun-darkened tough dapper Jonno. It's not the parley he will have with him that bothers Eneas, but that Jonno has come at all. There was a time when Jonno would rather have stuck pins in his eyes than stalk up that garden path. Even now he fancies he can see the effect of the lead in his old friend's legs. Possibly. They have reached this point because they have been faithful to different masters, and lacking in faith in each other. Many times secretly in his own private mind he has kind of laughed at Jonno for the seriousness of his beliefs. And here he is now invested with a fledgling power. People are choosing who they want in Sligo and who they want out. If Jonno were to draw a pistol and carry it up the path pointing at Eneas, how could he be surprised? It would only be natural. Only months before, he spotted Jonno marching with some others of Collins's crowd, drilling you might say up Main Street. Is this Sligo Main Street? It is, and the farther you go the meaner it gets. Then they were shouting and wheeling about on the Showgrounds, causing grief to the football players trying to train. They had been a joke really, put against a real army, but there is no one of the correct sense of humour to laugh now. The pity is, yes, even as the new man he is now, and after everything that has transpired, he does love his friend Jonno, and truly it hurts him to see the yards of the cinder path covered. He loves him. A madness. Because it does not suit the present world. He looks at this man approaching who has said all manner of terrible things to him, and he feels a love for him. And now he smiles like a dog and sticks his boots out from his bit of a chair. The dust from under the chair where the rain didn't reach folds back on his bootleather like pieces of lace. Jonno is clearly surprised by his ease and smile and has a few moments of blankness, where the dark look he has maybe engineered coming out from the town seems to lighten and evaporate curiously.

'Do you have a gun, Eneas?' he says.

'No,' says Eneas. 'Do you?'

'You're not so badly fixed out here,' says Jonno, who always admired a camp. 'Have you any ould tea? I'm parched. It's a long haul in this weather along the sea road. Thank God for the bit of rain last night.'

The tone of it amazes Eneas, considering the nature of their last conversation. You'd swear there was no civil war anywhere, that Eneas had never joined the peelers, and that all was right with the universe, except for the pleasant enquiry after the gun. Clearly Jonno has lost his marbles. So be it. They can be two easy madmen here in his Pappy's old garden. Jonno removes a finely laundered handkerchief from his jacket and smears at the smattering of dust on his forehead. His hatband looks tight and wet. When he removes the hat the hair is bright and jutting. Eneas gives half a snort but not of contempt. He gets up and goes back into the shed and fetches tea for his old pal. Jonno takes the cup and drinks the entire thing in one go like it was beer.

'Tea for thirst,' he says, fond as always of a good saw.

Eneas decides more or less to say nothing.

'Jesus, we had the gas out here in the old days, didn't we, boy?' Jonno stares about the garden busily then lets his stare fall pleasantly on Eneas. Eneas is not interested in a staring match and sits back into the chair. As a matter of fact it is an orange box from Venezuela. He found a broken chair-back behind Hanrahan's public house on the shallow bay, and banged it on to the orange box with a couple of old nails and the heel of his shoe. It isn't a throne but it takes his weight anyway.

'Is there any chance you know why I've come out?' There is a fine element of pleading here, of wanting to be let off his task. Maybe he is tired of killing and the plotting of killing and the going about and the shooting of former comrades in the moil and murder and foolishness of the civil war. Maybe he is a new man also. Maybe not.

'I'd have an inkling all right,' says Eneas, falling into the tone of it quite happily, and rubs the back of his right hand like the schoolmaster Jackson used to years ago. For some reason he remembers that. In fact his head is a riot of flashing memories because Jonno is exciting it. An electric storm. The friendliness of the man delights him and over-whelms him in the same instant.

'Well,' says Jonno, truly as if he had good news in a way, and he wedges half his arse on the old step of the shed, hitching the trouser leg when he has to bend a knee tightly, he doesn't look in the least comfortable, but he's acting comfortable, at ease, relaxed, a man confident with another man, 'let me tell you, Eneas, there's a section there, let me call it a powerful minority, that were keen as hounds to impose on you immediately the, the, you know what I mean, the old death-sentence, you know, in consideration of the black-list and the fact that you wouldn't go after the Reprisal Man.'

'The old death-sentence. Oh, rightyo.'

'Aye, you know, the chop, the finito, the End.'

'Yeh, yeh, got you. And how would they go about that, as a matter of interest?'

'Send out a few lads, you know, or just the one, like me today – sure you know how it's done. Weren't you a witness often enough to such matters when they were carried out during the—?'

'Murders, like?'

'No, no – I wouldn't call them that. During the struggle for, you know. Military operations, that sort of thing. Reprisals and so on.'

'Aye, aye, Jonno – murders.'

'Act the whiteman, Eneas. You can't call all that murders. Acts of war and such are not murders. A priest would say as much. No. Sure a murder's a mortaller, isn't it?'

Funny to hear the childish word applied so. Mortaller. Jonno is a changed man. The gloom and darkness is gone out of him. His very hesitancy and lightness are deeply inappropriate. Lunatic. He must have seen things, witnessed things, dark things, to be queerly lit so, no doubt.

'I don't remember anywhere in the good book, Jonno, where a directive shall we say from a group of bowsies to kill a man is said to be beyond the borders of murder.'

'Sure what are you talking about? Isn't that our whole point, boy? Aren't you after shooting men yourself, Eneas McNulty? You see? What are you going on about the Bible for? Jaysus, that's rich coming from you, constable.'

'Oh, as you opine, Jonno, I have fired off a few bullets in my time. I didn't hit anyone but I surely tried. Flogging about the countryside in your Ford motorcars and terrorizing bloody everyone. Jaysus, Jonno, a well-aimed bullet would have been too good for some of ye. And as for these present days, God himself couldn't keep up with the goings-on of you.'

Jonno rises up.

'You can't be serious talking like that. Don't you know I'm after pleading for your life. Your fucking life, Eneas. I'm after pleading for it. There's Stephen O'Dowd was rearing, rearing he was, to come out himself along the fucking Finisklin Road and blow your head off. And he could do it. He was very disappointed, Eneas, very disappointed about the Reprisal Man. Because, it embarrassed him. He wrote you a nice letter, the letter of a gentleman, and because you are a bowsie and an ignorant man you didn't reply. He's not a man used to getting no reply. And more to the point, you didn't act. It wouldn't have been anything to you. Hah? But you couldn't do it. You couldn't even try to do it, which would have been something to be going on with. I don't like the killing. It's for the sanitation of it, the new country. You know? There's a load of rats being killed now quick, executed, you know, quick and quiet and official-like, and there was an RIC officer done just last night in the midlands. Shot at his own gates, the bastard, in front of his fucking wife. For mistreating prisoners in Dublin, one night they were held without coats or food in the forecourt of the Rotunda hospital during the fight against the British. O'Dowd hates you, man, hates you. By Jesus, twice you were asked, twice. And sending your feckin mother up to him was low, boy, low. It embarrassed him. He hates to be embarrassed. We all do, Eneas. You know? We all hate you. And I pleaded for you because, I don't know why. I hate you. Now, you boy, you see what I'm after doing for you, even though you're a hated man.'

'Ah, it's kind of you, Jonno, it's kind. But, contrariwise, why don't you eff off now down that path and let me alone?'

Jonno's stunned. He wasn't expecting high talk, but he's getting it suddenly. Eneas is taken aback too, bizarrely . . .

The words in his head and his heart are in rebellion against him. It's the word hate from Jonno's mouth that has done something wild to him. Hate. I hate you. *We all hate you.*

'Fine talk to an old friend. From a bloody RIC man. Eneas, what in the name of Jamaica were you thinking of when you joined that shower? I could've found a job easy for you if you'd said.'

'Oh, yeh, killing, like.'

'Jesus, Eneas, it's like I don't know you. I always thought, I always woulda said you were a finer man than this, I woulda. Anyone asking I woulda said. Couldn't you have obliged yourself and your country by going after that feckin Tan? Of course, we'll get him now. He's gone off down to Brazil or somewhere and there'll be lads following him. He won't escape the justice due to him. If it took us fifty years, it wouldn't be too long for us. We'll get him, however long it takes.'

'I'll tell you what it is really feckin annoys me, Jonno, since you've come out so far to see me. It's that you have Viv warned off me goodo. Scared to see me. Terrified. You see, she's that way, Jonno, because your comrades gave their spake to her, Jonno, my hero. A tender woman like that.'

'It was me gave her the spake. I did it. Just like I'm out here with you now, giving you the spake. Because Eneas, this is how you have me, ever trying to prove myself to O'Dowd, after you went and fecked everything up for me. The bloody friend. Your friend McNulty, that's what O'Dowd always says to me. And I'm tired of it. I want him to stop saying it. I warned her off you. She was lucky she heeded me. Yeh, well, Eneas, no use looking like you're going to burst, we'd shoot her too if we didn't like the going about of her.'

This more or less ends the conversation for Eneas. He is giving a good stare back at Jonno. He doesn't know where the anger came from, well, he knows from where, but how he let the wild words rise up he doesn't know. You need a good cage for anger in a corner like this. He knows well it's a corner. A serious corner. Jonno himself is stuck for good words now, Eneas can see him beefing himself up a bit to say something good and vital, strong, ultimate, authoritative. He laughs suddenly in his familiar manner to think that once as a little lad he longed to call Jonno's name and fight him for the wild hell of it and be one of the lads to rob the minister's apples, to box the minister's fox. You never knew how things were going to turn out.

'You listen, Eneas, you pack your little bag because you're finished here now.'

Jonno seems very distant now to Eneas, unimportant. It's odd. And Jonno's backing awkwardly down the cinders like Eneas would go for him or something but there's no likelihood in the world that he would. Sure it's Jonno has the gun, he can see it making a hard lump in Jonno's waistcoat. He's a different Jonno now. Fearful almost. Hard to say. Probably more in fear of the words Eneas might say than the deeds he might do.

'You know, Jonno, you should go to California and secure a job in one of them horse operas, you should. Yourself and all the other cowboys of Sligo.'

'Right, right, Eneas,' says Jonno, veritably trembling he must be by the rattle of his hands. 'You think you're calling the tune. Fair enough. You've called it. You come from a family of fluteplayers. By the power vested in me by the council of Sligo . . .'

'Them roadworkers, do you mean, Jonno?'

'By the power,' says Jonno, leaning up the path towards him, lifting at last the weight of his task in the sight of God, spitting the words, 'in-fucking-vested in me, I order you, Constable Eneas McNulty, to quit this town and this district and this country by nightfall of tomorrow night and I put you under pain of fucking death if you do not, my bucko. And O'Dowd says to tell you, sweetie boy, if you step foot back on Irish soil, you're a dead man from that day out, if ever you try to see your people again or your town or your feckin girl or whatever you like, Eneas, we'll kill you. You can get up as early as you like, don't think we didn't know all your movements, we'll have you. And even if you get away from us, we'll follow you, and we'll kill you, and just like that Reprisal Man it don't matter how long it takes us, we'll do it, for the honour of old Ireland and her heroic dead. Got me, boyo? Pain of death.'

'Pain of fucking death. What a way with words.'

But Eneas's heart is sore, very dark and sore. Pain of death, pain of death. Hatred, we hate you, Sligo hates you.

'Go on, then, Jonno, me lad. Tell your comrades how you did with me. You can have your Sligo to yerselves. I won't linger. Sure there's nothing here for me now. You can tell them that. You can tell them that I said they were a pack of fuckers.'

'Right so,' says Jonno, in a lighter tone, inappropriate as ever. He has reached the gate and maybe he thinks things have gone worse than badly. Who can tell? Not Eneas. And he knows Jonno knows that his crowd wouldn't have touched him with a bargepole if he'd wanted to join the great revolutionaries, because of his stint in the Merchant Navy. Or he'd have had to shoot some poor bastard even then to prove his loyalty to the heroic ideals they cherished.

Jesus. There was going to be a lot of shooting for them to do now. Maybe Jonno didn't fancy shooting his old pal at this bridge of life, like your man, Ferdia, and the other man, Cuchullain, in the old story. Maybe he was sent out to shoot him, with the little gun in his waistcoat. Jesus, a lot of bodies in old Ireland right enough. Jonno lingers at the gate for a moment. As if in two minds, as if having second thoughts. Or maybe just to shoot him now there and then and be done with it.

'You didn't leave anything behind, Jonno? Like your hat – or your feckin honour?'

So he is gone then Jonno and it is all done. It is the high road out of here for him now. Pain of death. There is nothing humorous about it. No. He sits on at the door of his father's old shed with the ruined vista of grass and hollyhocks. He shakes his head against some weird laughter that rises in him. Guns, murders, reprisals, friendships in ruins, loves destroyed. What a way to live a life. Now he laughs in his chair. He has to laugh. Pain of death. He wishes he had been more astute with Jonno, and reasonable, but maybe it would have come to the same damn thing. One curse borrows another. It is no use sending a boy to do a man's job and it is no use sending a friend with the phrase pain of death to deliver, certainly.

But he knows that O'Dowd fella only too well, and it disturbs him immensely that O'Dowd has expressed anew, so clearly, so officially, a keenness for his extinction. The proof if proof were needed of his madness was the way O'Dowd had spoken to his Mam. O'Dowd is a mad bastard certainly, an auctioneer and as such a very dangerous person, used to getting his way and highly practised in the arts of the despot. And it would surprise you sometimes that

Collins tolerates men like him when Collins is supposed to be so fair, so normal, so statesmanlike – ruthless maybe, but fair. Many of the police in the old days admired Collins even though they were fighting him but you'd have to be very short of heroes and on half-rations mentally to admire the murdering likes of O'Dowd. Funny to think now that men of O'Dowd's ilk are driving the pony and trap of Ireland. Of course, if you need murders done you have to have murderers to do them, that's plain. And now the true effect of Jonno's words reaches him, strikes him, the vial of darkness opens in his heart, he is fixed and queerly shot by it in the chair made out of an orange box from Venezuela. An asylum, the whole of Sligo is an asylum now.

The hints of summer dark begin to change the old garden. The colour is being robbed out of the hollyhocks. First the lighter blooms are taken, and as the evening goes on minute by minute the darker ones, the purples and inky reds, are vanishing. At the last Eneas himself will softly vanish, softly vanish into the blackened canvas of his father's paradise.

PART TWO

9

IT IS A LONG TIME before he reappears as himself, if he ever does. In the meantime he is crossing the poor sea to England on a cheap ticket in the cattle boat, so called as a measure of the comfort and dignity afforded the emigrants thereon. He has suffered privately, severely, on the late train out of Sligo across Ireland, but despite everything he said goodbye fleetingly to his siblings, getting an unexpected kiss and prayer from Teasy, impregnable and absolute with her fourteen years. The kiss of his Mam and the different kiss of his Pappy both were similar sparks on his face, smouldering there he suspects with eternal intent, and even Young Tom and Jack embraced him uncharacteristically, all angles and bones – at close of day and end of all their own eldest brother. And there was a class of shriving in that moment of leaving, simplifying, a feeling he would have liked to carry with him at least as far as the blowing lights of the station. But it was not to be. In the carriage he dwindled like a spud fallen and forgotten behind the kitchen press. He talked at himself all night, the mails and parcels jostling in the secure van behind him.

Now he lies in the night packet to Holyhead amid the great bunks of three and four men each, the starlight closed to the sleeping minds by the tiers of iron decks. There's a tide of breathing, the different sorts of men a-dream you would think in unity. He watches the fishes of stray lights that wander the inky ceiling. At the rim of his composure wrestled from his hours mumbling on the train, there are Godless monkeys of fright, kept back maybe by the mountainous smell of feet and sweat. Safe among strangers, young, adrift, and in his homeplace hated. He can hear the enormous engine labouring nearby in the metal bowel of the boat. Now and then a passenger passes in the corridor with a lamp, coming down from the crowded halls or the wooden decks, moving across the streaming darkness. The tips of objects in the cabin are illuminated, golden, as if the cabin was a tomb of sorts, with precious swords and bowls put in to help the dead on their journey. But they are only the handles and edges of worn cases, or the metal attachments of workboots strung up on the bunks like onions.

Under the fragments of swimming light he lies close to three other men, sharing the ample bunk, two fellas from Donegal and another lad with a young wife in the women's cabin. The three are pleasantly sleeping, a little curled against each other for peace and warmth, though the cabin is not cold. Perhaps it is that the journey itself is cold, in its nature and necessity. He has a sense somehow of the waters beneath him, with whatever fish are favoured by the Irish Sea toiling, travelling also, and if his fears are Godless, all the same he prays to God that He might be perched above them after all, tremendous and impartial in the enamelled stars. He prays to his God that he might be rescued or, like those decrepit pens they used to find on their desks at the start of each school year, be given a fresh nib. The young husband stirs at his side, turns heavily, and throws a leg over him, and a long arm falls gently across Eneas's breast. He falls deep into sleep, deeper than the sea, down the long narrow well of dreams and explanations. The packet goes on in its bowl of weight, the bothered waves only tipping at, parting for, the iron prow.

*

England suffers the affliction still that brought the Tans to Ireland, there is work to be had almost nowhere, and the flotsam of men and women without employments spreads everywhere, pushed by the shallow sea of need. As he moves from town to town, as much a ghost as any English drifter, he marvels at the condition of the old Promised Land. For an Irishman might affect to hate England and love America, but they are both and were ever equal refuges to him. The towns seem to be rotting at the edges, like lost villages of the West of Ireland. Even the King cannot cure this palsy. The King is much talked of though, as a man suffering in spirit with the forlorn multitudes. He is seen in his dark suits here and there, commiserating, gripping hands, his face furrowing and darkening. He is like a creature going black from being underground, you can see him a little agape and peculiar in the newspaper, should a newspaper happen to blow by your feet. And all the clockwork and rightness of England is hurt and bloodied. And Eneas knows it is the war that did it, England has broken herself for those fields of France.

Maybe he sees England now through his pall of grief, his mantilla of bitterness. Truth to tell, as he sits betimes at some scored table in a charitable hall, listening to the sermons of sin and death and taking his stew, he is not a singing man, nor a light man. At such times the metal of himself is being beaten and bent over the anvil like something a blacksmith is trying to straighten. And surely the farmer will return in the evening to find the task uncompleted, impossible.

Still, out on a white lane, between lines of hops on their bulky poles, the metal suddenly comes now and then right, and the sheer tincture of beauty dropped into his darkened blood delights him, jimmies him up, makes him smile, alone, hated, but human on the ravelling road.

*

It's Grimsby, pretty far north right enough, where he finds a berth of sorts. He goes there by no design, because it is the next town merely, though as he has walked so long among the fields he has had a hankering for the sea, as any Sligoman might. Because a Sligoman misses the garnish of sea-salt on his skin.

First thing into the district, he takes up a position on the long stony beach that seems to fly in a massive arc out of the town, going away at speed from it into the unknown distance. He's pulling with his teeth at a decent enough bit of dried fish that a scrawny woman gave him over the wind-burnt castellation of her hedge, in a sea-garden with a corrugated house thrown up among the ratty dunes. And he spreads his legs quite happily, looking at the dun-coloured beach and the long granite lid of the sky pulled over everything, the black roofs, the small arms of the fishing harbour, the wide long ribbons of current in the mauve river. The fish he supposes is a mere sand dab, small, salty, bony, but it's fizzing and churning on his tongue, it's a pleasure. Like many sayings of his Mam, 'hunger is a good sauce' is proved again. Hunger is a good sauce, Your woman's a horse for the hard road, There's no hearth like your own hearth. They were almost songs to her, as much as the Irish jigs and American jazz of his Pappy. His belly bubbles and growls. And surely he's in need of ten of those dabs, with the waste of flesh on his bones. He's a big man a touch rubbed out by ordinary hunger.

Some of the stones of the beach are very small and round and green, a puzzle to him. He finds he can squeeze these queer pebbles with his fingers, they are not right pebbles at all. Indeed they are like little classroom globes strewn all over the beach, as far as he can see, all land and no water marked on them, some tremendous version of the world repeated eternally. He wonders are they stars fallen on to Grimsby, or maybe more likely that manna of the Bible story, to feed the wandering tribes. By Jaysus, he sees, they are peas. Mere peas. Placed there in such a multitude, evenly shared out among the true stones. Well, there's an ould fella creeping along the beach, keeping to a narrow band of sand where probably the tide turns, and Eneas hails him.

'How are you doing, mister?' he says.

'Day,' says the man, his share of thin hair as sere as the marram grass.

'Listen, tell us,' says Eneas, 'do you know at all why there's them peas all over the strand?'

'Eh?' says the man.

'The feckin ould beach is covered with peas, do you not see them?'

'Ah, yes,' says the man, 'of course, that's the factory.'

'The what?'

'The pea factory up the river. Don't the leavings of it come spilling down here? We're so used to them we don't see them.'

'All right,' says Eneas.

'You with the boats?' says the man.

'No, no,' says Eneas. 'I walked in. Do you think there'd be work in the factory so?'

'No, but, one of the boats might take you, if you knew boats. It's cold black work they do out just near the ice, they're gone for weeks at a time, poor men. Daresay you might get something with them, if you don't mind the hardness of it.'

'I'll go down and have a talk with someone so,' says Eneas.

'Why not,' says the man. 'Sooner you than me. Good day to you.'

'I'll see you,' says Eneas, in the lingo of his own place.

*

And that's how work is got in those days he supposes. And the Captain, Simon Cousins, takes him on as an experienced man, though the Captain has no sleek boat that would entice a boy to America, as in the time of Galveston, only a broken-lunged one-masted fishing boat that saw paint maybe when the old dead queen was young. And as the ould man had said, it is queer black work, but for shillings and grub. And a bed bucketing about, way over above Scotland near the ice-locked shores of Greenland, is better than a rainy hedge. And with the stretch of meat and fishes grilled on deck and such, the muscle goes back soon enough in the manner of the youth he is, and he is strong and good for the work, working the distant herring, away with the weather and the weeks. Simon Cousins is a man without much of talking and Eneas suspects that the man says little because his head is as empty as a little salt barrel when the haul of stilled herring has its petticoats and lace-caps of salt out of it. And he is glad to learn the ways of those three-week fishermen, the manners of their trade, and their silence.

Grimsby isn't too different from any western seaboard town of Ireland, there's many that go to America when they can, dragging pots and all behind them, and wives. Because the very poor bring everything. And the fishermen come and go, some with their songs, some with their bitter violence, some with their crimes and others with their youth, in the course of the scrappy years that Eneas spends with Simon Cousins, living mostly not two foot from him and gathering in that time no more than a yard of conversation. True enough, the stars over Greenland are so bright they are tiny tears of fire in the sky, and the unseen seals and ice-coloured bears of the flows are dryer than Simon Cousins and Eneas. And that's a thing to engender silence. But when the sea eases and the herring run into the exhausted nets, that is a season for joy of a kind in the blood and the bone of arms hauling and content enough in the frozen North. In time Eneas is master of the shoals and in the manner of a proper fisherman can smell the great designs of herring fanning and spreading under the pitch waters. They are regions where strange things befall them as by right, as by common occurrence. As talk is a scarce commodity, the words that might have been spoken seem to gather in the old brain, like very herring themselves, bright, thin, darting. And Sligo itself seems better described for Eneas, clearer, more tender to him. Out in that immaculate waste world of ice and sea and herring, with the companionable whales and rarely betimes a narwhal nosing past, where animals are black or white and only the moon and the Northern Lights themselves, extravagant and chill and high, are shadows, remembrances of colours, it is possible somehow to hold Sligo in his head, floating, particular. And the hatred his countrymen have for him is a class of signpost, a class of explanation for the ruin of their tenderness. For they are not tender people now. And savage years among a civilized people have done that to them, because when there is murder and murder, the heart is killed like a rat with poison, up on the sill of a farmhouse, panting, trying to cool its burning self. And away in those northern fishing grounds, the outlying fields and farms of Grimsby you might say, with their imaginary fences, he can feel at times something akin to love for Sligo, at least it sits there in his mind, his Mam and his Pappy and his toiling siblings, and all the turbulent citizens, Sligo, Sligo, and it strikes him that any person alive in the world, any person putting a shoulder against a life, no matter how completely failing to do the smallest good thing, is a class of hero. This is a fleeting thought, as temporary as the arc of an albatross in the passionless air, but it is there for a moment, and for another moment, and another. Of course, a person might say it is easy to feel no fear, no hatred, in a district without true land, and maybe so, Eneas allows that, yes. And thrown up again against the shingle of Grimsby, in the narrow adjunct to the Captain's house that is Eneas's land home, lying in the fixed dark, the room rooted on the sandy earth, oh yes, he can feel as much fear and hate as the next man, and lie awake with it spinning and churning there in his addled head, the names O'Dowd and Jonno Lynch heartily and blackly cursed anew. But by the grace of mere time itself or, sometimes he thinks, the peculiar clock of God, whose divisions seem both unending and brief in the same span, he spends a decade and more at that work, in which to catch the cold fish and douse his brain with the solemn rainwater of stars. It is true that such work repeated and repeated, with its circles of journeys and seasons, weaves a pattern as simple as a country bedspread that gives the years the sensation of brevity. If he were going from job to job it might have seemed an epic time! But tucked into this life on the edge of things, the edge of Grimsby, itself an edgy town in the greater world of England, a dozen years is a full, fast river of minutes and months.

And one time, as they are returning from the distant grounds, bearded and tired, Eneas sees a great ship passing to the south, whose name he can almost make out, it goes by so close. And it's not a regular ship taking its known course along the allotted lanes, and as such might be classed a danger to a small fishing vessel, if Simon Cousins and Eneas were so inclined to view it. And indeed Simon Cousins looks very black in the face at the sight of it, and Eneas can sympathize with his anger and distress, but is also more simply amazed by the ship. Because they see it in early morning, a good clear early morning with a cloth of light frost thrown over the little boat, and he can make out clearly lining the rails of the great ship hundreds, maybe thousands of people, looking out silently on every side, port and starboard. And they seem to him dark-clothed and infinitely sober, like prisoners beyond reprieve, like children being ferried far from hearth and happiness. And they take no interest in him, the shadowed man of Sligo looking in astonishment, as if some other picture is fastened over their eyes, bigger and perhaps terrible. And he wonders naturally whither their course is set, and whether they will land somewhere in Scotland, or are going round the ferocious isles of the North. Or maybe will turn southward for Ireland and her benisoned harbours.

*

And back in Grimsby he asks other less silent sailors what that ship might have been, was it a ghost ship well described in stories, or a passenger line on a new and foolhardy route between Europe and America? But he is told nothing about it, and has recourse to giving up a sixpence for a decent newspaper, to see if there might be a clue there. And indeed the *Grimsby Echo* can tell him in its dark print and chaste paper that the ship he has seen holds a strange cargo of Jews being returned to Germany, certain there to be imprisoned as enemies of Christ and country. That no port on God's earth would take them, and that they had lain outside Dublin port and been refused and Southampton, and what affects him strongly, not only had crossed the Atlantic to be refused by the President of America himself, but had anchored not far from Galveston in the Gulf of Mexico, the very heartland of emigrants and lonesomeness. For it is a cargo of hated people, all folk like those Finans of Sligo, with their perfect shop and their weather all about of foul remarks. As a hated man Eneas feels the force of their useless journey. And he thinks of that fella De Valera, now king of Ireland, piously refusing the ship entry, and it makes a racket in his noggin. Oh why exactly he could not say, but surely, he hopes surely, there is a host of other men and women who feel the same storm of disquiet and anger he does, in the mottled lean-to by the Captain's house. And he thinks the sighting of the ship has been a thing of terror lent to him, and he would have taken them all in the Captain's ship like shining herring if he had known, impossible though it would have been. For what is the world without rescue, but a wasteland and a worthless peril? He doesn't need his dreams continuously to see those dark men, dark women, dark children at the rails, because they progress now against the mirror of his mind's eye.

*

Employment ends when Simon Cousins has a rare thought and is thinking to follow not the herring no more but the bits of his family that have taken the ship to America, from the deepwater harbour of Killinghome Creek. Indeed and the herring are a poor show in that year and there is growing talk of the new war coming that will be fought mostly at sea, and Simon Cousins hare-brained or not has no desire to fish among fighting ships. He did not like that great ship of doomed souls bearing eastwards. He and Eneas and some other lads heel up the old boat in the yard above the fishing harbour, against a time when Simon Cousins might tire of walking the pavements of gold in New York and return to fish the darkest waters on God's dark earth. Then there is a curious and wordless party, with silent drinking of good Grimsby ale and a sort of truncated goodbye and fare thee well, with a hand as hard as a turtle placed on Eneas's shoulder, and a brief 'Good man,' briefly spoken.

*

'C' Company Depot
Berkshire

Dear Mam,
Here I am in my uniform writing to you and I hope you have received my letter of the last summer where I was letting you know of my change in employment. The herrings are quite gone out of the northern grounds they say because they know the war has come. I hope you are

133

fit and well at home and I read that you are all to be on short rations like the English though you do not go out to fight. Many here think the Irish President is a poor man not to help Europe but who is to have the say of that, not me. I am in the King's clothes again and God knows it will not help my case in Sligo but then I believe surely I am beyond help there. Please do write to me here as regular as you like and Pappy too if he has a mind and I wonder what Jack will fix to do in the present emergency will he join up or what. I suppose even Tom is an ould fella like myself and might do likewise but I know in other letters you say he is a busy man and well up in Sligo and why not. But I am thinking that there is work also to be done out there in France and other places and I will go there to do that. We are fixed to go shortly. Mam, you are ever in my thoughts and Pappy too, keep well and dry as they say, and remember your fond son always.

Love,
Eneas.

And out he goes indeed, ever mindful of those old fields of France, but also now of that strange ship he saw strangely gliding over the cold waters to Germany as if in the sunken morning of a terrible dream.

I O

AT LAST AFTER MUCH DRILLING and training and some understanding of the philosophies of officers, the latter the darkest task of all, he is sent with his new comrades to rescue France from the threat of Hitler. He is put in a high wide boat and he sails to the cherished shore as if upon a daytrip, except there is little ease, the crowd of men anxious or light-hearted as character dictates, but all itchy and steaming in the pitching holds. And France looks immaculate in her fields and towns, with her high skies and the heavy flush of flowers upon the thoroughfares. And he goes about with his companions whither he is urged by the flustered officer.

In the fullness and the dread of time the imaginary and tender line of Maginot is sorely broken, and Eneas and all the army of the King is driven back to the shore. And to reach that shore they pass through districts livid with fear and death, and through columns of lost people they pass, men and women without homes and deep in rags and, he supposes, an echo and a remembering icon of those perished souls along the Irish seaboards a hundred years before, when the hag of Famine showed her dark face and dripping bones.

There is only terror at the shore. Most terrifying of all, inducing in all his comrades and himself a sort of madness,

a ferocious dizziness and misery of the heart, is the heaving
and fantastically flinging and extravagant lobbing of bombs
and the deathly singing and whine of bullets, and when the
sand is reached at last, and he and his fellows are miraculously intact, it is a misery, a depth of horror, to witness the
broil of milling men, and death coming suddenly amid
clumps of soldiers, like children killed at the hems of their
mothers' skirts. For Eneas can see that there are a hundred
craft heaving on the pitiful tide, fishing boats like in
Grimsby days and other unnamable boats that look like
pilot-boats and estuary pleasure-boats and even dainty
yachts show gaudy colours in the white surf, and it is as if
some tremendous holiday, some longed-for visit of a royal
yacht, was taking place on the sea, and just beside it, on the
bloodied sand, the filthiest and most wretched of wars, with
nothing between but the unheard thundering of the waves.
And everywhere along the torn material of the tideline,
soldiers are trying to reach the affectionate craft, though the
seas ride high against them. And by God many a man is
drowned in the murderous surf, weighed down by his
freight of arms and kit, by the panic of his own soul. There
is the screaming of human extremity and the deepest caco-
phany of bombs and in all instances and through the gaps
of all, Eneas lends an ear to the weak music of his officer
ever failing to give his charges guidance. And there is sad
panic and blood torn out of bodies in a savage system of
fountains, the drops bursting and falling, slowly, slowly
they fall, and ravaging disaster. Eneas surveys the miraculous carnage and destitution of the beach, a shocking and
afflicted painting utterly without the mercy and wisdom of
women, and France is a field of fire and the German guns
wherever they lie make a firmament of fire. And when

a bomb, machined not for mercy, splits its belly open violently two hundred yards from Eneas, there is an extraordinary silence suddenly for him, he stops still, useless, dark, and stares into the bleakest silence. His companions are abruptly dying, their living forms ruptured, boys of England and Ireland are dying, the excited officer himself is erased by a shard of shrapnel removing his gabbling head, it lies on the simple sand complete with neat hat, there is fire, darkest fire, and then silence, and then deeper silence. Eneas stands on the beach arrested by this triumph of killing, with the orchestra of war soundlessly roaring.

*

And whosoever was not found written in the book of life. He is thinking these thoughts. *Was cast into the lake of fire.* Hours have passed. Eneas McNulty looks to the west where he imagines more ships may be, to bring home the ruined men. Perhaps no more will come. The living have been taken off the shore but the dead are left lying. His own face is a mask of dark putty. A thousand years of English ships bringing bright soldiers to these shores of France, and now, everything backwards and destroyed. Seemingly the saving of France was never to be done. A moon blowing like a flag hangs in the lower sky, clambering about you would think in the distant copses. A little acre of the strand is on fire from a leaky vehicle that got halfway down the beach and probably exploded. Anyway it is blazing away now. There is no smell of death exactly because all the boys are too newly killed. He wouldn't care to have a dekko at the faces in case they are late pals, but there is a hundred, two hundred must be, corpses set near him on the beach by death – in the places they found individually death. And all along the sand no doubt in the darkness are hundreds more. He has stood there fixed as a post for hours, and deaf as a post into the bargain. He feels queerly as if he has been away somewhere flying through the bright gold of the ether that glues the stars but truthfully he has not budged. Now in the lonesome aftermath everything is wildly still, and for all the world you might say that the sound of burning might be the moon herself, trying to get out of the tangled trees. Now she rises. He is standing near the slight lapping of the oily waters and surveying in a calm manner the burning beach and the ruined men. Liverpool, Manchester, London, Newcastle, Belfast, Sligo, Dundee, Cardiff . . .

The moon rises over Eneas's France. He is forty, no, he is forty-two or three, he can't say any more. Time is a dark puzzle, certainly. No sense saying he knows where he is because he does not, damn well does not. Even the name of the beach eludes him and when he heard the name first it had a Scottish sound to it but he has forgotten it now. Even if he could remember the name what help would it be?

He moves his shoulders in his tunic against the black chill of the night air flooding across the calmed sea. He checks in his head for a song but there's nothing going on there, in his head. Usually he finds a little music there, a little scattering of notes from his father's fading repertoire. 'The Lass of Dunloe' or 'The Merry Merchants' Reel'. 'Peg Vallelly's Leg' or 'The Nights of Armagh'. Looks like they're gone now for sure. He wishes these youngsters would rise up and shake off the wet sand and gather their clothes about them and he would go on down the beach with them in the absence of the broken officer. In the passionate but quiet fashion of soldiers. Everything had been against them, the food, the weather, the officers, their

138

innocence of the world, but nothing of that sort could have killed them. Eneas carries his own sergeant major's stripes on his uniform. They said when he volunteered that an older man was worth three recruits and indeed without a word of a lie he would lay himself down in blood and misery now if three of these young fellas might rise. Maybe another man might tell you that these two hundred souls are rising as sweetly as the moon through the diesel fumes and floating up against the colours of the moon and travelling away up into the darkening heavens like balloons that have escaped the hands of children. To go back to the points of light they came from, some eighteen, twenty years ago. What is a life, to be ended like this? What is a hundred? Eneas hasn't a notion. Nor can he allow that his own life has been worth saving. He doesn't even know what his life has been, whether it has a weight or a value. Any damn priest looking for his soul would say it had if he asked him, but Eneas is no questioner of that kind.

The fields of France, they have been killed for the saving of the fields of France. That's the why and the what of it.

Assured in his heart of the truth of that, Eneas turns about and, setting his back against the sea, walks again up into the selfsame France. In the caves of his ears he hears all the oceans of the earth bellowing with storms and crying sailors. Though he can see through his eyes well enough, yet he walks like a blind man through the remnants of confusion, and goes on into some lonesome woods by the mercy of Shank's pony, walking straight forward, like a small child in a meadowland or indeed a forest, straight, with some purpose unknown, and never looking back.

*

The night sky is bluer than a beetle's back. Now in a hayrick, growing ever more lonesome, he has a go at resting. The hayrick is very brown and damp from sitting there untended and the grasses at its circling base are tall, all a mockery of husbandry. The lasses who built the rick were maybe dead under the same grasses somewhere or gone away down the white road to Dieppe or wherever they considered a refuge. He thinks of the girls in some lost evening after a day or two of excellent driving weather – no, France had ever an embarrassment of that, he knows – but he thinks of them with their dresses tucked up into their fabulous drawers and their thick brown arms and their laughter and talk, there in a gap of happiness in the war, a hedgegap of happiness. Of course he is imagining the girls, maybe a mere man and his labourers built it, and set it up new and fresh when this darkened field with its hedges grown out like a simpleton's hair was cut to the very yellow stalks of the grass, deep where the sun had not reached, and you could not walk over it in bare feet for fear of tiny cuts, and all the weather of that day was lambent and telling the men lies of ease and hope as they worked. He is rustling in the rick like an exhausted dog, a dog that's been run too long through the hills after rabbits and such. He is afflicted now by these trembles. He nips out onto the thick grass and shits very quickly and neatly and is back in his nest before he knows where he is. Half of his thinking head is still out on the grasses, half is back in the hayrick. There's a big aching in the roots of his brains. He is like a poisoned man before the poison starts to make him sick – discombobulated and swimming in the head. The souls of his friends are washing against his face and chest like pigeons, they are kind of clamouring for his attention, he does not fancy it at all. Yet at the same time he is fervently spreading his arms and sweeping in the souls close to him to nurture them and to nurture himself, a blanket of souls. The night sky just some moments past so peaceful, so blue, is speckled with gold faces nattering at him, talking loudly, like travellers in a great station. There is fierce goodbying and waving and promises. He wishes he were not the fool in the hayrick but instead going off with the noisy men to whatever Dieppes and Dovers heaven could boast of.

*

The solemn night entirely perplexes him. He discovers that having seen the dead he can scarcely retrieve a sense of himself as a living man. The enduring grasses and the murdered daughters of the rick seem more real, infinitely so. The night breeze with its cargo of cold plays in the rick. There is purpose in everything except him, one of the saviours of France. Once as a living boy he learned the world, so how has he now unlearned it? Where is the schoolmaster of the lessons of this night? Backward lessons. The trembles stop and a decent moon rides up above the unruly clouds in the low night. What he feels is a pure panic. He wants to leap from the rick and gallivant about the ruined meadows, darting through the broken farms like a friendly ghost, a playful familiar. It is sickening in his belly with all the jumble of things in his rowdy head, he does not even feel he owns his head and belly. The things of his life gone by and the present push of the day just gone are ganging up against him. God help the wanderer. God help the trained soldier with his stripes, and this the pass he has come to. There was no particular training for disaster, annihilation and blind panic. With a proper leap he ups and drags out through the flying straws and waves his arms and jumps up and down with good bangs of his boots on the roasted earth. He twirls about like a bloody dancer. High in the lonesome batter of the sky the souls of his friends are well and truly departed. Then a demon comes at him through the murk of the field's edge, a veritable demon all small and hard and he gets a terrific blow against his head with a weapon he does not even see. As he goes down falling like a treetrunk he is laughing, never a man to forgo laughter. After all he is a living man amid the dead in the occupied lands and there would be no sense in a peaceable night in a hayrick, like a farmhand waiting for a straw-headed belle. Out, out go the lights of the dark.

*

Cocoa, sugar and cold water. You have to take these ingredients very carefully from their niches without your mother seeing. Now you are under the kitchen table in the safety of the shadows with the heat from the kitchen stove to delight you. And you mix the sugar against the cocoa and stir in a spoon of water and you eat it slowly, secretly, grandly, and are so overwhelmingly comforted that you don't mind now when inevitably you are caught, or the pilfering is detected . . .

He's deep in this dream of a forgotten safety, deep in it, all coiled and happy in it, when he hears against the brittle walls of the dream a voice trying he believes to wake him. The voice is like a hard old blackthorn stick to prod a cow along a way with. It's prodding him now, prodding him away from that precious concoction. He's struggling because the dream is excellent and the voice is nail-hard and real. Unfortunately now the voice is paired to a broken old face that looms up as he opens his eyes. For a moment he is at one with this mystery, contented, interested. Then his head booms about like a hungry seal on a ledge, there is a filthy tide rushing through his ears, and he sits up and throws up sudden bile from his empty stomach. The old man with the hard voice and the harder face hurls himself back. But the devil's laughing.

'Oh, poxy English, don't you do enough all week, shitting and pissing on my bed? You have to vomit on me now, you shitty English?'

So Eneas is blinking and wiping his chin and tasting the bitter stuff and gazing at the old man. He feels immeasurably better, but cold now, shivery. He's elated. He looks about at a decrepit old table cluttered with mugs and plates and what might be an ancient lump of ham and the rows of sunlike, moonlike rather, plates on the famished dresser. He lies back with a sudden weakness and sees that the ceiling is made of bamboo and rafters much hammered into with hooks and nails. His head goes back on a dirty folded cloth but he gives the old man another stare from that awkward position.

'Jesus, bollocks,' he says.

'Yeh, jees, bolloc,' says the old man. 'You got it, English soldier. Heh, heh.'

'Who hit me?' says Eneas. 'Some bollocks hit me.'

'No odder bolloc here but me bolloc,' says the old man.

'Any chance this being Chester barracks?'

'Chester, English bolloc?'

'You don't have to break it to me gently, you old shit. I can see this isn't any Chester barracks here.'

'Chester bolloc?'

'Don't start, Jesus.'

'You, you Chester? I calling Jean.'

'Buggering Jean, is it? Where am I? Where-am-I?'

'I know where you are ... You in my grasses last week, this week you in my bed.'

Eneas feels for a surging moment a kind of sagging away of his blood.

'I'd get up if I could.'

'I don't want you get up. I want you lie down, nice and safe, like the teddybears.'

Maybe it's dusk or thereabouts, maybe he smells the faint smell of burning wood, charcoal maybe, maybe he hears some birds just going to bed somewhere, maybe he catches that odour of late sky when it is marked by the rooks going high home, maybe ...

'You going make me rich man, you going make Jean rich man. Rich!'

'Eh? I'm not, my friend.'

'You not? You is, English, you is.'

'I feel like my arms are lead. Lead or iron or stones. Why's that?'

'What the western pictures says? Figure it out – figure it out.'

And he's doing some cavorting of his own, saying *Figure it out* in his stolen American accent. What picture he's stolen it from God only knows. If the bugger began to sing 'Lilac Time', Eneas wouldn't be surprised.

In the great and lonesome music-hall of this warring France nothing should be surprising except the everyday and the ordinary. Three seconds of being awake and Eneas doesn't like the look or the sound of this old monkey. Neutral monkey maybe, monkey of the Allies hopefully, but dangerous, dubious, too-friendly monkey. Bite your fingers off most likely if you put them too close to his sharp little mouthful of teeth.

'Listen,' says Eneas, 'if you got a drink of water I'd be grateful. I'm parched here, parched.'

'Hey, hey, water, water. I give English water.'

He takes a dulled silver scoop from the flaky wall and dips it into his water bucket at the door with its soft lid of damp muslin and puts the edge of the scoop tenderly or at least carefully to Eneas's lips. Eneas drinks in beelike sips, because he has to.

'That's good, that's good,' he says, in the midst of a sighing from the bottom of his stomach, 'that's most excellent good, my friend. Now, I'd see it as a favour, one man to another, if you'd help me up.'

But the old man only smiles at him and replaces the scoop.

'Now,' says Eneas, 'I'm going to have to get myself up.' Then adds, 'I tell you, the sorrow of many deaths is weighing me down,' half to himself, surprising himself. But he can speak like that because the man gives the impression that the room is empty except for Eneas. He's barely there because maybe of the curious effect of the broken English. If this old codger spoke properly he'd seem more there than he did maybe. Well he has a right, Eneas, to think nonsense after a whack on the head like he'd got just lately.

Sadly, while intending to rise and bestir the blood in his veins, he finds he cannot. He looks at his arms and his legs and he sees the rusty old shackles holding them. He looks up at the old man in surprise and anger.

'Why did you fetter me?'

'Ah, ah, ah,' says the old man, dancing about. 'Ah, ah, ah. You going make me rich, English. Yes, sir, Mr English.'

'You going to sell me to someone? Maybe to a German someone?'

'I maybe, if I like. I find you, you my.'

'I you, eh, you little piece of shite? I'll I you if I can get out of these chains.'

'You not get out, my buddy. Them is chains for my mules and my mules don' stray ever, not ever, so forget it.'

The geezer lights the farm lamp because the evening is upon them both in the boxes and shelves of shadows and half-lights that now grow in the old room. Birds beyond the walls add a sense of depth, of sea, of dreams, to the new shadows made by the ancient lamp. The old man Jean smiles at Eneas, quite tender again and strange. He trots over and strokes Eneas's bruised head.

'My buddy, I got to say, I never hit no man before this time. So I also say I not going to go sell you to any German man. Outside the farm is broken. My sons are gone into the clay. The city boys they kill first one, fighting there in the hill. The soldier Germans kill my second boy when they come into this place. They see him on the road at night and shoot, bang, bang. The farm is all broken. My buddy, I need your arms and hands and all strong to make the farm. What you say?'

'You going to lead me about with these on, for me to do the work? Old man, no one's going to do that for you. And if you take off the chains what will keep me?'

'I begin all wrong. Look. You be friend and help me with this land. I tell you, this land is with me and my fathers for three hundred years. Never has there not been the wine, never. Even for a war I not stop. I need friend, brother, son, father. You help because God says you help because you here now.'

'The war's going on all about you here, how can anyone farm in the middle of a war?'

'There only work here, no war. Never mind that war, Mr buddy.'

'Take off these feckin chains, old man. You got to take the chance. I'm not going to do anything without you taking off these chains. Come on, what's the difference? You're going to be the same madman before you take them off and after. I'll let you know how I feel when I'm a free man to help you or not as I choose. I'm a soldier, old man, in these badlands of France. Maybe I'll help you, maybe not. Who can say? Take these mule fetters off of me.'

So the old man after a half-minute to ponder and consider and chew the cud of Eneas's words stoops in and grapples with his precious chains.

'These good old iron,' he says. 'Don' you speak against them, my buddy.'

'OK, but take the bloody yokes off me.'

'I doin', I doin', you bolloc. Now you go-go dance down the road, hey, you bolloc?'

Eneas is free. Yes, he would like to dance down the road but maybe the road is full of Germans. Maybe he is a safe Eneas while he lingers with the old man, possessor he can guess of hiding places galore. And at least he has an interest in keeping him alive. Eneas has no ambition to go to a German camp or be a hero of the army and find an unknown spot to die on with a bullet housed in his breast. So now he is standing and very much looking down at the old farmer. Must have rallied all his strength to himself to haul such as Eneas into this farmhouse from the field with the rick. Right enough he had noticed there how old and ruined the harvesting of the grass was. This old bastard must be living on cured hams and cheese and whatnot. The thought of ham and cheese is a happy one. Christ and His Nails, Eneas is hungry. All the ache in his head's gone. He feels strong, good, reasonable, generous, clear-headed. What a thing, what a puzzle. You'd do things now you wouldn't bother about other times. War was a big orphanage or prison or lunatic asylum. You had to follow the rules of the attendants, the gods of this war.

'I suppose I'm the man to help you, after all,' he says, and the old man Jean suddenly lights as bright as his lamp and shamelessly embraces him, as much of him as he can reach. Eneas holds still as a tree. Then he hears the old bugger weeping into his stomach more or less. Gently he pushes the man back.

'Come on, you old bollocks,' he says. 'Let me go free, can't you? Jesus Christ.'

'I say, thank you, Chester, thank you. Now we see good times again.'

*

To be the husbandman of the vines of France, ever so briefly, to be dropped in on to a ruined farm as its sudden saviour, fulfils mysteriously for Eneas the dreamed love of his youth. Now in setting down shovel into clay, binding the vines, keeping them spruce and clear, bringing, in the heat-laden evening, the bounty of the small river into the dry irrigation channels, he knows he has put his very body close against his desires. He works for Jean not so much because it makes any sense to him but because as Jean's servant he serves his old dreams. He must take the letter of the laws of husbandry and believe them word for word as he has no information of his own. He is a child in Jean's fields. Somewhere up behind the house where they never dig, Jean's sons lie interred, waiting for the mercies of peace to be buried in the little bombed churchyard in the village of rubble across the near hills. At night as Eneas lies in the old linen of his bed under the gnarled rafters, in the swimming music of the owls and the stately snail-like progress of the moon up the high sky caught in the buckled window, he thinks of the lonesome bodies of the sons under the red earth, dreaming or dreamless he could not venture to say. As the weeks pass and many nights of these thoughts with them, he grows to love the poor sons in their permanent beds.

All night also Jean lies under his rafters. One evening when Eneas looks in he sees old Jean lying there asleep with his scored and clay-dark hands folded on his whittled chest like a corpse might have. The bed is narrow and tight. The body of Jean lies still and deeply sunken in the paths and woodlands of dreams. Whether or not the old man hears his wife calling to him there among the trees Eneas cannot say. But he knows that men when they are made widowers or women when they are made widows see in their lonesome dreams their vigorous dead in the cascades of the trees. Eneas can only guess at the sorrow of the old man who is living still thus while his progeny are eternally abed under their sheets of rotted leaves. Does it all trouble him less as he is old himself and soon to follow, or indeed does it trouble him less because Eneas is there to be the workhorse and the architect of the coming harvest? He hopes he is the handmaiden, the midwife, the messenger of the old man's happiness. But Jean is dark enough. He eats and drinks in this surrounding cauldron of a war as if he were a sparrow in a park of death, as if he were a songster in a boneyard.

Surely the massive war is all about. In the clarities of the night guns sound off at a distance. Formations of men are seen distantly also on ridges and raised parts of country roads. Often Eneas imagines he may be killed by a stray bullet or by some soldier firing on him from some high vantage. He does not feel secure on that afflicted farm. And yet the very isolation, lonesomeness, jollity and darkness of the old man keeps him at his post. And he is willing to fight the fight of clay and seed as long as he is allowed. To be the strange champion of the sorrow-beleaguered farmer.

*

In the evenings they drink from bottles of wine that date from some years back. Wine indeed that the dead sons saw to, and crushed with their dead feet and pressed with their dead hands. It is funny that the markets for wine are still virtually functioning, and now and then a vehicle comes and takes away a few crates. Neither Jean or Eneas knows who will drink the wine but it is more discreet and appropriate not to question. The few francs it brings are worth the mystery. But it astonishes Eneas that with no doubt horde upon horde of German troops all about, someone still furnishes the comfort of wine.

He is puzzled too by the absence of English troops or any other of the Allied soldiers. Unless some celestial magician has taken him from the glades of the earth he cannot think why he sees no one, hears nothing of anyone, and is left alone moreover to live with Jean. The van-driver asks no questions and no one else comes to ask them either. It is as if he cannot be found amid the soldiers, as if the war eludes him on purpose. Firstly he stood amid the dead by the edge of the sea and secondly now he works the rows of vines not so much as a living man but a vanished man. Of course he understands this is his natural condition. He is not required as a Sligoman and now he is not required as a British soldier. Jean calls him the English and fair enough. It has transpired that Jean knows nothing of Ireland, the vague island beyond England, with its black pools of disquiet and revenge. And sometimes he would like to tell Jean of the beauties of Sligo, the curiosities of its mountains, and the strange pull of its lonesome streets, visions and pestering remembrances that afflict Eneas betimes. Oftentimes in dreams he sees dark men of Sligo, dark fellows in black coats, O'Dowd and his cronies, following him, looking for him across the terrain of dreams. Yet he would like to talk of Sligo. He would like to describe that home place, but the words for it have begun to desert him, the pictures leap about in his head unhelpfully, he cannot grasp them. He is a vine uprooted, and the cold white roots are tarnishing in the swimming air.

*

It is tasty work, the endless breaking of the soil along the rows of vines, the tying of the new growth so there is no cramping or snapping, the quenching of the thirst that is like a star of need in each new grape. It is not like the growing of potatoes in the dark seams of lazybeds at home in Sligo. And Eneas feels his own father's hunger for the health of flowers and plants in the old garden in Finisklin in his own blood now, giving a strength to his arms that is both tireless and tender. With everything changed about, it is not unlike the fishing it seems to him, the same stooping, the same peering and care. The clay drinks the water he brings to it with almost a sigh, with almost words of thanks.

He might swear that in the tricky twilight or the pleasant ease of firstlight, when the watering is done, language itself, a sort of lingo or slangy stuff, rises from the drinking clay. And he understands the passion of Jean and why Jean tied a stranger down to make a worker out of him, for those human plants. And harvest comes, and there is the pride of that, and it's as if he has stood up straight for the first time in all those months, and he and Jean dance in the big stone basin and acquire the honour of their labour, treading out the juice, till they are like two strange men in the moonlight, dancing, with purple stockings.

I I

HEEDLESS OF BREVITY and longevity, of talk and stories, of guilt, of lonesomeness, of the ruined artefacts of the war under the simple sky, God brings Eneas again to the shore. He supposes it might be God Himself, fearing any other truth. He hopes it is God. He stands on the sandy headland surveying a tideless beach, in the remnants of his uniform, more farmer than sergeant major truly.

As this day came up over Jean's fairly pristine fields, Eneas was prompted to set out and did. It was something like the message that touches the starling in the town trees, touches the swallow, touches the goose in the fervent mud of the estuary. He couldn't for the life of him say what got into him. Maybe a sense that his promise to Jean, if promise it was, had been fulfilled. That he had given his word, and been as good as it, in the upshot. And the juice safe in the barrels. He put on his uniform and kissed Jean goodbye and walked away over the hill till the air got salty again and he saw the beach with the Scottish-sounding name unfolding before him like a drying watercolour.

Now there are no terrors, no troops massed in panic and agony on the empty tidelands. This time the slightly dancing sea, the waves you might say merely demonstrating a few steps, has no multitude of craft, no fishing boats and pleasure craft, incongruous among the acrid smells of the war. Sleeping humanity has sailed out from England long since to fetch the wakeful soldiers. They had been painfully, plainly, in need of fetching. Up from the chaos of running men and milling groups had arisen that terrific music like a choir gone mad. Eneas puts his roughened palms over his ears because although the beach is empty he heaves it suddenly again. He stands there and watches the deserted scene unblinkingly. What is he to do? He cannot go back into France.

With his palms fastened behind his ears, he turns half about and heads northwards along the beach, if it is true North, his boots crunching mildly the delicate sand. For a day and a night he proceeds like that, through the owl-freshened reaches of darkness and the long day. Wraithlike sand blows across the spaces. He climbs betimes onto cliff or field paths, understanding the wayward coastline of France, and when he hears noises he does not like, he hides fast in crevices of things, under abandoned machinery and indifferent hedges. Till he comes wordless and weird in his damaged uniform, his damaged self, to a small seaside town where he stands weeping on the harbour wall. And the fishermen come out of the dark café and hide this wretched man and take him out that night over the dangerous sea and deposit him softly on a murmuring shore of England. And in this way, belatedly, and many miles from the beach itself, and many months, he is rescued you might say from Dunkirk.

*

It's true that in barracks in Sheffield there are some incidents that he must regret as a generally peaceable man. He's ravaged in the nights by headaches, and even when he sleeps he dreams of his dead pals on the beach. Ordinary talking gets him excited in a peculiar fashion so he's leaping up and contradicting or shouting at his newer comrades and gabbling gobbledygook at them for small reason. He goes into the industrial districts and hears the deep thumping of the steel presses and hears like a ferocious echo the explosions they'll make when they are guns. They're not noises you can keep out by pressing your palms to your ears but he tries. He thinks of the enormous cauldrons or furnaces at the hearts of the brick factories, and the civilian men stoking them to ever greater temperatures and the waterfalls of molten steel cascading and sparking onto the beaten hearths. His own heart is consumed again and again till he's only a kind of shouting fool in the roads.

When his captain arranges for his discharge he spends some months in the mental home for military casualties. Now these formerly fighting men look diminished and ridiculous to him in their standard issue gowns. First the uniforms for blood and bullets and now the uniform for nightmares and shouting. There are swards and swards of pale green grass stretching into the distance towards the fiery town. At night from his window glowing with the moon he catches a fanning glimmer of the fires and imagines the greensward like a beach with heroic nonentities fleeing the slight incline down from the dark fare-thee-well of the German guns. He sees the shadows like forlorn twigs scuttering across the useless acres. He feels impelled to set hedges into them and rows of vines, and to harvest the swollen grapes and to drink the fresh wine in tremendous swallows. Sheffield is full of owls.

He writes at last to his mother and takes some solace from doing so in a manner he couldn't have imagined before, not of course being given to letter-writing as a remnant of his humiliations at school:

Dear Mam,
Here I am in trouble in Sheffield with my head but not to worry. I am back from France and it is a release. I hope the harvest was good for my friend Jean who I was helping there to save the vineyard. France is a holy place and I am glad I was there to see that. The beaches were sorrowful things. I lost so many of my pals that I was unhappy and am unhappy still. Look at me a madman like Pappy knows so well and you knew once when you were an unmarried girl. I do long to see you all the lights of the furnaces in the city are strange to me. I read in the paper that the river has silted up the Garravogue is this true and how will the ships get up to the deepwater berths now. It was always a worry for a Sligoman the state of that river and it is just another sorrow of the war that it must be blocked by mud. I think of the mud coming in from Oyster and Coney Islands but maybe it comes in from further out beyond Strandhill where no one knows what's what in the deep of deeps. What will happen to the great endeavours of the docks now I wonder do you know. It is hard enough here there are many misfortunate cases now the shellshock that we saw in the old war and the lads going about the town and screaming or falling down or eating refuse from the back of the hotels but a harder sort of madness from being so young and seeing too difficult sights. All here need rest and home and sigh for both you might say I am no different. The attendants are rough sorts and there is no seamstress to remind me of you with your needles and the flowers sewn into the linen and cotton. We are all in shifts of a sort and we are lucky to escape the famous

jacket that no one relishes but sometimes what can be done the man is dangerous to himself and everyone else. What will cure us all but time and perhaps when the war ends we can be merry again.

Your very loving son,
Eneas.

To no one's surprise his mother sends a reply immediately, proving if nothing else that the post office is still a credit to Great Britain and Ireland, because it seems to him no more than a day when he gets her little envelope with the writing crushed on to a single page:

Dear Son,
Your letter arrives safely. When you are better please come home. Your brother Tom is mayor for '43. Jack is made major in the Royal Engineers. Your father keeps well. I have sent Teasy for to be a nun in Bexhill-on-Sea. Her address is Nazareth House if it is not too much out of your way. You are twenty years gone next Thursday! Surely your old trouble is long put to rest. We are in a new house now on the Strandhill Road. We are a bungalow.

The river indeed is full of silt. How time flies!
Your unhappy mother,
Mam.

Order returns to his addled head, and God no longer breaks eggs there in the morning. As health returns he begins to feel a certain pride for all he has done as a soldier. What better thing than to spruce a French farm, better than maiming and killing he hopes. He is very proud about his brother Jack and tells the men in the bed about him. They are very cheery about it and offer their congratulations. One man says he is surprised two Irish brothers have given so

157

much for England. Eneas laughs and mentions France also, France also. The depth of feeling for France ... There's an old geyser in the cliff at Garretstown in the county of Cork, he tells him, a pocket of air in the rock. When the sea swells it sends up a plume of saltwater like a dray-horse's tail, or its breath in the cold fog. That is an Irishman's feeling for France. And as Eneas speaks he knows he loves England also. He feels a depth of affection for this queer England of flinty furnaces and ruined soldiers. For the weird papers that everyone reads full of high talk and blame and football. Chelsea, the Gunners, Leeds ... Maybe Sheffield aren't so hot, but who is to mind? There won't be proper teams till the war's over, they say. His fellow inmates are romantic about association football, but not like Sligomen are romantic about hurleying and the GAA. An English team when favoured might as well be a sweetheart of the man affected. It is mighty peculiar but attractive. It used to be said that a person's soul was revealed when he or she sang, whether behind a door for modesty or brazenly before the crowd. An Englishman's soul appears when he speaks of his favoured team. His soul materializes before you like a bird with lampy plumage. How locked away he is till that moment, how dark, how complaining, how filthy-minded really but then they are all mostly damned Protestants. Ashes, dirt, hurt fall away when the heroic matches are remembered. The souls of the women are harder to see because he does not know wherein their passions lie. Not religion certainly, not sporting affairs. That is all a mystery. He has seen no Vivs among the women, no straightforward passionate ladies. But he accepts that they will not reveal themselves to him, a penniless foreigner astray in the wits. Nurses, orderlies, chars ... All mysteries, jokers. When there's cruelty in the asylum it's as often the women orderlies as the men. They're in cahoots. The wicked are beaten just as quick by the women. The severest punishment is a buggering, but that of course is always the men. Eneas is as good as gold.

*

He goes south into different country through all the damped parishes by the Bexhill train. It's a bit of a detour on his homeward journey, but nevertheless. He sits up like a clean child just out of his sickbed, with the alien and intriguing air of the released inmate. And the fields of England look fresh to him, starched, sentinel, precise, but empty as a catastrophic site, empty as certain districts of Sligo where there is nothing and no one to meet except lone cows and hobbled donkeys. The people hide in the nethers of their farms maybe. Here he can't explain the absences. Nothing moves except the thrilling train and the sooty bushes of the cuttings.

His sister Teasy is a girl in a starched hood and a black habit as sharp as a boy-scout's tent. She's small as always like a wet lamb. They bring him into a parlour in Nazareth House to see her, and he waits at a table loaded with sandwiches and two fine cakes. It's like being at someone else's meal. But Teasy makes it clear that the meal's for him, as an honoured guest, the brother of a nun. After the cakes and the tea she takes him into the grounds to see the little marble slabs where the dead nuns are interred. Sister Benedict, Sister Catherine and a host of Victorian nuns from long ago. It's a mendicant order and these would be all very fit corpses in their day from walking the hills and valleys about Bexhill, begging alms for the poor.

'Poor old things,' says Eneas. The salt-laden sky rears above him and his sister. He feels very honoured by the welcome of the cakes, an unfamiliar feeling. It all puzzles him. He thinks Teasy has landed on her feet, in the right place for her maybe. He hopes so.

'You're all right for things?' she asks him with the deference of a younger sibling. 'You seem grand now, Eneas.'

'Sure, terrific, I'm terrific – that's an English expression,' he says laughing. 'It's a nice ould place, isn't it? Is the work hard?'

'It's not so bad,' she says. 'We have the poor orphans, you know, and they're good lads in the main. They're rogues, but it's like a family. I always wanted a family, of my own, like, you know?'

'Did you, Teasy?' he says, surprised enough. Teasy.

'It's the ould husband I wasn't keen on, you know,' and Teasy gives her howl of laughter. 'Not at all keen!'

'Why would you be, sure, they're all animals!'

'They are, by all accounts. Excepting the Da.'

'Pappy. Ah, yeh. Well, you can't call him a husband.'

Teasy laughs again though neither of them knows what he means.

'Was it hard getting you a place here, Teasy?' he asks.

'It was. Mam had to move heaven and earth.'

'Literally, says you. I see,' he says. 'Well, just so long as you're happy, girl. You're happy enough set here?'

'They say I'm the best beggar, I mean the best mendicant since who knows how long, that's what they say. It's a knack. You can go over all these hills up the back, you know, and the women come out when they see me and give me a shilling or so, for the orphaned boys. That's how we keep going here. The other nuns are regal. They're mostly regal! And yourself, Eneas, you're sure you're all right?'

'Tip-top,' he says.

He sleeps that night among the boys because of course he is a man and what can you do with a stray man in a nunnery full of innocent women? The lads chat to him in the shadowy dormitory, and one by one they fall into slumber. Even in their dreams they chat with their own dark selves, chattering and giving out. His bed is narrow as befitting a boy, and it's curiously restful being there anonymous and temporary. Better by far than the asylum. The boys are curative, a kind of balm to him. Some of them sounded pretty rough types to him and gruff enough, but he can sense the simplicity and the security of them. The nuns must be guarding them well. The older ones are apprenticed in the town and one of them works in the fairgrounds along the front, assistant to a candyfloss man. Another follows the manure cart of the city council, trailing the last of the horses. The war saw an upsurge again in the horses but they'll fade away, everyone knows. He dreams of his pious sister traipsing the hills of Bexhill, a slight figure through the years of summers and storms. In the morning the boys compete in farting like dogs and go off down the wooden corridors to their prayers, leaving him to dress in the slightly foetid peace. At the gates again he embraces his sister and they wish each other well, a little awkwardly. He knows so little about her, and she about him. But blood is a bond nonetheless. She's like bones in a bag when he hugs her. Rats of fear run about him for a moment. He hopes she wanted this and it isn't some plan of his mother's. He suspects his mother in the matter but maybe her plotting has had a good result. The best mendicant nun for who knows how long. A real accolade!

*

The Irish Sea though narrow still accommodates the most hectic storms. It is hard to see God's hand there unless He is a theatrical person. Eneas holds the rail on the steerage deck of the mailboat, scorning the teeming bunks below. But he knows the migrant men are sleeping there, four to a tier like one of those terrible military camps he's heard about. Men from Mayo, Galway, Sligo, all the ruined kingdoms of Connaught. If they are soldiers they have changed their uniforms in Wales and lie on their beds in their civvies, respecting the neutrality of De Valera to that degree anyhow. Perhaps it is a shame to have fought for the freedom of far-off places. Eneas McNulty can not claim to understand a fella like De Valera and feels no sense of his kingship in Ireland. He never read a word of sense that man said, but then he rarely took a newspaper. Since the demise of Collins who could they elect anyhow? It is just O'Dowds and De Valeras left.

And now he has said the old name in his head, O'Dowd. Can he really return home? Although it is so long ago he can remember exactly what Jonno Lynch said to him in the garden. Pain of death. Step foot back on Irish soil. But life is clearly short and maybe his mother is right, maybe the years have healed such matters. And yet something of that moment returns to him, lowers him, defeats his optimism, Jonno terrible and full of precise information in the garden in Finisklin.

He leans now on the mahogany rail not for a moment doubting its strength but wondering suddenly what it must be like to fall into that golden water. He expects that the force of the fall might knock a person out and that would be that. Or you might bob about in the chill waves while the air was in your clothes, till only your upturned face was married still to the sky. They might lower a boat if your cries had been heard and search for you in the glimmers and glitters of the sea, being careful not to strike you with an oar blade. On the other hand if you were quiet and chose an empty moment on the deck you could slip away and no one would call after you or rouse the captain and his men. He imagines the panic of being alone in the water but he has heard that a queer peace intrudes on the drowning man, sailors have told him that. Momentarily he too longs for that peculiar peace.

Towards wintry dawn, Dalkey comes up to starboard. It's lightly raining, spangling his overcoat. He must be drowning anyway because now a peace invades him like a love. The shock of the land invades him. Dalkey with its solemn island, the beseeching arms of Dunleary Harbour quickening the boat. He sees the little bathing places of south Dublin, Sandycove, the Baths, the Forty Foot, places he barely knows, maybe visited the once in the old days when his mother would bring him to the capital. They could be in Honolulu for all they meant to him. But his chest heaves with love, with peace, with pure need. It's the tobacco, the opium, of returning home. There might be angels standing on the rocky shores throwing out one after another bright ropes with grappling hooks to dig into and find purchase on his heart. One after another the arms rise like fishermen in the ancient days. Shortly he goes down riveted by this love, with the bolts of this love fastened into his skin, and eats a large plate of sausages and rashers washed through with dark tea aching with bitter tannin. The soldiers transformed by De Valera's wishes for Ireland sit about with heavy eyes, restored by sleep but still poisoned by beer, uncomfortable in their peaceable clothes.

In some manner to his surprise he sees sit down beside him a Negraman, perhaps he thinks a wandering townsman of Galveston, perhaps not. He wouldn't be expecting to see such a personage on the Irish mailboat, in usual circumstances. But these are days of war, and the war throws up all inhabitants of the earth in strange places, rearranging and re-siting its creatures. However this man with his hearty plate of breakfast is in old civvies though the face is no more aged than Eneas's. He seats himself with an easy groan and gives Eneas a matey wink and throws off his battered shoes under the scratched tabletop. A companionable smell of much-travelled socks wafts up, very much the smell of war. But there's no war in this old panelled eating-room, just tired humans stoking their stomachs.

'Good morning to you, brother,' says the Negraman.

'How you do?' says Eneas. Straight off he knows this isn't any Galveston man because he has no Yankee accent. His accent is not Irish or English but it dances differently to the Yankee all the same. This is someone new from somewhere new to Eneas.

'I'm always hearing about the Irish breakfast from the priest back home. Irish lad from county Carlow. I don't know where that is. But I think I do in another way. From all his talking. And it doesn't disappoint, I tell you. Very fine arrangement here of the sausage and the bacon. But you'll be saying rashers, ah?'

'That's it,' says Eneas. 'I'll say rashers now on the Irish boat. No sense saying rashers to an English butcher. He'll only stare at you. "What you want, Irish?" he'll say. Like you were mad.'

'Well, we're all mad to the English, that's for sure.'

'We're all mad?'

164

'You know, Irish, African, Chinese man, all the boys from far away . . .'

Eneas laughs above his emptied plate like a moon over a moon. 'Yeh! That's it, right enough. Never looked at it just like that. But, you're right.'

So the man eats, and Eneas watches him.

'What brings you to Ireland?' he says.

'Holiday! I'm always hearing about Ireland from that priest. Carlow. What's that like, brother?'

'I never was in Carlow come to think of it.'

'Well,' says the man, rising, 'I'm going to go have me a shit as the soldier said. Goodbye now, brother.' And he gets up and leaves the plate still swimming in yolk and a part-chewed but rejected rasher lonesome there.

Eneas gives him a nod. He's worth a nod all right. Seems like a very pleasant person. But he's gone, his untied shoes whacking gently at the metal floor up the deck a bit. How quick they come, how quick they go. Friendship. Oh, well. God sails his boats on the pond of the world and at fall of darkness goes off through the rubbed-out roses with the boats under his arms like a fabulous boy. The clock is the terrible high clouds fleeting to some unknown meeting. In the city encircling the park of the world lives are lived quickly, the admired baby soon the dreaming old bastard in the narrow suntrap under the lee of the church. Quickly quickly everything goes.

*

Mid-morning they are released out past the barricades and through the railway entrance and on to the bare seats of he mailboat train that signals somehow to the returning men that now there's a pause to the music of an exile's heart and for a time they may think of themselves as natives in their native place. Eneas rides again the river of home like a broken branch. He feels that old sense of power that comes from being fit and alive in his own country, as good as the next man. Perhaps after a minute or two he feels only a modicum of that power. Perhaps now with his boots on Irish soil for a good half-hour he's not so sure of things. He has assumed that, as he has suffered in a mighty war and lain ill in a great asylum of England, his old sins will not be set against him. Now he's not so certain. He smells Ireland outside the window of the train, and she smells very much the same as always, as twenty years ago she smelled. Trouble, trouble. In the sights of the railway, the Victorian stations, the pleasurable monuments set up beside the curve of the bay, the swimming baths, the backs of good houses, the mottoes of factories, the aching spread of the city with all its numberless children sprinkled on streets and in rooms like specks of gold, with its gangsters and respectable folk rubbing shoulders in the bleak thoroughfares, in the sudden luxuriance of the Liffey from Butt Bridge, the tidy cargo ships tight to the wharfs, the high cranes peering into their innards, the beaten-out surface of the river thick with salt from the devious tide, the thrum of the moiling salmon in the secret depths, the filthy prams of generations fixed in the muddy undertows, in the huge silent racket of history seeping into the very blocks of the river walls, the pocked custom-house and everywhere and on everything the ruinous effects of the rains, in all these things he senses as he sits in the knocking train the old strains and presences of trouble, even there, four hundred miles from Sligo.

12

HE DEEMS IT PRUDENT to take advantage of the early winter dark and prefer the edges of the buildings and move carefully and keep his hatbrim tugged down over his eyes like Edward G. Robinson or Bogart himself. The joke of being an outcast in his own town isn't lost on him as he passes the Gaiety cinema just as the women are lighting the bright foyer for the evening custom. The joke is he's twenty years away and he can't recognize a soul, let alone prepare against attack. Would anyone attack him, just like that, on the strength of an order of long ago? But nothing more current than hatred. He must for the moment go softly.

It's the town he recognizes as an old friend. This surprises him. John Street, the Cathedral, the Lungey. If his father's new place is on the Strandhill Road, he has a deal of a way to go. He wishes he could cross the river and peer down into the Garravogue again but he's all the while going away from the water. Perhaps this nostalgia is a treacherous river all of its own, and river enough to be negotiating for the moment. Dangerous love. And he remembers Mr Jackson the master explaining in his batlike voice years ago that nostalgia means something hard and tricky in the Greek, not a pleasing feeling at all, but the *sickness* of returning home. And how Greek mariners, Homer's or just mariners of the wide and ordinary world in old epic days, suffered it, feared it, answered it, were led into the vales and isles of death by it, *where nothing is as it seems*. And yes, he understands it now, that mysterious claptrap of Mr Jackson. How wise he was after all. Here they are, the streets and houses of his boyhood, answering the roaring sickness in his blood. Memories and thoughts flash out of dark lanes, beam down from pub signs and chemist shops, leak from the doors of butchers with the slight stink of blood and sawdust. He thinks he remembers the butcher in John Street right enough, wheeling about all red-faced and rotund in the ship of his shop as Eneas passes. The fact is a butcher never grows old, he is eternal like the boatman at the river of death. This is a cardinal fact of life that he has often noticed. A chemist grows ancient, old and frail like mortal women. As does the grocer and the lady in the post office. Only the butcher goes forth into the centuries like a veritable vampire. It's all that red-blooded meat he devours in the back parlour.

As he leaves the shops and the people of Sligo whom he no longer knows, the old exciting smell of the sea begins to lap against him. He strides now along the Strandhill Road, and maybe there's a touch of the cock-a-hoop to his step, just a tincture. Look at him, in his black suit none too new and his slouched hat and not a soul in the world to call his wife nor a child to delight him and yet there it is, a touch of the cock-a-hoop to his step. Oh, he may be outcast, he may be taking his life in his own hands or putting it into the hands of others by being there in Sligo, but it isn't how he thought it would be. He is heartened again by that sense of not caring, of not being as afraid as he had feared! The fear of fear is a mighty afflicter. The thought of seeing his mother makes his heart bang in his chest, he wants to take his father in his arms and cry out for love of him. It is insane. Surely he needs another and a longer spell in the asylum.

He feels quite buoyant enough to ask a man going back up the road where the McNulty house is. The man knows instantly in the fashion of Sligo people, but Eneas doesn't think he is recognized. Perhaps after all he has been changed so much by life in the normal way that he can be another person here now, no longer the outcast of his youth.

At last he stands at the verge of his father's little kingdom. Indeed and it is a bungalow, quite a decent one. Even in the poor light of the moon and the stars he can see, almost feel, the order of the large gardens about the house. He knows straight off that his father has bought it for the bit of land and not for the appearance of the bungalow. It is a style of house come out of the East perhaps and one of the offshoots and fruits of Empire. If it is really designed to accommodate the sun and the monsoon of somewhere far off, it suits also the lonesome dark days of the Sligo weather. Certainly in sunlight it must perk up the place mightily. It is the perfect Acropolis to the little Athens of his father's garden. This is his euphoric suspicion anyhow as he lurks there alone at the gates. About him in the glooms all is composure, perfection and vegetables in a mighty order, he can be sure. His father's garden will have the humility of parsnips and the pride of hollyhocks. The bit of land must have knocked the old man sideways with excitement, his own bit and hopefully paid for. The band must be doing well for to furnish a place of this amplitude. With excitement not dissimilar to his father's, Eneas surges forward towards the rosy door.

*

'Sit you down,' says his mother, 'sit you down. Poor Eneas,' she says, 'all the lovely colour gone from your hair. But, God help us, you still have a head of it, grey as it is.'

His father keeps to the fringe of the carpet in the sitting room, as if he doesn't want to intrude too soon, as if he might do a mischief to himself or Eneas by leaping in too quick. He looks mighty wound up. He must be well into his sixties Eneas reckons and he has every year of his life worked into his bleached face. You'd say he was like a piece of pork that was washed out by water a few times, putty grey and soft in the skin. Neither of them thought to embrace Eneas and now already he's in a decent sort of a chair and stuck somehow, at least as far as embraces go. The room might as well be an army of savages the way it has a go at him. His mother has sewn flowers into cloths and draped them over the set of seats, a sofa and these stiff, clerical chairs. It all looks like a priest's parlour. His father is maybe afeared of the great cleanliness, of the great strangeness of it all. In John Street there was a lot of peaceable dust because things were old and nooks and crannies abounded. Here there is a fighting newness, a smell of newness like a fresh deal coffin. Of course there are a few winter pansies for colour as always which is familiar. He desires to kiss his old father's face, to touch it at least with a hand and make sure for himself, for his own reference, that his father is truly there with him in the peculiar room. He longs for his father to drag out even the cello and press a tune upon him, but his father only lingers there like a hungry bird afraid to encroach while the humans are in the garden. He has a sudden terror of time, that time is robbing him, that the river is pulling at him too fast, too strong. He's

170

speechless with love and remembrance. Perhaps they are too, or without the words you'd need for to conjure up those notions, perhaps the three of them are in the ruination of time, betrayed, betrayed.

'There'll be a good match on Saturday, there will be,' says his father. 'How long'll you stay, Eneas?'

'As long as ... You know. Is Jack home?' he asks his mother.

'Oh, yes, Jack's home, son. Sure aren't they expecting the third child? Imminent. Oh, yes. They've let him back for that. Compassion, do they call it? But he was only in England, you know, liaison officer for the poor Yanks in Leeds. It's the uniform I can't get over. Not that I've seen the creature wear it. But photographs. A lovely brimmed hat and all very smart trim.'

'Christ,' says his father, 'there's no touching the British for tailoring. You should see our crowd, the poor buggers going around in little better than sacks. I might have made them myself, in my heyday! Thank God for neutrality. We'd be the laughing stock of Europe.'

This might be a great joke but Eneas is so taken aback he forgets even to pretend to laugh. His mother certainly doesn't laugh.

'And Tom, how is he getting on? Mayor, you said, in your letter. Mayor, no less.'

'Tom's doing well enough,' says his mother grimly.

'How so?' says her husband. 'Well enough? He's king now!'

'Right,' says his mother, 'king. We brought him through a bit of a mess just these months gone by. King he may be, Tom, but he's still a fool in some things.'

'Ogh...' says Old Tom.

'You'll see him later, son,' says his mother. 'So you will. He's staying with us at the minute, like yourself.'

'Is he not married? I mean, I thought he would be by now, a musical man like him...'

'Well, he is and he isn't,' says his father.

'He is and he isn't?'

Old Tom gives him a silencing look, pleasantly. What's not familiar at all is the mire of talk he feels himself to be floundering in a little. He needs a good lamp to light his path.

'We don't like to...' says Old Tom, dark as a ditch. 'Your mother...'

'You saw Teresa?' says his mother.

'I did. I did,' he says. 'Oh, she seems right set up there. Really set up. The very best at the job they do there, going about and seeking alms for the orphaned boys. I never saw her look so, so – well, set up is the word I fixed on at the time.'

Old Tom gives a grimace, a private sort of a grimace that maybe speaks its own volumes. No, you'd need more than a lamp for this. A lightship maybe. A good moon. A midday sun better.

'She was sure of her vocation, so I didn't stand in her way,' says his mother.

Old Tom snorts ever so quietly.

'I never knew anyone before nor since so pious anyhow,' says Eneas, on safer ground he hopes. 'I'll never forget her praying for Collins that time in the old days. I suppose Tom'll be for the other crowd...'

'Well, he's no blueshirt, if that's what you mean,' says his mother severely, but devoutly.

'Blueshirts. Fascists, you mean, Mam?'

'You don't know the half of it,' she says, and another warning glance from his father. 'Anyhow, your brother's for the other lot. I wish it was more than whiskey and land.'

His father raises a hand as if to prevent a torrent, but his mother subsides.

'Any hope for the Garravogue? Any sign of the silt being dealt with?'

'Maybe your other brother will have a go at that when the war's done with all that engineering he has.'

'Sure, maybe he will,' says Old Tom reasonably. 'Let's get ourselves into the kitchen for to be dealing with that nice bit of lamb, Mary. Why don't we?'

*

In the morning he lies low in his room and feels no inclination to leave it. Instinct dictates. He hears children playing below his window and for a moment thinks it must be Teasy and Young Tom. But of course he realizes then that he's back thinking of twenty years ago. Young Tom is a big man in the town and Teasy is the finest mendicant nun in England.

He parts the curtains and finds two round faces peering in at him. He's surprised to see how near the ground is to the sill, because the bungalow is dug into the sloping lawn behind the house. The children shy away from the glass like they've come face to face with a monster and run off away around the house, screaming and laughing. It's a little boy of about five and a big long streak of a ten-year-old girl. He expects they must be Jack's kids if the wife's in stir having the new baby. His niece and nephew no less. If he was a real uncle he'd have brought gifts. As it is, he must seem mighty strange to them, lurking in a darkened room at the very prime of the day. It's not a thought that brings him comfort.

By the time he dresses and goes out into the kitchen, Young Tom has long left to attend to his no doubt magisterial duties as Mayor of Sligo. For a moment Eneas is unexpectedly offended that his little brother hasn't gone in to greet him after all these years but then he is the stranger of strangers, the vanished elder brother. He can't mean anything to any of them really. But there's Jack all right at the square kitchen table, looking very smart in a sleeveless gansey and big puffy shirtsleeves gathered at the biceps with silver bracelets, if that's the name for them. He looks like a sharp-eyed cardshark or the like, keen and sleek anyway as a shark, with a rich head of red hair pressed down with oil, shaved as a seal and scrubbed red by a pumice-stone you might think. He's drinking tea mightily, legs crossed, good brown shoe-leather gleaming, deep in the *Sligo Champion*. Down goes the paper with a little catastrophe of salt-cellar and teacup.

'Eneas, Eneas,' he says, leaping up, clasping a hand with comradeship and fervour, businesslike, absolute, overwhelming, 'How goes it, brother?'

'Oh,' says Eneas, 'You know . . .' His hand is shaken for some time.

'Great to see you back, boy. Will you stay? Get yourself fixed? Why wouldn't you?' He surely spots Eneas's hesitation. 'Sure all that ould stuff is over now. No, no, all done and over. These are new days now. Look at me, a major in the Engineers, and they haven't shot me yet!'

'They'd never of wanted to shoot you, Jack. You've a touch with people I never had. You're liked.'

This seems simple and good to Eneas, but nonetheless it causes a sort of obstruction in his brother's talk for a little. Jack takes a pinch of the spilled salt in his fingers and throws it over his left shoulder against bad luck. They both sit down at the table and smile at each other and his mother silently pours him tea in an excellent blue china cup, the like of which he's never seen before. The band must be doing bloody well all right.

'Thanks, Mam. My God, the great style in everything these times. The band must be doing well.'

'Not just the ould band,' says Jack heartily. 'Sure Young Tom has everything stitched. Land deals, whiskey deals. You've no idea.'

'That's enough of that talk,' says their mother.

'Ho, I tell you, brother Eneas, it might be wartime for Joe Soap, but for Young Tom it's harvest time. Petrol, oil, chocolate, sugar, soap even – all legal and above board, of course. Nothing ever passes through his hands. It's just – he accommodates the free flow of goods. In the interests of the town, the corporation. These are hard times for everyone.'

'And you're married, Jack? And were them your children in the garden?'

'Aye, little Des and Annie, you saw them? They weren't tormenting you?'

'Not at all.'

'The wife's up in the hospital. Ah yes, quite a little brood for ourselves. Wonderful.'

Their mother sets down a fry for Eneas with some vehemence.

'No, it's grand, Mam, it's grand.'

'Grand my eye,' says Mary.

Eneas smiles at them both in the manner of a stranger

wandered into an intimate conversation and with no wish to know what it's about. Nor does he. He wants suddenly for his family to keep their mysteries to themselves, to keep their eruptions well lidded for the nonce.

'Where's Pappy?' he says.

'Oh, in the garden, where else,' she says.

'I'll go out to him,' he says, scoffing down the remnant of the bitter fry.

*

His father's digging like a maniac, like a soldier under fire and not a trench to his name, in the further reaches of the garden where the bare black ground is, for the vegetables. At first Eneas stands and watches without greeting his father, astonished that he is forty-four and his father God knows what, yet he might after all be but the child of old gazing at his tremendous father. The old man still digs with the selfsame ferocity, the selfsame need. The rich dark sods turn away over at his flashing strokes.

'Hello there, Pappy,' he says gently.

'Eneas, oh Eneas, I didn't see you there. Like a ghost.'

'Like a ghost indeed, Pappy. The garden's a credit to you. More than that, a wonder.'

'Fine soil's my friend here. Didn't we have the high times, you and me, in the old place under Midleton's?'

'We did, Pappy, oftentimes.'

His father sticks the spade into the earth and lets it be. He comes over the ragged earth like a man walking on black waves and suddenly grips Eneas's arm.

'I don't care what they say about you. As long as you've got your health I'm happy. You're my son. My eldest son.'

'Right, Pappy,' he says, taken aback.

'And look here, don't mind what you hear about the house here, don't mind what they say, what the bloody carry-on is, this is your home as long as you want it, Eneas. To tell the truth, if the others were as little trouble to me as yourself I'd count myself a happy man.'

Eneas looks into his father's face, says nothing.

'Now,' says his father. 'There you are.'

*

At nightfall Eneas brings himself up as much as he can to the standard of Jack's clothing and, spruced and combed and polished, ventures out into Sligo. The few bob of his disability pension jingle in his britches pocket. Though only five o'clock the swamp of darkness and rain lies over the sombre town. Men are walking home along the shining pavements like soldiers scattered in a defeat. No one greets him. He passes the looming dark of the Showgrounds where the association football is played these times, the empty stands looking brittle and odd in the downpour.

The eight windows of the Victorian town hall are glowing out on to the black tar like eight bright shields of yellow bronze. On an impulse of brotherhood and love he enters the building. How strange to think his brother is master here, if that's the term in democratic Ireland.

He asks the little withered lady in the hall where the mayor might be, but the answer is so chill and unwilling that he has to add that he's the mayor's brother. Maybe she doesn't believe him but at any rate she brings him up the marble stairs to the principal offices. They stand outside the tall oak doors and he gets a powerful sense of two schoolchildren waiting to be punished by the master within. The old dame sticks her head in the door and he doesn't hear what she says but she indicates for him to go in.

The room is peculiarly bare like a policeman's, with a desk frothing with wooden carvings at the edges, and a veritable heap of papers and dossiers and files and pens and calendars quite neatly stacked and arranged. Behind the mound of important work sits his little brother, a red-faced person with a lot of healthy-looking fat on his face and hands. The backs of his hands are like a turkey's legs. The hair is black as an octopus's ink and in the black suit his brother Tom seems compact and perfect, like a painted advertisement in the station. He looks like he owns a brushed hat and a new car anyway, he looks like he knows his way about the alleys and lanes of official things, competent, secure, with a gold watch to top everything, solid on his thick wrist. He gives a huge impression of likeability and humanity, and indeed he gets up from his labours and floods about the big table and just embraces Eneas like the brother he is. It is a most remarkable thing really. Affection and enthusiasm and precision pour off him like good clean sweat. The man is a marvel to Eneas.

'I heard you snoring this morning, you divil,' says Young Tom. 'I haven't heard that sound for many a long year. Well, Jaysus, we've missed you around here, boyo. We have. Maisie, dear,' he says to a timid-looking girl in the corner, 'go please and fetch my brother Eneas some tea. He'll take four sugars, isn't that right?'

It's long enough since Eneas put sugar in his tea but he knows that Tom is remembering some important detail from twenty years ago and he's not the one to dishonour such accuracy.

'It is indeed,' he says, still frankly amazed by his brother. 'It's really good to see you, Tom. I'm delighted you're doing so well.'

'So am I! It won't last much longer. I won't be elected next year the way things are going. You'll remember Jonno Lynch. He's the boy now. Bloody blueshirts, excusing my French...'

'I do certainly remember Jonno Lynch.'

'Yeh, I'd say you do all right,' says the politician.

'I wonder does he remember me?'

'How do you mean? Sure you knocked around as kids, didn't ye? Oh, you mean, the other thing. Listen, Eneas, I can't be discussing that. You know.'

'That's all right, that's all right, just wondered if there was any word on it, you know. Sure you were only a kid at the time. How would you know anything about it. I forgot that.'

'Well, I'd know what's going on as mayor, but that civil war isn't over yet, if you follow my meaning, and it's best to keep a sort of lid on all that. I will tell you, because you are my brother, that a lot of things are still being settled that you'd think they wouldn't bother with now. Long memories, those lads. You'd always be hearing of fellas being shot, even now I'd be careful, very careful. I don't know what was said to you twenty years ago, but from what the Mam and the Pappy was saying the other night, the night before you came home, I'd tread warily and watch my back. If I were you. Which, thank God, I'm not. They sat up into the small hours with me, and they were very upset, very upset, wanting to see you, and worrying themselves to death about it. They're old, you know. I don't really know anything about your case,' he says, with a vaguely official air.

'Ah, sure, why would you,' says Eneas, head going down.

'Ye see, I didn't have half the fun you did, Eneas. I was tethered like a nanny goat. The Mam wouldn't let me out of her sight. Because of you and all the trouble you got yourself into.'

'Yeh. You've turned out grand anyway. The band must be doing well, I'd say?'

'Flying. The band's flying. Jesus, we have two hundred people out there in Strandhill of a Saturday. Mad to have the dancing. They can't get petrol, tea or chocolate, but they can still have the dancing. So they're all walking out early Saturday afternoons. And when the tide's out you'll see fellas coming over the strand past Coney and Oyster Island, their girlfriends' skirts all bothered by the winds. There was three men nearly drowned trying to cross from the Rosses a few weeks back, in an old bathtub of a skiff, the strong roar of a tide that there was in the deep channel. They're all mad for the dances, mad. It's something great.'

'Good for you, Tom.'

'And yourself, Eneas, how's it going for you? You were in France the Mam says. Fighting I suppose.'

'I was over there right enough.'

'Did you kill any of them Germans?'

'Nary a one.'

'Well,' says Tom, laughing too, 'Jonno Lynch would be pleased. I think he fancies them Germans in the days to come. The United Republic of Germany and Ireland or some such, with Jonno for gauleiter maybe. And me strung up from a tree, I shouldn't wonder. More power to your elbow, brother. Well done. You had the guts to go out there. Me, I'd rather stay and make a few bob, line the old nest. You'll have heard about the wife?'

'No, no, I didn't hear a thing. I know you're married now. I asked the ould fella about it. It's good. You haven't the few kids yet?'

'No, no,' says Tom, all reddening up, 'and I won't have them out of her now at any rate. No, sir. Not the best business for the bloody mayor's wife, you know.'

'Well, sure, you'll sort something out.'

'Oh, Jack warned me. Of course I wouldn't listen. Love, you know. Of course it's a regret. I don't like to think of her – stranded. Well,' and Tom leans close to him as the girl comes back with tea, 'say nothing.'

Eneas couldn't have said anything anyway because he hasn't the slightest notion what his brother means. Tom tucks himself back behind the desk and gestures to a splendid-looking chair for Eneas.

'That used to be the Ombudsman's chair. We got him a new one. He's only four feet six and he was lost in that yoke. You fill it well I must say. You should be in politics.'

'Do you want to get a drink out somewhere?' says Eneas. 'When we've this nice tea drunk. Will you have a pint with me?'

'No, I haven't the time. I'll see you later this evening. I've all these papers to sort through, to process as the new word has it. You'd never think a little town like this had so many transactions. They never rest. Scheming away. Never resting.'

After a few minutes Eneas feels it's time to relieve his brother of his presence. He rises to go softly. He understands his little brother, and the wave of work that builds against his neat form each day. He likes him. He doesn't care if he's a rogue or not. He seems like a decent and a pleasant man. For all he knows he might be as straight as a die. It doesn't matter.

'Eneas,' says Tom, as Eneas reaches the ornate doors, 'Jonno, your man Jonno, he drinks in Hardigan's with his mates. I suppose for the sake of peace you won't want to go in there. It's not the public house it used to be anyway. Gone downhill. Your friend O'Dowd will be sitting out in his big house at Rosses Point, wonderful great mansion he has out there, he must be a feckin millionaire that lad, so you needn't fear bumping into him.'

'Rightyo,' says Eneas, even as a keel. 'OK, Tom. Thanks.'

'See you tonight, big brother. Welcome home.'

13

THERE'S A TRAGEDY up at the hospital because the little chap born to Jack's wife doesn't last but the few hours. There's a great colloquy of misery, silence and dark looks in Old Tom's bungalow. The two children, Des and Annie, are taken out of their room and put into a back bedroom beside Eneas's as if they might be in danger too, as if Death mightn't know his way about the back of the house. The bereaved grandmother keeps muttering about the baby being weakened, being weakened by ... But she won't say what she thinks weakened the poor mite. Her mouth is twisted all the while she mutters in her chair, turning over and over the pages of a large scrapbook. The grief of Jack is palpable, visible too on his smart face. There's the queer stench of fright and grief off him. The little creature is buried in the graveyard under a wall plot for easy finding, and Mary declares she'll be buried at the end of all beside that unhappy scrap. Old Tom can jump in with her if he likes. They'll keep the unfortunate child warm.

It's terrible for Eneas to see the suffering of his brother. He knows there's some story there with the wife but he doesn't ask for such information. As far as he's aware the wife is a very fine woman from Galway that Jack adores, whose father was quite the gentleman living out the Grattan Road. There's something else that no one can tell him, but he has no desire to be enlightened. His brother's grief is terror enough.

The birth has ripped the guts out of Jack's wife, so she lingers in the hospital. She can't take a bath for herself apparently without the help of the sisters. You'd think marriage was a sort of war with its own alarming injuries.

He goes out, Eneas does, to escape the turmoil, as far as the dance-hall at Strandhill. Frost covers the dune grass in a futile net. He stands at the water's edge near the little shuffling of the waves and remembers France. He also remembers Viv but he puts her aside from his mind sorrowfully. He asked about her in the public house the previous night as lightly as he could but one man said she was married in Lisdoonvarna and another man opined that she was gone long since to America under contract to a shipping company. He remembers with force the high set of her backside and the insane glory of fucking her. These he feels are not noble memories or a credit to himself but nevertheless they are the memories that rush at him like flighty bullocks. There's little noble in a man's mind he must believe. And yet he would rather be king of his own nature and think of her nobly. So he puts her from his mind instead. How long ago it is, how far, and even so the strand looks exactly as it always did, with the same sense now in winter that the storms of winter have cleaned the place, scrubbed out the stains and outrages of the holiday crowd in the high summer.

What can he make of it all? He's very sad about the little baby. Very sad. That's not right to be happening. He wasn't able to comfort his brother at all. He didn't, he discovered, have the key to his brother's distress. But that is no wonder considering the great stretch of time spent away. He doesn't possess the key to any part of his brother. Nor worse of his mother and father, grieving there in the bungalow as if they had been robbed of their perishing souls. The size of grief astonishes him. The grief of France was immense, the grief of this small child the equal of it.

*

He comes up the high road towards the upper village of Strandhill on his way home because the tide is deeply in and he cannot think of crossing the estuary. The sea has oppressed him and he's glad to be among the salt-streaked houses. You can paint them as much as you like but the black stains are only months in the making. There's a fine house on the left side of the road with a castellated wall. To balance that on the other side someone has built a corrugated hut with a bit of fancy woodwork under the eaves to give some grace to it, but not much. A strew of roses blazes in the winter light beneath the tumbledown veranda. It must be someone's beloved holiday home but it's a queer one right enough.

Then he sees that over behind the intricate frozen roses there's a woman standing in the deepening shadows dressed in a light summer frock of cotton or linen. He didn't see her straight off because of the new dark and the pattern of large tea-roses on the frock. Around her shoulders she has a fur stole of some quality and her bosom is pleasantly high and plump. She must be icicles itself in that rig-out and no mistake. She looks for all the world like she's prowling there, prowling like a tigress.

'Jack,' she says.

'No, it's not Jack,' he says surprised, 'it's Jack's brother, Eneas. I don't think you know me.'

'I didn't realize there were three of ye,' she says. 'Do you know who I am?'

'No, ma'am,' he says, 'I don't.'

'Well,' she says, 'you ask Tom who I am. Ask Jack if you like. Then you can come calling and I'll brew you up a pot of tea, next time you're passing.'

'Are you not perished with the cold there?' he says kindly. 'You should go in maybe and warm yourself.'

'It's all right,' she says. 'It's safer out here. Did you ever see rats stealing an egg? I'm just after. One of them puts the egg on his belly and the other drags him off through the hole in the wall, you know, like a sledge in the snow. That was for me tea that egg. But the rats got it. They won't get me. I'm walking up and down like a madwoman to keep warm. That's what your mother says I am, you know. A madwoman.'

'My mother?' he says.

'Yes, your sainted mother,' she says. 'Your brother Jack has other names for me I hear.'

'Well, I better be getting on. I've a long road to go.'

'Yes,' she says. 'You come back some time when there's daylight. I've no light here in this place.'

'I will,' he says. 'Take care now.'

'Don't worry,' she says. 'I know what to do.'

He nods his head and passes on through the dusk, turning left past the Protestant church with its handsome yews. He has a right old walk now because of the state of the tide.

*

'Who's that woman there in Strandhill at the top of the road, do you know, Pappy?' he asks his father that night.

'Which woman?' Old Tom says.

186

'Woman there in Strandhill, I passed her, she was, you know, not all there, but she knew Jack and Tom all right. Thought I was Jack, in the dark, you know.'

'Oh, bless me. That's Tom's wife.'

'I was thinking maybe she was.'

'Oh aye. Roseanne.'

'What's she doing out there in that cold hut?'

'Well, they're not, you know, together now these times.'

'Why don't you get a proper place for her?'

'She's not interested. She likes where she is.'

Eneas doesn't know what to say.

'Aye.' Old Tom gets up creakily, and away with him.

And Eneas lies in the pleasant sheets. The world of Sligo is a deepening puzzle. Perhaps it always was. Perhaps there was always something deep in the water, pulling at the force of the stream, twisting it, like a drowning, or a trapped branch.

*

'I've to head back out into this damned war the day after tomorrow,' Jack says at breakfast, 'and I don't mind telling you, Eneas, it doesn't cheer me up.'

Jack was like a little sealed box mostly and you didn't know what was in it. Here he is now more uncontrolled with his red hair starting to stand up in places from the catastrophe of the last days, prising up out of the Vaseline like orange peels.

'Your wife will be out before you go then, Jack?' he says.

'No, no, but I have to go back. I have to go back.'

Maybe there's a note of relief in Jack's voice, maybe so. So far Eneas hasn't heard her alluded to by name which is a curiosity.

'I hear you ran into Tom's wife there the other day,' says Jack.

'Yeh, I did,' says Eneas, 'I did, Jack.'

'What you think of her?'

'Very – handsome.'

'Yes.' A very peculiar yes. 'The Mam moved heaven and earth, heaven and earth to get Tom out of that. Jesus, when I heard in India that he'd gone and married that one. Roseanne Clear! Jesus. Look, there's a serious problem out there in that corrugated hut. Mental.' Jack looks up impressively at his brother. 'I knew her in the old days before the war, before I married myself.'

'Went out with her?'

'She's not the sort of girl you'd go out with, as such. She'd be around the dance-hall, you know.'

'OK.'

'That doesn't shock you?'

'No,' says Eneas.

'Well it shocked the Mam. The Mam was shocked, the Mam got her way.'

'Wouldn't he be better off being with his wife?'

'Eneas, you've lived away from here a long time.'

Eneas sits still and watches Jack eating, like a person might watch a bird drinking from a tin in the garden. One move and it vanishes, with a blurring of fierce wings.

His brother is a creature he cannot intrude upon.

*

Then it comes. It comes though the letterbox as ordinary as you like and it is addressed to Constable Eneas McNulty. His mother brings it to him with a cup of tea. When he sees the manner of the name he hopes it is some official communication, but against that he can see that the envelope is too small and paltry-looking for that. There's no crest or crown or nothing like that, nor even the harp of the new state. His Mam with her narrow face, more shrunken than before like those heads from Borneo, but still the face he has carried so long in his dreams while he wandered, sits onto the edge of the bed silently. He rips the envelope and has a dekko into it. The message is typed in black and occupies only a brief space on the lined paper. There's no dear sir or yours truly, just a plain bare streel of words:

Sentence of death now invoked.
You will be hunted down wherever you are and slain.

'How is it?' his Mam says.
'Not so good.'
'Give us a look at it,' she says. Then after a bit, 'Might be a, you know, a prankster. Give you a fright.'
'Well, it's worked.'
'Oh, son, this is so hard for you.'
'Well.'
'Drink your tea, boy, and let's call it a prank.'
'Aye.'

*

He goes down to the river hoping to see salmon caught above the bridges of the town. In the old days salmon were a rarity because they didn't like the work of the dredgers in the river. If a salmon senses the least scattering of dirt in his home river, away out maybe in the farthest skirt of the estuary, he will not deign to enter, or she. The salmon is as clean as a pig in its nature though unlike the pig it will not lie down in the dirt that men force on it. Though the decay of the docks, the deep-water berths filling with the river's natural silt, is a terrible story, yet the return of the finicky salmon is a slight wonder to set against it. Fishers are taking salmon now of twenty, even thirty pounds, long big brutes of silver that are more like calves than fish. He would like to see that, so down to the river he goes in mid-morning when the tide is on the turn and the great engines of the fish will be clogging the rushing channels.

He enters the park named in memory of a local priest. It opens out and out along the riverbank till Eneas might expect to see those famous Indians of Texas come running out of the simple hazel and oak. As always among trees he feels a sense of danger and a sense of safety. Refuge and place of ambush. He admires the long ropes of dashing silver that the river is, seen through the slim branches. A cold bronze sun sits hooked in the tree-tops.

He looks back in the silence of the trees and to his great surprise there are three or four men in black coats coming along the path behind him, some fifty yards away. It is so like his dream of O'Dowd and his comrades that he stops on the crushed wood and mud of the track and stares at them. Much to his disquiet the men stop also. He even considers raising a hand in greeting, but if they are only walkers like himself or fishermen it will seem daft. He doesn't think that coats like theirs are the coats of anglers. They're more fellas you'd see in a bookie's office up the town putting ten bobs on nags in England and standing around as though wires tied them to the radio speaker on the wall. What's fear to him that has seen his fellows die on the beach in France but all the same the bottom falls out of his bowels almost and the muscles in his legs weaken. Because the sort of death his enemies might mete out to him will not be a simple one, will not be an efficient shooting or a good sincere cutting of the throat. Men like those will fumble his death, they'll be clumsy and vicious at the same time. He's seen reprisals and they always used to make the worst corpses, the bag over the destroyed head and the few bullets put almost insanely into places that wouldn't kill a creature kindly. It isn't easy to kill a man cleanly, it takes training and talent. Those four men standing in Father Moran's beautiful park would not be masters of murder, he's sure. And twenty years rusty at that.

The difficulty with walking on is it will take him further from the town and deeper into this curious wilderness. Of course that's why they've stopped. They don't want to kill him here. But look how he's leapt to this conclusion. Maybe they're not his assassins. Maybe they're feckin seminarians from the college on the hill. Maybe they are some of those wild men he sometimes heard about on ships that prefer the company of their own kind, and he's an intruder on their pleasures in these woods.

He presses on without looking back and when he turns a decent switch in the track he runs like a hare. He runs like a bollocking hare and his arms flailing and his coat flying back. He's a bit long in the tooth for this sort of running but he runs like a youngster on this occasion. It's by no means a warm day, but fresh sweat pours down his face and it tastes in his mouth like whiskey. The surface of the track is poor enough for running and his English boots keep sliding an inch here, an inch there, till he's almost skating.

At his back clearer and clearer he hears the other men trampling through the mud in fierce pursuit. He has no need to consider now if they're lovers of each other or not. There's a terrible huffing and puffing, and he knows they like this scrambling along as much as himself. Maybe the thrill of the chase enlivens them. It must be a crazy thing to go galloping after a human person with intent to kill!

Not expecting anything but an eternity of this running, he comes out abruptly into a more open section of the park. There's an iron railing to his right with a little iron gate all bent by boots and shoes and across the river he sees a hunting lodge with a jetty. There's a man fishing calmly from the toe of the jetty and another two men in a boat, one fishing and the other keeping the prow straight in the current with an anchor in the manner of salmon gillies. He sees all this with the clarity of hours, but really he has four seconds to take it in. His pursuers are just behind. He jumps indecorously in the air in the manner that would shame a boy and cries out across the pouring river. It's not in flood but nevertheless the music of the water is loud and complete. He gets no joy at all from those flaming fishermen. Why didn't he go to feckin Enniscrone for a seaweed bath if he was so mad to be out in the daylight? What are salmon to him? He hates the taste of salmon! He rips at his own black coat, its buttons flying off him like little bats, and plunges forward into the Garravogue. He loves this river but its chill is deathly. He has often wondered what the river felt like in winter and now he finds out. It's like shoving your whole body against an electric cable. His heart nearly stops in his terrified chest. He hopes the bastards will leap in after him because the river will surely electrocute them. It's bloody electrocuting him!

The ice, the deep pure chill of melted ice that is the river, like some liquid strained through a glacier in the far Arctic North, tightens down the screws of his senses with a violence indifferent to his life. Air balled up in the folds of his clothes seems to be life-jacket enough for the minute, though he dare not move or roll, and all the while he goes buoyantly in the fast tearing of the channel, the river's temperature knocks at his very blood and soul, wanting entry. He has a wild sensation of flying, soaring above the river, of being an instrument that cuts with awful blades through very rock. This salmony world is devouring and spitting him out at the same time, destroying and remaking him!

At Buckley's old ford he hits the ancient shingle of rocks and stones and tries to stand in the strong smooth mowing of the water. He doesn't know why he isn't dead. He might as well have torn out his heart and flung it to a lion in Dublin zoo as a means to save himself. He sees the roofs of Ardoghan House up to his right and staggers towards the mucky shore. Through reeds he goes, lifting moorhens out of their secret standings in clumsy sequences of splashings. They weren't looking to the river as a source of men but the demon shore itself.

He has to pass through the old estate as discreetly as possible and then get on to the town road beyond. There's not much a man can do to disguise half the river on his person. He tries to squeeze out his trews and jacket as he goes, but the heavy old cloth is agin him. He's so chilled he's bizarrely warm. Again the few magpies and winter birds he startles in the woods of Ardoghan seem to be made of fire and light, rocketing up through the thick black branches. So wet, so water-logged, so charged with the river, yet he half expects for smoke to burst out of himself as if he was a creature of fire.

The object of open amazement he enters the midday town, parting the crowd at the junction of O'Connell and

Grattan Streets like a veritable leper. This is some way to keep his presence in Sligo secret, never mind the marauding murderers in the park. Maybe they think he's a drowned man come back to walk among the living. A pretty pass to come to, the object of dread and astonishment in the streets where he followed his mother about as a child, from chemist to butcher, from the Cathedral to the Café Cairo ... Without pause or further sideways glance he strides into John Street and on up as speedily as he can after such an ordeal towards the desired, the much-desired Strandhill Road.

He doesn't want to have to explain his quandary to anyone in his father's house so he flits around the back in as much as a large man like him in a drenched suit can flit. Flitting is his aim, making his way from merciful rhododendron bush to generous larch. He suddenly feels colder now, knocked by a dull hammerblow of exhaustion as he nears his refuge. He has no idea how he will dry his clothes, but it will be enough he reckons to get into bed and try and recover. Grilled by cold he is now, as he searches at the back of the house for his room, one of these four windows near the ground. He grips the frame of the first window and peers in like a bear upright and ferocious, his face wild with weather and river.

He sees a sight that unexpectedly hurts him. His niece Annie lies on the little bed and his brother Jack sits there at the edge. The lamp on the bedside creates one fierce cone of light that is as present as a third person. Jack cradles a book on his lap and is reading boldly from it, and his daughter is agog, as if visible words were falling, flying and leaping from her father's mouth. Eneas cannot hear the words, so the scene has the force for him of one of the old moving pictures without sound. Indeed his brother in the grandeur and excitement of his performance is not a mile distant from the methods of the old dead wizards of the silent screen. Only the wind soughing in his own father's trees at the base of the garden provides a music.

He sees his niece and his brother and feels the bareness of his own life. It could be Old Tom with himself years ago, and he is distressed at the empty rooms of his own progress in the world. No children, no wife, no picture house where human actions unfold and are warmly enacted. He can barely remember why his life is so bare, he is that used to it, the bloody life of a lone seal out in the unknowable sea, dipping down for mackerel and feckin around generally in a lonesome fashion. Here before him is the achievement of Jack, despite whatever trouble was upon him, here is the child and the father and the book, here is the living scene more holy and sacred than any official ceremony, for which all wars are declared and every peace manufactured.

Oh but, what are those fierce flecks of gold and silver streaming in the little room? He must dry himself and rest or he'll have a fever to beat the band. He lingers, he lingers. What are those fleeting freaks of gold and silver light, and why is his brother's body like a brave flame, a handsome flame against the roaring of a wind? How does that wind of gold and silver not destroy his human brother and strike him down and make the earth forget him? The child smiles up at him like a lonesome bud among brambles, a rosebud, a rosebud, in the depthless sanctity of a daughter's love. It hurts Eneas, it hurts him, worse than any bullet of O'Dowd, but he admires it also more than gold.

*

He goes round in his state of dismal vision to the front door of the bungalow and throws himself on the mercy and intuition of his mother. He doesn't know what else he can do. He hasn't the love or the energy to break his way into his own bedroom. She undresses him like a child and lends him a big white nightdress of Old Tom's and feeds him full of stew before the fire and gives him a few measures of whiskey. He sits there like a pilgrim who has been ambushed far from Mecca. He shakes his head at the leaping flames.

Jack comes in later and drinks a whiskey at his elbow, but Eneas can't look at him easily, a trifle guilty about watching through the window. He can't even answer him or join in the talk but perhaps they accept his awkwardness as characteristic.

Jack heads off to the hospital and Eneas is left with his mother. He tells her in scanty detail about the men in the park, and she agrees with him that he has to go away.

'There's little point being killed in Sligo when the whole wide world lies before you,' his mother says.

'Mam,' he says, 'I doubt in my heart, you know, that I'll ever come back again. I hoped to settle down here with a job and such but it isn't to be. Short wars and long memories. I know Jack has his troubles . . .'

'He has,' she says candidly. 'His wife is up to her neck in drink the whole livelong day. That's the situation.'

'I know, but, truth to tell . . .'

But he can't tell any truth he knows, he barely knows it himself as yet. He fears his fettered mind and the recent madness he has endured in England. He doesn't know if his own eyes show him the world, or a different world that isn't there.

'Mam,' he says, as the whiskey thaws his heart, 'do you know, if it's a sad life, it's a bloody mysterious one too.'

'It is,' she says.

'I will always cherish the days,' he says matter of factly, 'when you and me were pals and went about Sligo like brother and sister, brother and sister. When you and me were pals.'

'Ah, sure, yes,' she says, smiling.

'But those days are gone and a lot of water under the bridge. Mam, I don't understand the world, nor think I ever will, our going into it or our getting out of it. I am forty-four and none the wiser. Why is that?'

'It seems to be the way for us both. A bit of happiness here and there. Throw out your leg now and then and be dancing. Otherwise, a crooked way. Though your father, you know, he's always happy, always was, with his fiddle and his whistle and his band. He'd be happy stricken in the fever hospital if he could still concoct a tune. You and me, maybe, are not, you know, the happy sort. We're the sort that don't know our arse from our elbow when it comes to happiness. Me, I had hard beginnings, but many a girl had harder and was happy enough . . .'

'Those hard beginnings, Mam . . .'

'Yes, Eneas.'

'What were they exactly, Mam, if I might ask?'

'Ah . . . It's just ould stuff. It's not important now. Least said, soonest mended. Telling won't help it. Silence is the job. It's a great thing, silence, when you can engender it in a town like this.'

'I'm not coming back, Mam, and it might stand to me if I knew.'

'I don't know how it would.'

'I did always wonder when I was a child if there was a mystery there.'

'No mystery. I'll tell you, child, because surely I love you and you're going away from me. I was reared up by the Byrnes, by your grandparents as you used call them, and surely he was a good enough sort, an army man formerly like yourself, batman to a gentleman in one of the old regiments. This gentleman, by name of Gibson, married a woman out of the music-halls in England, well, you know, an actress I suppose. But it's said she died after giving birth to her daughter, that is, my own self, and Gibson went back into the army in India and the child, that is, me, was given away for to be reared by his former batman, Mr Byrne. That's why you used to see me go down to Athlone every Saturday in the month. I'd be going to the solicitor's office there to draw my stipend that was established for me by the Gibsons.'

'Christ, Mam. And did you ever meet this man your father or know the family at all?'

'I never saw him in my life, though he's dead now these many years I believe. His family want nothing to do with me, naturally. I'm no better than a dropper to them, though I'm told my parents were married and all in the proper way. That's my secret such as it is, and it's a common enough thing in this benighted country of hypocrites and demons. I had a wicked time of it as a girl with the whispering that went on around me like a nest of sparrows.'

'I'm sure,' he says. 'I can imagine. Does Pappy know any of it?'

'No, and he doesn't, and what good would it do him? He's as deaf as a plank to rumour, you wouldn't get an innuendo through to him if you used a crow-bar.'

'No,' said Eneas laughing, 'you wouldn't.'

'That's your mother's story anyhow. It's a cruel ould thing to be called a bastard and you just a little girl. But what odds. They wouldn't risk it now. Your mother has told that to no one but yourself. I hope you still love her.'

'Oh I do, I do, Mam. I do!'

'Nothing ever meant much to me before I had my sons. It's my sons that keep me fixed to this earth. I'd kill for any of ye, and kill anyone to preserve your lives. That's the true story of Mary Byrne, and the devil take the story you can do nothing about.'

14

IN THE MORNING his mother hauls in his heap of dried clothes. She's had them above the range all night, and they're stiff and dry as salty sails in the Tropics, stiff and oddly scentless. They no longer carry the odour of his journeys. The old clothes are unfamiliar to him. In her frugal way, she has gone down to the riverbank in the sparkle of dawn and retrieved his coat and restored its buttons. She gives him some boots of his father's because his own will never, she says, be right again after their ducking. One time in the Gaiety the winder for the film or whatever they used, the projector, was it, went wrong, and the picture they were showing slowed down, and horses and riders surged and fell softly and slowly as in a dream. This is how he feels now, as if he is slowly and softly engaged in a lonesome dream. It terrifies his heart that he must go again. The mountain of going is twice as high as ever, he has got a taste of the world he prefers for all its maggots and mysteries, the queer element that suits him as a creature. His family puts the wind up him mightily in many regards. Yet he would rather not be gone. Be gone he must. His mother gives him lamb sandwiches in greaseproof paper like he was going out for a day's labour somewhere, not a life's labour in the wilderness of the earth. He looks at the sandwiches and wonders half-humorously if they can carry him across the burning midlands of the world, if he has the heart to be a mere wanderer again. There's a seed at the back of his mind that suggests that leaving is still an adventure, but it's only a seed. The great tree of hope and energy is no more. He hopes it might grow again, somewhere in the wastes of this strange earth. With his sandwiches as perishable talisman he accepts his mother's kiss and she accepts his, and he heads away into bright Sligo with his soul as simple as a salmon's.

*

At the station he discovers a wealth of hours exists between now and the Dublin train, and he is stumped there, in the wooden world of the ticket office, with his scratched case. He's not a man to suppose that this gap of time has been lent him for nothing, and indeed at the back of his mind ever since their meeting his conscience has been raising the spectre of Tom's wife, mad as marram grass out there in Strandhill. He has taken good heed of Jack's words on the topic but all the same there is another instinct that is greater than his brother's words – his own plain word as a human person, given freely as the corrugated cottage hastened into darkness.

The poor old Jarvey Tomlinson whose father was killed in the sappers long ago runs him out in the battered Tourer. Where you could tour in a conveyance like that was a question. It was just luck that got them out as far as Strandhill. He commissioned Tomlinson and his epic vehicle to wait on the top road beside the old graveyard where a quiet smoke might fill the time, and off with himself down the sun-speckled road to the hut. Strandhill was afflicted now by a miserable sun all salted by a little bladed wind. A person would need a proper greatcoat for this fierce class of a season, especially a person that had taken a long swim the day before in the Garravogue. Never mind, he wraps his decent coat about himself and stands in under the veranda of roses and has a smell of them. Roses always make him glad to be alive, the strength of smell they enjoy.

'That's my Souvenir de St Anne's,' says someone behind him and he knows it's her before he turns.

'I was just calling on you, you know,' he says. 'I'm leaving Sligo and I just thought I'd call on you like we said.'

'I'm just back from my shopping,' she says, swinging a string bag at him softly, 'not exactly pearls from Macy's but it feeds the old maw.'

'It smells good, your rose,' he says, as she sticks her key in the door and starts to disappear into the interior blank to him as Africa. If a lion roared in the distance down on the beach it wouldn't startle him, she is that strange. She certainly has a beautiful back in her slight cotton outfit, and the most tender-looking hips and backside. Oh, yes, he's hurting now, and a little tic has begun in his left eye the way it does when desire afflicts him. He will never forgive himself if he goes on in this light and he feels confident that it was not the purpose of his visit to ogle her, or that Jack's intimations about her stirred him at all.

'Do you know,' she says, 'I actually prayed last night that you might make it back to see me. I don't know why.' She sort of casts her shopping adrift on a pleasant wooden table in the dim room. 'Don't ask me why, brother.'

'I won't stay long,' he says. 'I have the jarvey waiting up by the Protestant church, and my train's going in a couple of hours.' She doesn't seem to have much interest in this. 'From the station, you know,' he adds desperately.

She goes with terrific grace into the back of the hut, and

he hears the strong rush of tapwater and he's surprised she has water on tap, and she comes back in and hands him a glass and says:

'Champagne?'

The stuff is fizzing mightily, and for a moment he thinks Tom must be treating her royally what with the rationing and all that even though he's mayor, but one sip tells him the truth. He can't think of the name of what it is. He's afraid to ask in case she believes it's champagne in her madness. There might be a terrible rudeness in it too. My heavens, the things that people call eggs and cream nowadays were only shadows of those things, and maybe she has just taken things a little further and this is indeed in her perished mind champagne. He sips at it brave as an actor.

'You're better looking than Tom though he's a mighty man in the doss, but I suppose your brother Jack is the Valentino in your family with his face and the red hair. I was up one night a while ago at my father-in-law's place and I was looking in, you know, through the windows, and I saw Jack there in his uniform and I thought, well, the poor creature, he misses wearing it out on the street, the poor man.'

'You were up at the house?'

'Oh yes, I was going to beard the lion, but, my courage failed me. I can't stay out here for ever and I thought I could talk to your mother or something.'

'And did you?'

'Not at all, amn't I telling you?'

'You shouldn't be looking in the windows, you know, at the back of the house and all.'

'Oh, is that right, and did you never do it?'

He says nothing, how can he after all?

'Go on,' she says, 'what else is left me, but listening at doors and spying on my in-laws. Sure, child, they've made a madwoman out of me and worse. I should have your brother shot for a start. You know, I've been around with some pretty rough fellas and there was a time when I could have had that done, like that, snap your fingers, oh yes.'

'Ah,' he says, 'do you know, for an educated man, I don't know, he's my own brother, and an officer, but, he doesn't know women, anyhow.'

'You do?'

He flushes like a fool.

'Ah no, I mean it,' she says, 'Jesus. I'm not trying to be smart with you. You've knocked around yourself. You know the world a bit. I tell you, better than me. I never been beyond Sligo much. I was in Dublin once for a horse show week, that a fella brought me to. He was to bring me to the Isle of Man after. But you know.'

It's true now that he's perplexed enough not to know what to say any more. She's too big for him, too expanded. Neat as a rose, she is.

'Were you telling that that rose out there, now, has a name, or some such?'

'Oh God, yes, they all have names, boy.'

'What is the name of it?' he says lamely.

'Souvenir de St Anne's. Dublin, you know. St Anne's Park? Where the Guinnesses lived one time. No? Ah, sure, you Sligo men. I have to take them in at night in their pots, like dogs, or the frost would stop them quick enough.'

There's another silence.

'What is it, boy?' she says.

'I don't know,' he says. 'I'm flummoxed.'

'Flummoxed? By what?'

'Yourself,' he says, helpless.

'Listen,' she says, putting down her own glass anyhow.

'What?' he says, startled, like the glass had been his shield. 'What?' and showing the whites of his eyes maybe.

'OK,' she says, 'look. Life is brief, isn't it? That's what the philosophers say anyhow.'

'That's the story,' he says.

'You want to climb in the old bed, in there, with me?'

It's his brother's wife. It's the woman his mother reviles. Jesus, he's thinking, she's like something out of the Bible, Book of Revelation, no less. Babylon. He never saw a Babylon so sweet and hard, like a sweet nut in her dress. Breasts on her as soft as twilight and you'd say she was burning there in the half-light, alive as a God. There is more to her than meets the eye too. Her talk really obliterates him. It would be sinful to touch her, not because any human religion says so but because ... He doesn't have a because. He wonders suddenly why she said 'Snap your fingers' instead of actually snapping them but maybe she doesn't have the gift of doing it like some people can't raise just one eyebrow and most people can't jiggle their ears. Who was the Englishman says we are all from apes? Not this lady. His heart's gone on him now because she can't snap her fingers but said 'Snap your fingers' instead. That's danger-ously endearing. Now if he was standing in one of those fancy cocktail bars in London or some place swank such as the crazy officers in the asylum used to hanker after, he'd know the word for her he thinks, and that's charming. Maybe she is also a madwoman in a cheap dress, but youth in the world is everything. Lovely – glad as a rose was the phrase. Even as he thinks these matters he understands how rusty all these sections of him are, and Viv comes back to him and truly has not far to come, just up the hill of cold sun and sharp wind from the forgotten breakers beside the hill of sand below.

'Oh, you're far away now,' she says. 'A penny for them.'

'Not worth a penny,' he says.

'A halfpenny then,' she says, and takes three strides to him and sets herself in against him. She reaches up both hands like she was going to take his head down from a shelf and takes the head and he feels her hot hands on his cheeks. And she gets her lips on to his and kisses him not unlike Viv used to years ago, with her tongue as lively as a snail.

'Oh,' she says, pausing for breath, 'you're crying.'

'It's been a while,' he says. 'The war and everything. You know.'

'I know,' she says. 'Come on,' she says, 'you can get another train, surely.

'OK,' he says.

'In the morning.'

'OK,' he says.

'Go up the blessed hill and pay off Tomlinson, for God's sake.'

'All right.'

So he goes to the door.

'What's that we were drinking?' he says.

'Alka-Seltzer,' she says.

'Mighty good stuff,' he says, and hurries off like a veritable Don Juan or a cowboy or some fool playing a cowboy or whatever but as happy as Larry, whoever Larry was.

*

Morning comes colder and clearer, the gulls rocketing over the iron roof and racketing like maniacs, he has slept like a caterpillar in its hammock of silk. Now she doesn't speak but feeds him a veritable crust of bread and some tea with a taste that must mean the leaves are old and secret in the scullery. She's neither angry or gentle but absent. She dresses him like a child, firmly, neither gentle or angry. And puts him on the road like a grown son. He feels inclined to speak himself, to thank her even, but he knows better. She picks bits of dirt off his coat, and now he feels like a husband. And she turns about and leaves him on the graceless tar and leaves him to wonder and go up the road with the high gulls and the salt of the sea blowing up from below where the ghost of Viv seems still to be in his dark memory, and this is an hour of ease to him, a cherishable hour, with its own confusion maybe, but a right confusion, yes, certainly, and he is aware then of his prick, damp and sore and small in the nest of his trousers, and gratitude does not describe what lights his head, nor yet love, but he knows he'll carry the demon of that single night with Roseanne into the tiding reaches of the coming days, and greet that demon ever with a dark and conspiratorial greeting, and he hopes in his heart he hasn't done for the blooms of her roses, that stood out all night in the foul drench of the frost and the darkness, and were never taken in.

15

THE ATOMIC BOMB brings the men home from every quarter of the earth because the war is not so much over as stunned back into history, and Eneas must be nimble and quick with the employment columns in the newspapers and smell out something to put food in his belly. He's getting older no doubt and his illness is on his army record so there isn't a kaleidoscope of happy jobs open to him. At length he finds a job digging in Africa.

Africa in his Sligo head before he goes to Africa is a strange little tinful of fourpenny thoughts. Darkness, but when he gets there, a sun brighter than the creation of the earth. Primitive, but after a few days in Lagos it's a sort of a Sligo, but bigger, and alive as a Yankee port. So his fourpenny ideas aren't worth fourpence.

He belongs now the while to the East African Engineering Enterprise Company, with his contract signed and sealed in London, and his next three years indentured more or less to their efforts to bring water into regions catastrophically dry. For if there are to be farms, proper farms with proper European crops, fantastically long canals must be constructed by the EAEE and its indentured men, weird straight canals and bizarre twisting ones joining Muslim districts to Christian and Christian to pagan, good water crossing borders as swift and covert as flightless birds. Men of strength are needed, who can dig like blessed dogs, and have eyes in the backs of their heads like Grecian mythologicals for whatever tremendous dangers might bear down on them. So Eneas is told at each official juncture, at each signing and briefing and, he might say, preaching session. For Africa makes Bible spouters out of everyone, even the passionate engineers of the EAEE.

He wakes one morning at normal cockcrow in his wooden quarters in Lagos. Already he feels after a mere few weeks of tin cups and strong wine like a Lagos man, and it is just as well. Because this day is the day of his ascent upcountry to the canal works. Into his sun-stiff shirt and simple trousers and on with his stout shoes and then shaved and then a bit of already familiar food and onto the rough trucks and away. In the fashion of a human man.

At his heart, not diminished by the space of time banging about London, or the long sea-miles of the sea voyage, leaning on rails, playing poor cards in the steerage spaces, engaging in endless spieling talk about nothing with a variety of unlikely passengers bound for a hapless Nigeria, at his heart, a soft bird in a nest of dry moss, Roseanne, the flash of her linen dress, her dark easy breasts, every door in the mansion of her good self flung open, and a veritable bevy of owls and wild birds bulleting in and out, rattling the sashes with such screeches and yells of love, by God . . .

The elderly truck leaves the dwindling city. He's in mostly with a bunch of Lagos men, so there's seven pairs of shoes tipping against another seven, each side of the vehicle. The road throws them about familiarly, but it's not minded, there's laughter. On top of the truck ride the bound spades as new as gifts, jostling slightly. And the tin container of water bangs about and surges where it hangs from the tailgate. Eneas is missing Roseanne surely, but against that is the wide freshness of this southern clay and the sky so soft and clear it's a sort of happiness to look at it from the darker shelter of the awning. He suddenly thinks of himself running into the Garravogue and passing drenched through Sligo and he laughs out like a madman. It isn't taken as madness but more likely spirits as high as the other men's spirits.

For a good long while after, Eneas is examined by the quiet face of the man opposite him. It's not offensive.

'Well, I've seen you before, brother,' says the man finally, almost striking one of his own knees like in a music-hall skit. 'Do you remember where that was?'

'I should,' says Eneas, 'But . . .'

'It's not so long ago, brother,' says the man. 'A year maybe, maybe more.'

'Is that so?' says Eneas, but he can't recall it. As a matter of fact his head is addled in the matter of recent days, and those days further off are in a general state of rebellion.

'Yes,' he says, 'don't you remember? On the boat to Ireland that time.'

'On the boat to Ireland?' Eneas says, incredulous.

And any of the other men listening laugh at his surprise.

'I wasn't expecting you to say that,' he says.

'I suppose not. Don't you recall it?'

'I don't . . . I should . . . These are hard days. The old head . . .'

'Of course,' says the man. 'How come you're riding here with us, going digging?'

'Have myself indentured now to the company for three years, whatever's in store for me, I don't know.'

'Pretty tough work but you look like you can handle it.'

'I hope so!' he says, and the other men laughing again.

'Snakes for breakfast, fevers for lunch, and savages for tea. That's what we say.'

'Savages?'

'Well, we're all savages, truth to tell. What's your name?'

'Eneas.'

'Not so common.'

'It's a Sligo name.'

'Sligo would be your home place?'

Eneas finds himself considering this.

'Not your home place?' says the man helpfully.

'Well,' says Eneas.

'My name around here is Harcourt, because I was born down there in Port Harcourt, if you know that place.'

'Yes,' he says. 'Big shipping port.'

'That's it,' says Harcourt. 'My father, he is a piano tuner and soon after I was born moved to Lagos to be near the pianos of the rich' – now the other men are listening with their faces turned plainly on Harcourt – 'and raised me up pretty good, sent me to school even, drove those Christian values into me. All with the shillings he earned, going from house to house, piano to piano, bigwig to bigwig. Not bad for a blind man.'

'Not bad,' says Eneas. 'My father was in the music business too as matter of fact.'

'Yes?'

'Yes – dance-bands, you know.'

'Sure, brother,' says Harcourt, and the truck takes a dip and bangs the men about for a few seconds. 'Don't know how we got talking about fathers,' he says, laughing.

'Well,' says Eneas.

'You play yourself?'

'What's that?'

'You know,' says Harcourt, 'you play anything, tootling, or the like?' And he fingers an imaginary trumpet for further illumination.

'No, Jesus, no,' says Eneas.

'Ah, well,' says the man. 'I don't tune pianos.'

The truck weaves on across its chosen course. The men are content to sit with their hands on their cotton knees and their bodies as loose as they can make them to accommodate the rolling and the toppling. Short deep-red bushes flash by in the torment of heat outside. Burning, burning, but the high yellow sky amiable, kinglike. Must be a fair strain on the axle, Eneas thinks. The truck is British-made, simple and robust, all perfect childish angles thrown against the chaotic terrain, the tyres uniting both, yielding, leaping, simplifying the elegant empires of rocks and burning bushes. Now he looks at the men one by one, wondering at their stories. Every face a life of words. Mothers' sons. Maybe in trouble some of them like himself, because truly to go out into Nigeria to dig is pretty nigh kin to prison work. Only a desperate man, or a crazy, would go out. A three-year sentence of solitude, and hacking at the earth – thank God. In the Foreign Legion you'd be shooting at local men, here you could dig with them, ear to ear. He saw that film one time on a cold afternoon in Chester, Laurel and Hardy, and poor old Hardy rubbing his foot for ease and finding it was bloody Laurel's foot! Almost a recruitment film for the Legion that was, the fun they had.

'That's – astounding now,' says Harcourt. 'Me meeting up with you again like this. Who'd put odds on that? But that's how the world's made, you'd have to conclude now and then.'

'Certainly is,' says Eneas. 'Maybe I do remember you . . . The war years – only hash in the head now.'

Eneas wonders for a moment what the man Harcourt might have been doing in that far part of the world in those years but it isn't a thought that bothers him. Every last thing was topsy-turvy those times, nothing in its place, people finding themselves in all sorts of queer localities suddenly, homesick maybe, knocked about, half daft in the head . . .

'Hey, Eneas,' says Harcourt. 'You know how far it is to camp?'

'Haven't a God's notion.'

'Me neither,' says Harcourt. The truck fumes on a half-minute. All crimes and sorrows, all mothers, histories, are hidden in the afflicted smoke. 'That's how I like it!'

Laughter again.

*

Moonlight brings Nigeria closer to Ireland. It might be Ireland because the night is still and quiet as a stone. The camp receives them with a mixture of officiousness and good humour. They have their bunks assigned to them and their hours explained and it is just the same as anywhere in the world except Eneas does notice the clash of wit and easiness between the new men and the old hands. The talk is very speedy and he doesn't catch the gist of much of it and he knows these men would have the same difficulty if they were to find themselves of a sudden on the quays in Sligo, one single Negraman among a few dozen dense-speaking Irish. But he's glad now to be among the grubby tents with the toiling ditch of a canal reaching back up the night-encrusted plain. He eats some kind of vegetable stew with them, and they turn in like sailors on a becalmed sea, and it seems natural enough that Harcourt, the nearest thing to a fellow Irish, lays himself down on the bunk adjacent. Soon the room is a parliament of fireflies, the soft intensifying and dwindling whorl of cigarettes.

Harcourt gives Eneas a pleasant smile for himself. A few of the men gather round a candle stub and flick a pack of grubby cards about. One of the players has a bruised face, three or four dark-blue flowers of bruises, a week or two old. But the storm of violence seems far distant from him now, because his wrecked face frowns and mutters over each shining hand of cards.

'So, what were you doing there, in Ireland,' says Eneas, 'that time I met you?'

'What did I tell you I was doing?' says Harcourt, the ash from his cigarette beginning to gather unheeded on the chest of his long johns.

'I don't know, since I don't remember it . . .'

'You know Rice's public house, at the top of Grafton Street?' says Harcourt.

'In Dublin?' says Eneas, a little disorientated to hear those names out of God knew where in Nigeria, from the friendly mouth of a Nigerian.

'I think I told you I was on holiday! I think I did. Yes, I did. And I think I told you that the priest at home, at home there in Lagos, because, though born in Port Harcourt I have to call Lagos home, since me and my father lived there so many long and busy years, but I told you that already – what was I saying, oh, yes, the priest – can't remember what I was going to say to you about him . . . Well, brother, Rice's. Now that's a fine establishment. But on the first

floor there of Rice's was this little office of Army Intelligence. You won't have known that, anyhow. I hope not!'

'Army – which army?'

'That's right, you got your own army there in Ireland,
don't you? And it's not like the army here, which is really
belonging to Britain and His Majesty himself. No. But,
during the war, and secret, as secret as any secret between
girls, you know, well, His Majesty's army kept a little office
going there in Rice's, for the gathering of information
generally, in your sweet neutral country, information of
invasions, and such like. And me, I was assigned, due to my
indubitable talent for eliciting information in an easy and
decent manner, I was assigned to travel between Belfast and
Dublin on the trains and talk to servicemen in their civvies
and the like and to talk to any foreigners, you know, that
might like to be talked to and have information they might
or might not be aware they had.'

'By God – and did you gather much of interest?'

'Of interest ... I heard sad tales of wives deserted, of
children displaced, I heard tales of love, and history. Men
told me small dark secret things that would mean nothing
to anyone but were eating them away. I heard of great
things done by ordinary people, kind of astonishing things,
lives rescued from districts of hell. I heard of women's
breasts cut off and I heard of things so terrible I don't recall
them, I don't retrieve them from those times I was told
them. Up and down on the Belfast to Dublin train, on the
Dublin to Belfast, the friendly man, the madman, listening
and I tell you, sometimes crying like a child, more often
laughing, think of it, what an occupation. Yards and yards
of things of interest, but, nothing of use ...'

'Just as well maybe – in Ireland . . .'

'I don't know what you mean maybe, but I know what you mean. I was long enough there to know what you mean and not know what you mean. Yes, sir, brother.'

'There are many strange things about that war, and that's another strange thing you've just told me.'

'Haven't you noticed how out-and-out strange as a rule the world is, Eneas, man?'

'I have.'

'And how so little of it illumines anything at all. How so little of it shines the least light on the smallest penny of fact or truth?'

'That thought, that could be something in the Bible, Harcourt.'

'Most likely is, brother.'

'So how come you're out here for the digging yourself, Harcourt?'

'Eh?'

'You know, Army Intelligence like you were, how come you're digging out here? You know, you asked me the same question in the truck.'

'Did I? See, force of habit. Put me in a moving vehicle and I ask questions I should maybe leave alone.'

'Oh – I wouldn't pry. God knows, a man must keep his own counsel. Goes without saying.'

'Anyhow, Eneas, why I'm here is another story. It's no mystery. Fact is, I was invalided out – even before the war ended, blast me. I always had – well, this medical problem. But I was able to keep it hidden for a long while. Then one day I failed to keep it hidden, hidden anyhow from the eyes of my officers. They were kind. But I was out, and then home after a while, and you know what the situation is now for work, and I couldn't find any work using my head such as it is, so I'm out here using my body such as it is, and God help me ...'

'A person's got to feed himself.'

'Well, a person does.'

'And this ailment of yours ...'

'I tell you,' says Harcourt, 'there's worse things than buggering ailments and being fecked out of the army. It's not easy to be at home. I didn't want to hang about Lagos. Things have changed there, brother, it's not my town any more. My father's like an old cracked cup now that won't hold water. Some days, my father, he thinks he's the king of England. Confused old man he is now. He's got the notes all jumbled in his head and he's no use for the piano tuning. A sad sight. And that always troubles a son. Maybe I should be looking after him. But Lagos is full of wild men these days, wild-talking men. With the war over some men want great things, big things, and especially that big thing you have in your sweet country, and I'm talking about independence. And those sort of men don't like my father's sort and they don't like me, who was in the army, you know, and leads a quiet life, and takes things as they come ... Death-threats are all the fashion now in Lagos, let me tell you.'

'This is a familiar story,' says Eneas.

'Yes?'

'Familiar.'

'Well, so maybe you know what's going on for me so, I don't know. You say it's familiar to you. Good. That's good.'

'I wish I didn't.'

'Ah, yes. We all wish that. Goodnight, brother.'
'Goodnight.'

*

The house of the chief engineer looks like the drawing of a house that a child makes with a door in the middle and a window each side of the door, except the roof is flat and the fact is the whole house can be dismantled and trucked on to the next site across the packed dry earth. The chief engineer has a houseboy in a fine suit a little dusty that has belonged in the past to the engineer possibly and is a cast-off of sorts, but finer than any clobber of Eneas's. And the great man drives a big motorbike at the greatest speed he can muster, revving the throttle across the thorny spaces and creating in his reckless wake a wonderful flower, a bush of red dust. And indeed, the engineer's greatest pride is a pot of roses that stands at the door of his movable house, and is watered and kept shaded from the worst ovens of the heat by the houseboy. At night when he looks in Eneas can vaguely see the waves of mosquito curtains billowing and the chief engineer is at that time of day decked out in his mosquito boots and fair play to him. The canal already exists on careful charts in the house which are brought down to the site hut in the mornings, rolled underarm like large batons. And such expertise is wielded you might say against the strange blankness of that district.

It happens that this person is an Irishman called Benson from Roscommon, so in the first week Eneas is sought out for news of home. Benson has style to him like a polished stone, an ordinary stone off the roads of Ireland, but polished. And he has great politeness, Eneas immediately notes, and is agreeable and not satirical as the jumped-up species of Irish or any people can be. Eneas is stopped in his digging and brought up to the hut and given a mug of best tea and it is as refreshing now as a bathe in asses' milk, if that is refreshing, not just beautifying, as in the tales about Cleopatra.

'So,' says Benson, 'another Irishman, McNulty, you say, well.'

'That's it,' says Eneas and he notes in himself less of an ability to talk to this man than to Harcourt, still below sweltering with a ready shovel.

'Yes, yes,' says Benson, 'you know, I worked with a man called McNulty some years back, from Sligo, when we were both employed up there on the Gold Coast. A very nice man he was. Jack McNulty, an engineer like myself. I don't suppose he's any relation of yours?'

Eneas is on the cusp naturally of saying my brother, but he doesn't say it. No, he doesn't.

'I don't think so, sir,' he says, a little army fashion, a soldier speaking to an officer, a hint that Benson catches.

'You were in the war?' he asks.

'I was.'

'So was I,' says Benson. 'Bomb disposal. The engineer's lot.'

Eneas is about to say, 'Like Jack,' but catches himself in time. He doesn't know why he has denied his brother, as the saying goes, but he had better stick to the denial. Sure enough Jack did do some bomb-disposal work as far as he knows. You needed a quiet hand and a stout heart for that.

'What did you do yourself, McNulty?' says Benson.

'Not much is the answer. I was – taken off the beach at Dunkirk. Well, in a kind of way. But sometimes, I don't remember it.'

'Where did you come from this time when you came out here?'

'London.'

'Poor old London. I hope they can rebuild her. And I say that not only from a professional point of view. Thank God the war is over. Thank God.'

'Aye.'

'You see that rose? Isn't it a beautiful thing? "Peace", is the name of it. It was bred in France and launched on the world on Armistice Day. Every rose has a name, you know.'

'I expect.'

Eneas has that sense of his answers getting shorter and shorter but he can't help it. He feels he said too much when he mentioned Dunkirk. It gave him a fright to say the name. Maybe he hadn't been at Dunkirk and certainly oftentimes he knows he wasn't. Just as surely at others he knows he was. Looks like he has a choice of memories for the same times here and there. Not so good. Anyway, discretion, discretion. Of course he thought of Roseanne when the topic of the roses came up, but what would be the use of mentioning Roseanne to Benson? He would like to answer Benson like a civilized man but he can't afford to. Roscommon after all isn't so far from Sligo in fact neighbours it and if he has travelled so far for safety he must play it safe with Benson now. Maybe he doesn't altogether like the mother-of-pearl buttons on the man's shirt and the well-cut jacket and the general air of power and happiness – well, whatever the general air of the man is. Poor old Jack, with his mountainous problems, there was a time when he would have been proud to acknowledge Jack, educated, officer, and to talk about Sligo to any man who could share an understanding of its beauties and dangers, but somehow something has changed. He still sees instantly the grievous bulk of Knocknarea rising massive and elderly in a filthy rain, or the rain-browned pavements of the town, when the word Sligo sounds like a holy bell, but, something nevertheless has changed. It isn't just the famous threats of Jonno and O'Dowd and those hurtling shadows along the riverbank, but some inner urge now to privacy, to peace even it could be said. He doesn't believe any more in one man fishing fact and remembrance from another man. He's happy to drink the tea. He's happy to say nothing. He couldn't care less whether anyone followed him out here to shoot him. What an achievement that would be, to trail him across half the world, traipse upcountry here and execute the notorious enemy of the Irish people. Well, his blood would freeze and he would shit his pants if he saw them coming, because fear is an animal that lives in a man separately, and pokes its head out at will. No, it is that fear so long endured and the nature of his life with that fear as his companion animal that seem to have changed him, altered the man himself. Eneas McNulty. Maybe he should change his name he thinks, except it's very hard to trust a forged passport and anyway he believes that this fear long suffered has changed his face, changed the lines on his hands, his fingerprints, the imprint of his very soul pressed temporarily on the earth. The fear has become something else, could he dare call it a strength, a privacy anyhow. A sort of privacy private to himself, a house with a private garden.

'Maybe you should get back to your work,' says Benson kindly when that odd minute of wordlessness passes, kindly, at ease even, but with that strange definite air that an employer can always muster, even smiling a little. Let him laugh at him if he wishes, if he thinks Eneas McNulty is funny. Well, he is funny, a forty-six-year-old creature with a bleary face that can't answer a pleasant question about Ireland and denies his excellent brother.

'Yes, sir,' says Eneas, grateful for the tea and grateful to be gone. An oddity. A singular man. An anecdote for Benson.

*

Curious old earth they dig from the first wild talk of the birds in the thorns to the deeps of silence when the rackets and whistling and cheering of the insects stops and sheets of darkness plunder down over the plain and claim the numbed countryside. Day by day the new spades gather hoards of scratches and scores and grow old in their hands. Nevertheless there is pride in Eneas for the strength of his back, and he digs as if carelessly or careless of the task but he's fit and good for it. Harcourt not so much as he because Harcourt is really a head man. It's Harcourt's brains that are his pride. Eneas must conclude that Harcourt is truly a wise man in that he speaks elegant as a judge and opines on many a matter and has driven already the shadows from some dark questions bothering Eneas these dozen years. Harcourt believes that as a person is but briefly on the earth it behoves him to look about and understand the nature of the great puzzle of life. That a person could never know for why he is upon the earth and yet he might for a moment feel the light of heaven pierce down upon his head, for a moment, a moment, and have a little suggestion, a little touch of the sugar of heaven. Harcourt evidently scorns religion and priests after all despite his early comments though he has a broad knowing of them. Because religions and priests offend his idea of heaven, in the main. And he is fond of displaying to Eneas in the privacy of their near bunks the various amazing and ancient practices of some of the more lonesome people of Nigeria. His own mother, it appears, came from a group of excellent people that until the arrival of the British into the then private districts of her native realm – sometimes chopping off hands and heads for the sake of discipline and terror – were wont to give the credit of greater life to the dead ones, and called themselves in fact by the names of the dead and believed themselves to be mere shadows and the haunters of the huts of the Great Living – to wit, the eternal dead. Stances removed by the ascendancy of Harcourt's family into the colder and notion-less regions of the piano-owning classes of Lagos. And also that human life was a sort of first death before the great death, to wit, Life itself.

Eneas lies in the sunken dark of the tent and listens because Harcourt pleases him and he is greatly affected by the friendship that Harcourt bestows on him, him, an unwanted or extra Irishman as it were. Though Eneas has his own weeds of pride quite proudly growing about his soul, yet his simpler heart needs the balm of another person's bountiful friendship, which he thinks is the nature of Harcourt's admirable and continuous talking. Some slight academy of interesting and twisting thoughts takes place under the starry tent, and if Eneas is beyond healing truly, yet he settles further into peace, and things in his head find their places, hammer to its niche, sextant to its shelf and box, and he is fiercely content to dig the canal for Benson of Roscommon, and hear wisdom from Harcourt of Lagos.

16

THE DAYS OF LETTERS are well gone now, and the only touch he has against his mother must be in dreams, and truth to tell his dreams are poor things really and he has a contempt for them. But now and then some nights she flits through in strange guises, whether as the avenging crone of old dreams, or the bright flame of an aisling that he has no need of, and rises unbidden from the paltry bog of his sleeping brain. He knows that she and all her world will die, and her secrets too, and he knows that all traces of even his own days will be pulled from the streets of Sligo, and the names of the shops will change again, and someone's premises here and another's there will suffer the great iron ball, and he knows that in that sense he is already dead, that time has already taken care of him. There is the living breathing world of Ireland with De Valeras and the sons of powerful men taking power as they come to age. It's all the old story over again except this time the rich man is themselves in a motorcar and a house on a respectable road. Well, he must not worry about politics, he's beyond them now. He has never been for politics, only the flotsam of its minor storms.

And he thinks back a little over his life and where he was born and he wonders did he make such a hames and a hash of it after all? Didn't he just live the life given him and no more side to him than a field-mouse as God's plough bears down to crush his nest? He thinks maybe it was a mistake as such to join the police that time, but what else was he to do, hang about the corners of Sligo and harass the widows as they went by? By the mere fact of being willing to be killed for his 'crime' he is beyond his 'crime'. Enemy of the Irish people. He wishes he could keep in touch with Teasy away there in Bexhill in her convent and the wonderful network of roads about for her to beg along, but ... He loves that Teasy, though, he believes.

But he wishes, ah, he wishes now sometimes all the same that he had been born a simple farmer's son far from the devious town and had taken that farm to himself in due course and farmed it and got the grass off it yearly and been good at the work, yes, and married a lass of small means, and rowed through the winters with her, and brought up his sons and daughters, giving out to them the while, and trying to set a path of stout wood across the dreary bogs and verdant meadows of a life. And when he wishes for those things his body feels heavy against the digging, and Africa's colours leak from her, and he might be a dog locked in a lightless room without water or food or walking.

Then his brain really rattles and he has to dig faster to fling out the demons from the red earth, so dry and deep in the channel of the canal, whose water waits two hundred miles upland still locked in the bright waters of the lake.

He knows Benson dreams of the day when the locks at the lake are opened and the water bursts forth and fills the trench in its three hundred miles and carries rich moisture down to lands that will fall back into fertility from the shock, lands that know only segments of inches of rain betimes, or great crushing sweeping deluges that last an hour or two and pass away higher to the Muslim districts. He knows Benson dreams of that because he himself would if he had the gift of those drawings, his own brother's gift indeed.

And in his heart somewhere between sleep and waking, in the dark pit of his heart, he senses to his grave discomfort the moil and torrent of the distant water pressing somehow to be released, impatient and mocking. He knows the water lies far north of him and his blessed heart, but it's a confusion so peculiar that he half believes he is a sort of Nigeria with northern water and southern drought. And when his mind latches onto dryness, he sees there, dotted about, the dirty backs of mountain sheep in the hammered reaches of Sligo hills amazing his inner eyes – so there is worse confusion, bareness, wet, dryness, Africa, Ireland. And it isn't so pleasant when the mind won't put things in their correct places, dragging such dirty sheep into an African day dream. And now being wordless more or less apart from a grunted thanks or a hello, even bit by bit, hour by hour, with Harcourt, his poor head becomes all the more afflicted not by visions, not by things that John of Patmos might have cherished in his visionary cave, but by useless fragments of past and present, as if a joyless hammer has struck the template of his head and partly ruined it, bent it, buggered it up rightly.

Thankfully his arms and legs and such aren't too heedful of his difficulties and they swing and settle and do as good as ever.

The mystery to him is, though they slap his back and watch him and even converse hotly or mildly with him if one or other happens to be working by him, his fellows don't pass remarks on his condition. Indeed he sings betimes whatever he has of songs, wordless tunes of his father's, or bits of things he has heard on his travels, to give himself the appearance of self-command and normality. But even if he were to spend the day on his head and hands he doesn't believe these men would find it remarkable enough to mention it. The condition generally shared is a certain physical strength, and as long as Eneas does his share of the digging he remains part of the curious sphere of the work-force, tracking back and forth across the clay in all the thousand journeys and mutations of a day. In this way every man is a vagrant star following his vagrant and allotted path through the firmament of the camp, though there may be no plus and minus to explain him.

*

And though his discombobulation grows indeed apace, and he can sense it always lurking inwardly, he searches for means in himself to ward off the rising of it. He imagines beyond the material of the tent a high blue-stricken Sligo sky, an autumn sky, fit for passing fast above the withering branches of maples and oaks and roaring out of it the story of Sligo, the thousand stories, the million, the countless, the numberless stars of the stories of Sligo and in that eternal Babel betimes he finds the sweet nut of rest, the ease in his limbs, the eyebright womb of proper ease.

And digs like a demon.

And Harcourt becomes second nature to Eneas and digs like a demon. Harcourt grows strong as a donkey and he digs, you have to admire his digging now. And the dry earth mounts each side of the channel and their canal lengthens southward. And when Eneas is worse than troubled, when the stricken part of his head worsens and in worsening forces the head downward onto Eneas's chest like the neck is broken or under fierce strain, it seems to Eneas that Harcourt is digging for him, for his health, digging for it like a pirate digs for the gold on the bleak island of adventure.

'What troubles you, brother?' Harcourt asks. 'Can you say anything at all in that silence of yours, brother?'

And Eneas barely can. Fear afflicts him, silence abets the fear. Sometimes he lays down his spade and shivers in the lengthening ditch, he shivers with an ague like malaria but it isn't so simple. It isn't mosquitoes are ruining Eneas, but the pressing down and piercing up of a life. He's being run through from many an angle. Sometimes he yearns for the refuge of an English madhouse, for the refuge of youth even, of a fresh start. He is mortally exhausted sometimes by being this Eneas McNulty. The wicked idea strikes him that his would-be murderers were in the right, that there's nothing to recommend him, that his life has been ill led, that he deserves tremendous and afflicting punishment. When he thinks this he trembles worse. He's lost in a childhood state and he fears the displeasure of God the King of good and the Demon of evil. He lies fast in the bed of himself with the starched sheets binding his legs, and the ministers of God approach the bedroom of himself and will be in the window like a fiery bolt to accuse and torment him and he feels it will be well merited.

*

It's Harcourt that brings him back to the simpler world. They go out one morning as usual to the digging area with spades on their shoulders and cardboard visors against the sun. The birds of Africa angrily call. All as usual, daily, the now familiar newspaper of sounds and sights that each man reads for himself in his own way. A day indeed when Eneas feels his own inclination to silence as a half-decent thing and he hovers on the ragged border of contentment. And they dig as is their wont and work and it doesn't seem so pointless a business after all to be striving to realize the great dream of Benson. Or maybe it isn't a great dream but a natural job of work, and if Benson was building a wharf in New Ross it would be all the same thing. Maybe it occurs to Eneas he makes too much of expert work, maybe he should lose that strange part of his soul that envies and worships the expert man. As he thinks this, suddenly Harcourt stops in the digging and begins to tremble. Now this could be Eneas himself and Eneas is doubly startled, and thinking he knows this ague lurches to embrace his friend. But Harcourt won't stop at trembling but goes down on one knee on the brittle earth and leaps up as if kicked by the earth and falls about and then bangs back on the crumbling ground and shakes all his limbs at once, and a nasty looking bile or foam starts to bubble and froth from his lips. And Benson leaps down into the ditch and hauls off his own belt and shoves the thickness of it into Harcourt's mouth, startling Eneas. The other diggers have stopped and are staring down at Harcourt silently with their chins at still angles as if all movement has gone out of the world except for Harcourt's twitching and gurgling.

'He's having a fit,' says Benson. 'I've seen it before in one of my aunts. Epilepsy or the like. Mustn't swallow the tongue. That's the main thing.'

'No, no,' says Eneas, and he imagines Harcourt's tongue going down the throat and into the belly to be digested as if it was the edible tongue of a cow after being boiled and skinned by his mother years ago in the house in John Street. 'Mercy, mercy.'

Now a number of the other men have climbed out of the ditch and are talking softly to each other and shaking their heads because it's an ill sight and possibly an evil one. They're saying the clay is dangerous or the water or the company food maybe, the same thought going through Eneas's mind, unworthy but unbidden. Now Harcourt is quiet enough except his eyes are up under his lids somewhere and occasionally he gives a massive jerk. The heads of the workers shake at each spasm. No, no, no. And then Harcourt is up with a jerk and the fit is on him again and he waves his arms and flails his legs like a dancer, like a dervish, and you'd swear, swear he knows the dance, and even likely hears a personal music proper to the dance, and he twists and leaps with tremendous poise and balance till he's down on the clay again and spasming and gurgling as before. And the leather belt has flown out long since and Harcourt is struggling now with the depth of his fit, and Benson has his hand in Harcourt's mouth and is trying to hold on to the root of the tongue to prevent it turning back on itself in a murderous rictus and stoppering up the precious breath of Harcourt. Then the wretched fit passes away, and Benson holds Harcourt's exhausted head in his lap and strokes the fevered face and seems to be talking to him gently with all the terrified susurrus and low voice of a mother. Eneas watches and thinks of his brother Jack reading in sacred privacy if that is the term to his daughter in the night-swallowed bungalow in Sligo. And such evident tenderness, accidental, necessary tenderness in Benson towards Harcourt, sweeps against Eneas also not hurting him as Jack did but roughly illuminating him. And the engineer stroking the face of the afflicted man quells the demon momentarily that feeds at the core of Eneas. In an hour Harcourt is able to stand with assistance and go back shaken and solemn with sometimes trailing legs to the speckled tent.

Harcourt lies in like a ruined man on the thin yellowed pallet of his bunk, lies back still at last and lets out a breath as lonesome as a mountain peak.

'Easier for you now?' says Eneas. 'That easier?'

'It's easier now, brother, don't mind me. Just a broken donkey of a man.'

'That's a wicked thing was running through you, Harcourt, man.'

'It will not be difficult for you now, brother, to see why I was let go from the English army, with this sort of carry-on afflicting me,' says Harcourt, not without relish, relishing also some deep breaths, a deep well of gladsome breaths rising to flatter him, to inflate his life.

'No,' says Eneas. 'No. But all the same, a man might expect better of the King's army.'

'No one minds illness invisible. If a foul cancer were eating my heart, and my face was fair and open the while, it would be no matter. But with this leaping and foaming disease ... Wasn't always so violent. You could charge money in to see me now when it's a-hold of me.'

'That Mr Benson seemed to know the drill.'

'Well, is that so?' says Harcourt.

'He didn't scorn to comfort you, you know.'

'I'll thank him for it.'

'I'd better get back to the ditch. I'll see you later.'

'Maybe I'm in the right spot after all.'

'How so?' says Eneas, turning, turning.

'With you and buggering Mr Benson to look out for me...'

'Maybe so...'

A clearer head and a quieter heart engines Eneas McNulty back out to the delving and flinging of red clay. Whether things are good or bad he cannot say, but at the least his eyes are seeing true, or so he hopes and trusts. Better the world as it is, than other worlds his mind may prefer. That he knows. God keep Harcourt fast to the rocky earth, he prays, nonetheless.

*

He sits, Eneas, at the mouth of the tent where Harcourt has been consigned, for the sake of safety, religion and fear. A poor lamp burns within and makes the old material of the field tent into a larger lamp, sitting like a bubble of light in the limitless darkness. And fireflies occupy themselves in the ragged dark and echo the ferocious display of stars. There are too many stars for comfort, and the extent of the world has no limit. The tent is moored to the extreme of the diggers' camp, and the great blank of night starts at the lips of Eneas's boots, he feels. He hears Harcourt breathing lightly in the mercy of sleep.

Someone, a pair of someones, is causing a ruckus in the middle of the camp. Eneas is disturbed as a nurse might be, watching over a child ailing in the worrisome night, or a person needing quiet for some secret function, a prayer perhaps. Two tall men half lit by the wayward lamps and half concealed in the old cloths of darkness. Whatever light there is celebrates the shouting faces. They are too far away to understand and anyway he thinks it might not be English they are using to orchestrate their fight. Now the matter passes from words to deeds, and the men punch at each other, softly at first, pushing really, then firmly, then fully, then murderously. Other men come out into the domain of light and watch. Eneas fearfully regards them, fighters and watchers.

Oh and he remembers passing through a town, in the county of Roscommon, in his policeman days. Seeing in the wide market street two tinker women fighting, just like this, with sluggish intent, landing the most hefty punches on their breasts carpeted in vast and ragged cardigans. And he sailed past in his Crossley tender. Because the trouble of Roscommon was not contained in those two women contesting what question he did not know. Their punches were not political. And they are fighting still in the silent picture-house of his addled head, on the wide market street of his lonesome fears. Harcourt sleeps on. The stars fire down their brutal spears of light, making the old bowl of night a destructive spectacle.

How dark and hurt and deep the world.

*

And when they come to dispel Harcourt from the world of the camp, not because they dislike him but because they cannot bear the mystery of his illness in their midst, they find Eneas asleep or seemingly so on the half-broken chair. And indeed he has slept under the dying stars and Sligo dogs have barked through his dreams. They give him a few slight and reasonable pokes to get him awake. But he is already awake and needs only to open his eyes. He knows a purposeful delegation when he sees one. It is the time of the little peace between dark and sunrise where the insects seem to obey some strange law of silence. Eneas smiles at the seven or eight faces and glances back into the tent where his friend Harcourt still slumbers. There are two bruised faces among the intent group, and Eneas assumes these are the battlers of the night before, and as only one of them speaks he assumes this man is the victor and the desirer of Harcourt's departure. The man speaks quietly and decently and it seems to Eneas religiously and perhaps it is a religious scruple that excludes Harcourt, or a rightful alarm at a diseased man being amid a closed camp of workers. Eneas asks in the same level tone for Benson to be fetched and the matter settled by the engineer. The speaker expresses doubt that a whiteman can understand the complexities of the matter, but Benson nevertheless is fetched for fairness' sake. Now the tremendous population of cricketlike creatures begins, adding their aching volume to the dispute. All is elegant and courtly because the speaker for the delegation senses the strength of his position and so does Eneas. After all, this is their spinning world, this patch of toiling ground, and the force of public opinion, tiny though the public here may be, is a thing so violent violence is not needed to carry it.

Benson arrives looking distinctly unenthusiastic. He tries to explain that Harcourt and Eneas too for that matter are under a three-year contract and as such are bound to fulfil their terms. And as Harcourt is able to work when not in his fit then there is no true reason for him to be sent away.

'And where will I send this man?' says Benson. 'There is nowhere he can go and fulfil his contract. Will I send him to Lagos where the company may proceed against him for breach of contract and most likely imprison him?'

'This is not the matter in hand,' says the speaker. 'If he

was God himself or King of England or boss of the company, no luck or fortune could attach to his staying. He is afflicted and as an afflicted person should not be seen among other men or work at their sides.'

'He's just a poor man with epilepsy. What trouble would you like to bring on his head, Joe? Epilepsy's neither contagious, nor against religion. Can I not convince you?'

Eneas stands under the sun without hat or safety and is reminded of his brother Tom. The vaguely oratorical turn to Benson's speech is the same. It is the politician talking to the voter, the owner of the mother tongue talking to the native with a measure of grace. Yet Benson is an Irishman. He is trying in some ancestral desperation to enter into the idiom of the African. But in borrowing only the tone of the speaker called Joe, Benson betrays his condescension. It would not be important except the speaker called Joe gives up suddenly and walks away with his companions.

'I don't know,' says Benson to Eneas. The tone remains intact. 'Unless you're willing to fight for Harcourt with your bare fists I don't think Harcourt can stay here.' Eneas after all is a digger of Benson's earth.

'What will you do?'

'I suppose I can send him back to Lagos.'

'I don't think he wants to be in Lagos.'

'They'll put him to work somewhere. Warehouses maybe.'

'He wants to dig.'

'These men here won't let him stay. If I oppose them they'll wear me down like a riverstone. I need them for this mighty work. Anyway, look at it this way, as an epileptic gets older the fits get worse. He could have choked to death yesterday.'

'Maybe he doesn't care. He wants to be here.'

'He can go back on the truck this evening. If you want to go with him go with him,' says Benson and turns away. 'I have a canal to make.'

'You put him together yesterday, Mr Benson.'

'All the king's horses, McNulty,' says Benson, without looking back. Eneas thinks this engineer from Roscommon is not much use to Harcourt after all. Or temporary use. He thinks maybe he should run after Benson and grab him by the shoulder and have it out with him better. He can see himself doing it as he thinks it. But it's too immense a task. Instead he goes into the tent to tell Harcourt the plans other people have made for him. For them both.

17

LIFE IN LAGOS turns slowly slowly into a diminishing epic of drinking the astonishing drink of the district. How this could be so for a man heretofore not ferociously interested in drink astonishes him. Certainly he has known others dedicated in practice and principle to the devouring of alcohol at all possible times and to the detriment of many another pursuit. He wonders sometimes as he wakes in the busy panic of a Lagos morning what matters in particular have awoken in him this consuming vice. He suspects too that it wasn't only political demons that haunted Harcourt in former days but also this easy catastrophe of bar, bed, and beg. As befits perhaps a man on the edges of the desert of death Harcourt is thirsty.

The good hours of the day are given to the warehouse of the company. Eneas and Harcourt truck in the lofty piles of wood and stone that will one day be gates and locks of the canal. The great granite blocks look soft as butter with a thousand gentle chisel marks on every one. They're heavy as houses. Eneas learns the principles of the block and tackle and sees in the long piles and avenues of materials the raw kindling of the fire of civilization itself. He is not agin it. In the long murks of the warehouse he appreciates it like a man might a song or a great painting. Someone is slowly painting over Africa, fellas like Benson, shoving out great confident lines across impressive distances like a child with chalk. It is exciting, and all the more reason for drinking the pleasant liquor. All the more reason for scraping a few cents together for a fierce bottle of the stuff. Him and Harcourt and civilization and Africa.

Sometimes they shack with Harcourt's father. Not often, and not so much because the drinking is a bleak sight for a father, but because the father himself is decrepit and that hurts Harcourt. The old man prances about heavily and begs to be called Your Highness. Mad as stones. Harcourt would prefer to think of his father as the dandy servant of the crown going about putting right the pianos of the blest. But all that is behind him. Now the deep woe of age is upon him and heaped on his blindness is a small madness, a kind of tuppenny halfpenny madness. Neither grotesque or dangerous, but from minute to minute a dance of despairing hope and babble.

*

'The trouble of the world,' says Harcourt – this on one of their untenanted nights, in the dusty black ruckus of a back lane – 'is we're not long enough in it, that this famous life of humans is brief and lasts only the flick of a London sparrow's wing, and still and all, brother McNulty, we're not suited to it, and even this short scatter of days lies heavy on our hands.' At this he examines his own hands as if he might see time itself lying there, heavily. 'Oh, my brother, we are not masters of this life, as it turns out. In the upshot, peeking into the book of men's lives, we are not masters. Our names are not written there. We're for the high jump.'

'Maybe so,' says Eneas, in such a manner as to attract the eyes of Harcourt.

'Maybe so – maybe so what, brother?'

'Just, maybe so . . .'

'No, no, no, brother – you've something more to say, so you say it. Please.'

'Maybe we're not written in the book of life, as you say, Harcourt.'

'Yes?'

'But that's not the trouble, the trouble is . . .'

'Well, what is it?'

'We have no mate.'

Harcourt is stirred, he rises to his haunches. 'You mean, you and me, friends, you mean, we've no friends, I'm saying, not friends, to each other, is it?'

'No,' says Eneas. 'No, sir. You're surely the finest friend I've known but, no, not mates like that, not mates the way the English say it, I mean, mates, wives, we're solitary men, solo men, on our own, nothing to us but ourselves, no women, no babies, no childer, as the Dubliners say, no blessed offspring, Harcourt.'

Harcourt sinks back into the slight nest of dust. He stares as if stupidly before him, as if into the blackest darkness possible on the perilous earth.

'Brother, brother, that is the trouble.'

'I knew a fella one time,' says Eneas, 'fella by the name of Bull Mottram he was, quaint sort of a man, a sailor. He told me one time that the place for old sailors was the Isle of Dogs. That there was sanctuary there.'

Harcourt looks at him patiently.

'Yes, brother?'

'Sometimes, now that I'm old, how old I don't quite know – what year is it?'

'Can't help you there. If we got our hands on a newspaper we'd know, certainly, my brother.'

'Sometimes anyway I'm thinking of the Isle of Dogs, as a place of rest for a weary sailor, which I surely am.'

'Don't be old yet, brother, don't be old yet.'

'Sometimes I'm thinking of that, Harcourt.'

'Be thinking of it, be thinking of it – but don't you be old yet.'

And some roisterers, some weekend lads, spilling out of a drinking house distract them, because Harcourt and Eneas are not shy to put out their hands to the passing men, and ask them in worsened voices for the price of a celestial bottle. A broken-hearted whiteman and a broken-hearted blackman of still working age aren't much of a pull for money. They get nothing but puzzlement.

'My sister Teasy, she's the finest mendicant nun in Bexhill!'

And the moon is a barrel seen from the top, with the nest of water showing a grieving face.

*

The years themselves go on and there are groups in the streets now with whittled sticks for guns, now and then a true gun, if old and pulled back into service from a long retirement. What's afoot is freedom, that dreaded thing. He recognizes the passionate alarm of the smart police as they drive all tooth and nail through the major boulevards. Little peaceful backyards will suddenly mill about, as he passes, like a mob of woodlice with their stone dragged off. Harcourt's mind acquires all the slim alarm of the emergency. Better a broken drinker now than an army man. There is no trace of uniform or employment about him. Their company contracts are long done, and they scratch for their shillings where they can. Better so, when the patriots are trying to tear the old Britishness out of Nigeria, erase the men and emblems of the very Queen herself.

Nevertheless Harcourt's father reports some midnight visitors at his little shack, looking for Harcourt and very pushy and loud in the looking. New heroes of this trouble, but old foes and contemptuous enemies of Harcourt and his imperial ways. Imperial! Imperial dossers! Harcourt's father, as an old servant of the crown, is happily too mad to be properly alarmed. But it behoves the two younger men to be as dark as lice, as secret as birds. And keep to the cracks and nooks of darkness. Which is doubly awkward, as Harcourt has some buckets of potatoes fermenting nicely in his father's abode, only a few weeks from drinkability.

*

'Did it ever occur to you, brother Eneas,' says Harcourt, 'that Lagos is almost the same word as Sligo, give or take an i or an a?'

'What help would it be, heart, if it did? It's a long road to Sligo. I saw yesterday in the window of the Asian tobacconist that we're in nineteen hundred and fifty-eight. I stared into the window amazed. What year did I come to Nigeria? How long am I here? Fifty-eight! If the year is fifty-eight then I'm fifty-eight myself and an old fella like me can't be seeing home in every town he goes to. I don't know where I am, but it isn't Sligo town.'

'OK, brother. Brother?'

'Yes?'

Harcourt halts him in the cindery street.

'Does that mean we're eight years going about?'

'I don't know. I'm not looking into it. A lady doesn't like to count her years. An old Sligo bastard likewise.'

'Right.'

Past they go, the spick-and-span police, in wagons very like to the Crossley tenders of yore along the rhododendron backways of the county Sligo. Roaring then through poverty and grandeur, blackbird and peacock. Beloved Ireland. Disastrous freedom. These fellas, the Nigerian police, are just like them, in the wrong suits to please the patriots.

'Eneas!'

The final wagon nearly skims a slice of ham off of Eneas's cheek.

'What, what!'

'Don't step out there, brother.'

'Just looking at them. Just looking at something familiar to me. They don't know. I was once like them. They think their strength's going to be a protection for themselves. But the only creature that survives the world is lambs. Those men'll lose their Vivs and their Sligos. I can smell it.'

'What can you smell, Eneas?'

'Freedom.'

*

The shopkeepers' eyes have tiny lights of terror dancing there. In the gloom among their tins and costly European goods, the relics of decency, items calling out to Eneas their longing for punctuality, trains on time, order, starched clothes, they harbour in their eyes the minuscule constellations of fear. And whereas only yesterday they awaited the tread of the stranger's foot on their thresholds with professional interest and attention, now in this new day they cannot altogether rule out that same tread as the tread of a killer or an agent of retribution. Eneas and Harcourt find their formerly efficient ruses for begging more or less defunct, and few things are more frightening it seems than two bedraggled codgers stumbling in at a shop door. They can wholeheartedly curse this political turmoil, just as much as the flunkey in his endangered nest, or the imperial officer all tense with braid and doubt in his.

Nigeria is rising like a bird, dragging a little of the lake with it on its white feathers as it strikes out for the last light of the west. The swan follows the light with longing, leaving even the harbour of the blackening lake, letting the pearls of water fall back into the darkness. Perhaps freedom cannot be won because a man is ever a hobbled beast and is not among the beauties of God's old catalogue of animals. The violent chill that rushes in behind sunset blows against the bird but inside its coat of feathers it's as hot as a hearth.

'I think a bit of dancing is required of us,' says Harcourt. 'I think a bit of side-stepping. Getting killed by the patriots of Nigeria is one bloody thing but dying of thirst is altogether another.'

'Certainly,' says Eneas.

'I'll go to my old father's house with all due caution, brother, and throw my bits and pieces together. If there's anything of yours there I'll bundle it likewise.'

'OK, Harcourt.' He doesn't like to point out the obvious – not a farthing will there be.

'I'll bundle it likewise and say goodbye to the old man and we'll step out on the road to – to wherever a train still goes. How about Kenya?'

'All right,' he says.

'I'll meet you at the stockyard before nightfall.'

'All right. Where the wandering men sit drinking in the evening.'

'That's the place. Only this time we'll leap the train.'

'We will,' says Eneas, his throat as dry as fire.

*

He hurries to the stockyards and sits in the agreed place as obediently as a child.

An hour or two pass and as it is towards evening now the familiar wanderers gather on the scratchy slopes with their bottles garnered from a day of begging coins.

Eneas has no helpful, human bottle and his stomach is starting to shrink to a nut. He can feel his ribcage bending at all points like sixteen ancient bows. A yellow sweat emerges on his hatted head. He grips his old knees and tries to squeeze the little pain out through the wall of his stomach. Well, he can wait for Harcourt but he doesn't believe he's fit for travelling. It's a while since they've lacked their evening drink and now ounce by ounce his courage is falling from him. An old man is a sad bugger of a sight truly. Now and then in the filthied sheets of dark a train toils enormously up the gradient, its lamp out front as bright as a moon. Hurry on, Harcourt, for the love of God, he mumbles. The courage of your pal is waning. Hurry on. Hurry on. Hurry on.

*

In the upshot he's a heap of moisture. There's no charity in it. His head is a roar of sickness. Maybe somewhere indistinctly he understands the true nature of these ravaging DTs and accepts their plundering. But Eneas McNulty, all the same, man and boy, seems to him to be extinct suddenly in the petty maelstrom of nothing to drink.

At the very pit, the very doom of disquiet, he stands abruptly and staggers off back into the dark quarters.

Movement and purpose allay his panic. With old legs flashing along, sparks and smoke fuming from his trousers, he thinks, he heads for Harcourt's father's shack. He must pass through empty quarters where the moon is the only watchman with his broken stare, and old buildings aping the buildings of the London docks disintegrate under the pinny stars. The building of himself is no better now, a little Sligo lean-to collapsing, collapsing. Sligo, Sligo. Tuneless song. Harcourt, Harcourt, rescue your pal.

*

There's no handle to the old man's door, it stands open, showing the dark room inside. The foot of the door scratches on the dusty boards. The smell of something akin to alcohol blusters about. But maybe he imagines it. There's a dishonest stillness about the shack that is new to him. Surely the old father lies within, astray with his own addled brains, in the back room where his grimy bed is set.

'Harcourt,' he says, like a praying man, 'Harcourt, for the love of God . . .'

He doesn't believe there's a blessed soul to answer him. The smell maintains itself, to his surprise. The room as if magically lightens as his own eyes are altered by the deeper gloom. He sees some of his own scant possessions knocked across the filthy floor, and a white hat of Harcourt's well-known to him. This is a poor job of packing certainly. He suspects instantly that Harcourt has bought a bottle, and that is the smell he smells, and he can surely forgive his friend that weakness, because he would swallow a bottle, glass and all, himself. By Christ and His Nails, he would.

And he pushes on amid the bushes of darkness to the second room and he has to open that door. This room takes the moon from the gable window and after the dark assumes the brightness of a theatre. Harcourt's father as expected lies on his miry cot, as neat as a porpoise. His bulk fits the dip in the poor bed perfectly, by long tenancy. It would be a comfort to Eneas but for the stench being twice as violent in here, a stench as hard as shit but with that axe of potatoes through it. Someone has shoved a tin funnel into Harcourt's father's mouth, and the old piano tuner seems to bear it carelessly. He forbears to struggle up and shout and communicate to Eneas – his son's companion – his outrage. Down his cheeks and onto the mattress thin as soda bread, a yellow liquid lies, as if cooled like lava into rock, and Eneas puts out a hand and scoops just a hint of this stuff on to a finger and sniffs it and tastes it. Puzzling, primitive, like something you might put in your mouth as a child. His wild blood recognizes the rats of alcohol leaping into him like he was a sewer.

Harcourt's father is stuffed with the oaty stuff. Somebody has stuffed him with it. There's a knocked-over bucket by the bed with the remnants evilly spilling. Another unmolested bucket lurks in the miry shadows. Harcourt's magnificent attempts to create alcohol, to create joy! But a murderous joy. The sorry liquid has been spilled in winglike splashes on the dusty floor, and here and there the thick mess from the bottom lies like cowpats in a Sligo field. Even in the angry grip of his need, he resists the urge to scoop up the foul leavings and gulp them down. He knows a thing to kill him even in this extremity. Suddenly suddenly he is infinitely sobered, quiet, austere as a funeral. He's jolted into calm. The angel of addiction leaves him and another angel of calm possesses him like a changing of the guards.

Poor murdered Harcourt's father. Poor murdered man.

Not by Harcourt murdered, he knows and trusts. Not by himself murdered. But by some ferocious forces unknown. They have killed the old man with the stuff of his son's addiction, drowned him with it, whether by witty intent or accident who can say? For a moment Eneas reels with sheer sobriety.

He knows, as an ex-policeman, that he does the Lagos police no favours, but he cleans out the old man's mouth and wipes his face with a vest he finds abandoned on a chair but folded as neat as a sand dab of yore, and tries to arrange the corpse in a fitting manner. He pulls the still-warm arms up across the diminished chest and shuts the eyes firmly and wishes for a moment he had two Irish pennies to lodge there, one in each eye, to stop the lids possibly popping back open, but immediately decides not too great a degree of style is needed in these circumstances. Then when all is as shipshape as he can make it, he kneels in like a proper countryman and blesses himself and tries to make a prayer for Harcourt's father. And his prayers might be as ancient as a forgotten tongue for all the mastery he has over them. Only jibs and jabs of the Lord's Prayer are at his command, sputters and shards of it. And jagged, terrorizing fire-brands out of Revelation that follow him always. Will be cast into the lake of fire. Whoever is not written in the book of life. Our Father who art in Heaven. Will be cast into the lake of fire. Hallowed be Thy Name. Will be cast into the lake of fire. Give us this day our daily bread. Will be cast into the lake of fire. Will be cast into the lake of fire.

In the moony dark he weeps. Then he kisses the old gent once. And uptails and goes out into this difficult Africa.

*

What does a man do in these circumstances? His instinct and need is to find Harcourt but he fears the forces that have descended on the quiet shack and he fears the killers with such apt imaginations. If he can just scoop up Harcourt quickly and be gone anonymously, uniquely. Harcourt has left no pointers. Harcourt has left no clues.

And he is suffering now in these suburbs of the moon, his body is a-shake. He's walking indeed like an epileptic. Well, there's a thing. His only true notion is to canter back to the embankment and search for Harcourt there. Indeed, Harcourt may well be waiting there. For certain. But nothing is certain now. Bloody politics! Deathly, killing, seducing politics. Feckin ould freedom anyway. He feels his bones bollocky in their coat of skin. They're loose in their sheaths of muscle. It's not good. He fears it is not good. He fears this bloody life of his, with its ferocious sights, Dunkirks and all. A little farm the back of North Mayo, where he could turn the swaths to the sun in the August, and break his fast with a fortunate wife ... Much wiser, much better, than this lethal African gallivanting. He prays God as he reaches the railway sidings that he will see Harcourt's cold silhouette, maybe impatient, maybe broken and lonesome, no matter if only he might be there, against the embers of the moon.

*

But lonesome Harcourt is not there, nor materializes out of the shaggy dark, nor does anything that Eneas urgently needs him to do. The embankment is indifferent to the emergency. Little despairing fires are lit here and there towards morning, drinkers trying to beckon warmth into their comfortless arms. Eneas trembles not with the cold

248

but the submerged shark of fear at seeing death. The shark of fear lurks in his gut. He's too fearful a man! Gobshite, dosser! Without Harcourt he is as small as a halfpenny star. Without Harcourt as a matter of fact he is bollocksed. His backside is hard as stone on the damaged clay. He feels old and calloused. He hunches there, his coated back bowed, his hands open and lying palm upwards. Unimpressive man, disappeared man. He thinks of his mother mightily dancing on the hearthstone in the unlikely stone-age of his youth. He doesn't really believe he was ever that boy. Loved, and his father crazy and desirable with his broken tunes. The tunes are gone, the names are gone, the face of his father . . . His hands are the hands of a useless man, they lie there uselessly. There should of been a life made from those swollen hands. He should of kept at the sailing or the digging or stuck it out in Ireland and let the buggers shoot him if they had to. A bird without its bush wasn't much. The whistles go out of it, and the blood. Yet all of Africa is strewn with men like him maybe, from Dar es Salaam to Cape Town, the yellow beaches of Cape Town. Lads from Southampton, Cardiff, Mullingar. Men without kids or sweethearts. Poor, rain-ruckled, diminished men. Like himself. Not as good as monkeys even. Rubbed-out men in the ravelled empire of the Queen.

PART THREE

18

HE TAKES A WORKING BERTH on a steamer of low standing, carrying God knows what from Lagos to London, its rivets so rusty the boat screeches its passage northward. He carries the hoar of the Tropics now around his heart, the little mottled frost of time alone. He looks at the stars, but they're scrap to him.

The journey is a kind of sea fever, a lengthy dream of iron racketing in the great depths of its ribs, of mash and fruit delivered up to the sailors like ambrosia or lotuses – and, as ever, fierce, close work is a mighty balm, a soft medicine, as good as a confab with a dextrous leech. All living people, Harcourt, his tuneful father, Roseanne, become for the voyage mere rocketing planets at the back of his mind. The work goes deep into his arms and into his much-pickled brains, as the iron ship passes through meridians and bucketing sunlight and finally, sleet and the true frosts of France and England.

From London docks he hurries through the Isle of Dogs. His great idea now is the War Office. It's an inspiration. To the War Office, yes, to enquire after the state of his pension. Perhaps long ago they removed him from the honoured roll of disabled veterans, but it gives him a sterling sense of purpose, moving in his sea-soiled clothes through the famous streets of old Bull Mottram.

There's an exhilaration suddenly being back amid the red and yellow bricks of this eternal England. The hoardings make no sense to him but the begging sparrows do, and the affectionate decrepitude of the houses. He may be an old ghost scurrying along but he enjoys the handsomeness of the young men – youth itself is handsome – with their white shirts rolled to the elbows, and the growing grandeur of the city as he passes out of the poorer kingdoms. It's nothing to do with him but as a human man he can rejoice. London lies under its tender sun and it seems to him that lonesome angels would not be out of place resting in the fabulous niches.

*

Truly he does not set much store by his pension being in existence nor would he put a decent bet on it. The little row of wooden booths is quiet. There's a spittoon as big as a figurehead. His number is fetched against his travel documents by an elderly clerk. Maybe the clerk is younger than himself indeed, but Eneas feels no more than twenty. There's a clattering of drawers and a scratching of a nice modern pen.

'You'd be a veteran of Dunkirk yourself then, sir?' says the clerk, which degree of courtesy is remarkable, given that Eneas isn't exactly dressed for a tea-dance.

'That's the story,' says Eneas McNulty.

'I have a special regard for those such,' says the man, 'if you don't mind my saying so.'

'Oh, no, I don't,' says Eneas.

'And you haven't been drawing your funds at all, I see, sir. Not for some ten years or so . . .'

'Been away in Africa.'

'Ah, yes, sir – do you know, a lot of veterans tend to go overseas, sir. I sometimes surmise I know why. I don't want to speak out of turn. But sorrow, I think, it is, that drives them away. That drives you all away far from the shores of your country.'

'Do you know,' says Eneas. 'I never considered that – but you might have something there. Yeh.'

Next thing, given the great politeness, he's expecting the clerk to explain why there's no money to be given out, this reason, that reason, and very understandable it'll be, Eneas is sure. But the clerical officer issues him with a chit.

'That's all checked against your documents, all legal and above board. I haven't crossed it, sir, to facilitate you, having been away for so long . . .'

'Oh, right, yeh,' says Eneas, and glances at the cheque. He grimaces and sighs through his yellowed teeth, the ones remaining anyhow.

'All in order?' says the clerk.

'Well,' says Eneas. 'Are you sure and certain this is right? For me, right, the cheque, I'm saying?'

'Believe me, sir, that's a cheque will pass muster in any bank in the British Isles. By heavens, sir, you could go into a bank in Gibraltar with that or Nairobi, and you'd find it honoured in a twinkle.'

'Oh, I'm sure, I'm sure. No, it's a beautiful cheque, indeed it is, it's just . . .'

'We could have sent you your money anywhere in the world poste restante, if you had authorized us, you know.'

'All right,' he says, not secure on the meaning of the foreign phrase.

'Do you have an address currently, sir? Or will you be coming in in person again?'

It seems as dangerous a question as ever. But this is not a killing man. This is a friendly man, a man as courteous as a king, or a king's servant. Eneas is reluctant now to be mysterious and rude with so elevated a character. In possession of this miraculous cheque. But he has no address, just the eternal address that forever lingers in his head, Sligo, Sligo.

'Sligo,' he says, 'whatever you called it, the bit of foreign talk, and Sligo.'

'Poste restante,' says the clerk. 'You just sign here, sir, and I'll see you right. You might as well have your money regular, sir. You earned it, God knows.'

'Well, yeh,' says Eneas, remembering the great labour bestowed on Jean's farm, in those vanishing days of war. 'I expect every man that went to that war earned his money. I expect.'

'That's certainly my impression,' says the noble clerk.

Now Eneas is a touch stymied by such immaculate contact with officialdom. He sees himself again as a young sailor, passionate and hopeful on Avenue 1½, in golden Galveston. Politeness is a sorry thread leading back to youth, for a young man expects politeness wherever he wanders, and knows he will always deserve it, by force of valuable character. Eneas is silenced. He would like to express something to the clerk, something vague in his mouth, something about things being made up for, about a heavy heart lightened, oh, he knows not what. The clerk's little lightless face stares out at him over the polishless wood.

'Well, no matter,' says Eneas, 'and thank you kindly, and good day to you. Be seeing you. God bless.'

And out into the parsimonious sunlight with him, and the sparrows eking through crumbs, and such like. Gobsmacked. Twelve hundred pounds.

*

Comprising, he must surmise, the accumulation of the weekly stipend. He remembers this sum as being so small that for it to add up so magnificently flings him into a dizzy panic. He grips the chit. He marches along like a foot soldier against the fiery guns. He thinks of the mighty efforts of Harcourt and himself over so many years to acquire the few coins for a drink. And all the while this monstrous sum was building and being added to in his name. He sticks the chit into his clothes, checking it repeatedly as he hauls himself through the light of tawny London. Even he, the master of pennies and sixpences, has full respect for the terrifying piece of paper against his breast.

Of course he might drink now if he wished and drink hard and remove the pleasant terror that way. He trails into a park and seats himself with all the dignity of twelve hundred pounds and a backful of rags, and a better plan strikes him. Indeed, having given his address in reflex action as Sligo, can he not return to his Sligo as a man of wonder, a returned man like one of those Yanks spick and span as turkeys, a new man anyhow, an ordinary man but a distinctive one, a man with the gentle responsibility of – twelve hundred pounds? He could always imagine O'Dowd and company shooting a penniless man, but a bugger with twelve hundred pounds ... He might sit with his brothers and swap knowledge of the world and buy a – well, whatever his mother felt she lacked, and likewise his father.

He is not expert in the matter of gifts. He doesn't remember ever giving a gift to anyone since the days of Viv.

And maybe, now he puts his mind to it, and most importantly, there'd be some application of the money possible in the great and dark matter of Roseanne, queen of the iron shack. Roseanne Clear. He has been remiss in thinking about her, perhaps he has forbidden himself to think about her. Perhaps it is so long ago it is foolish to think about. And yet now when the matter of gifts arises she rises too, quite plain and clear in his head, bright and needful as a painting. The years are a row of dark houses and the man he is stands next to the man he was when he left Sligo for the last time, and there as close as summer heat is Roseanne. Human time is a curiosity, no doubt.

Ah but it's true that in the first bank he finds he has trouble with the doorman. By the mere process of not looking, he's trying to gain entry to a bank of particular swank. Nevertheless, the warrior in gold epaulettes relents when Eneas explains his business in his murky Sligo accent – the doorman is an exile from Clare.

Once inside – and here indeed are ranks of angels in a long sentence of niches, white and naked as the world found them – he finds wealth a tangled puzzle in itself. When they are satisfied so tattered a man is connected legally to the chit, they recommend to him a bewildering sequence of actions. In the first place he must surrender the marvellous chit to them, a moment of low panic and sadness, then allow them to open an account and issue him with a little booklet. There is honesty here at least, he surmises, and they have faithfully noted his fortune on the first line inside. Still and all, the booklet to him lacks the romance of the fine little cheque, wrecked though it is by the grip he put on it in the street. Of course he has had company cheques in the past and he knows such a thing must be surrendered but all the same he is flustered and boggy in the head from these immaculate dealings. At last he is equipped and reassured and sent out into the difficult world of wealth and infinite purchases.

*

He is full of inspirations like any other person burdened by a windfall. Buying comes natural to him. Perhaps in the upshot it's as old as swinging through trees. And at any rate hasn't he had almost matchless practice with his Mam in the old idle days of childhood, rushing through the palatial streets of Sligo with the rain-bedappled parcels. Oh, yes.

Into a simple haberdasher's with him, and isn't it the bee's knees of a suit already made up and hanging tempting as ice-cream on the racks. Now that it comes to it he has wished all his life to get his hands on a brilliant readymade suit and not be all his life having something made for him by a seamstress. You'd be in terror years ago in the yards of the school that some fella'd spot the hand of a seamstress in the stitches of your trousers. Or worse, far worse, your own Mam. Readymade even then in the dinosaur days of Sligo was the ticket.

All the blessed rage is the suit, he is magnificently informed, bang in new from somewhere in the East End of London, maybe the work of a rajah or a emperor of the Indians – that you'd see going round with sheets wrapped about their gleaming hair, princes and the like, so it is said. Now he is standing foursquare in a London premises with the cold assistant measuring him and then putting the jacket of the suit against his chest, and the trousers sort of shaken at his right leg, for the fit. What a spectacle and a wonder.

The power of money is immaculate, like the Virgin herself. Maybe the blue has the glimmers of the Northern Lights about it, like the wing of a magpie gazed at sharp like, but all the same – fashion indeed. Maybe the crotch now that he puts his mind to it has a bit of a feisty handhold on his balls, but all the same – dandy enough. And then nothing will do the assistant but sell him an acher of a shirt with a black tie attached to it permanent with extra stitching – no extra charge, though. This strikes Eneas as very handy in a rushed morning – the assistant is full of praise for the ingenuity of the Indian tailors. At this point he shares the fact with the assistant that his own father and mother were tailor and seamstress and met in the Sligo lunatic asylum, but it all falls on deaf ears, even such magical information.

Well pleased with himself and the world, he issues forth under full sail. He expects naturally to be the object of admiration, but truth to tell no one gives him a second look. Of course he appreciates that he is in the capital of tailoring itself. If he was to take a bus to Folkestone or Bexhill or other rural and coastal towns, he knows he'd be the best dressed man there, surely.

And so he comes in his thinking to his sister Teasy. No use going to Ireland straight off now without a visit to the finest mendicant nun in Bexhill. He feels the responsibility of the brother with money. It's a mere shade of a feeling, but nonetheless forceful for that. By his clothes shall you know him, don't they say? He wants Teasy to see him in his new clothes!

Prideful and simple as a boy he takes the Bexhill train from the old palace of Charing Cross.

*

A little ghostly perhaps, he waits for Teasy in the convent in a room speckled by a windy sunlight boisterous outside in the tarry garden. The tall vigorous nun who showed him in has looked at, he imagines, his suit with proper wonder. A ferocious contentment takes a hold of him. He waits minutely, intently, like a visiting king. Young as an apple. Bursting.

But the woman that comes in to him seems far from Teasy, divorced from the Teasy of old. She walks wordless to the very limits of his shoes and holds out a hand of bones and grips his own shoe-hard hand with extravagant force.

'Eneas,' she says. 'Eneas, good man, good man. I thought you were dead.'

'Oh, no, Teasy, no, indeed, not at all.'

He rises up and kisses his sister. What's up with her he doesn't know.

'How have you been keeping? Often and often I asked the Mam where you might be and it was divil a bit she knew about you, you poor wandering man, you.'

'Oh, sure, Teasy, I was wandering, no doubt, but, as you can see, I'm well fixed now, and heading home, and I was thinking there in London, oh, I couldn't go past England without seeing you.'

She sits him down like a person might an old man and sits herself down adjacent where the strange sunlight, divorced from the wind that blows it, moils in the dustless room.

'They're terrible old now, the old people, you know,' she says, 'but, I never hear bad about them. Jack comes the odd time to see me, you know. Says they're hearty enough. The old man still riding his bike!'

'Mercy. Is he?'

'He is. Oh, isn't it yards and yards of years since I seen you. Oh, Eneas, well, there's certainly a darkness in our poor family, with such gaps of years.'

'Do you think?' says Eneas. He's shocked to find it so. The gap of years seems less to him. But of course, when you're traipsing the backroads and the hillroads of Bexhill through all the four seasons, maybe a year is a longer affair.

'I'll tell you, Eneas, I always had a great grá for you, and I often worried you didn't know that, and so kept away thinking I wasn't much to you, but . . .'

'Ah, but, girl, I always did know that. Certainly.'

Round and round the cheerful sun, like so many dolphins turning in the bluest ocean, the deepest, the bluest.

'Well,' says Teasy, 'it's been a time of it. And I expect I've been thinking and thinking. More than I would normally.'

'Why, Teasy, dear?'

'Arra, man – have a gander at this.'

And she hoists her black skirts up her girlish-looking legs, past the stop of her black stockings and on to her bare thigh. Then a peculiar thing happens. Some cloud wedges in between the sun and the lonely earth and the light alters in the room and to his surprise the same yellow colour of the sun remains on his sister's pleasing face. She's yellow as the beak of a blackbird.

'What, Teasy?' he says, in the grip of the moment, his sister's chaste thighs revealed to him, for all the world like a merry harlot's in some other place entirely, which stills him, still as an alerted mouse, and his heart is banging, banging in his chest, banging.

'The lump there,' says Teasy.

And her right thigh indeed is adorned you might say with

a swelling, sitting there maybe on the bone itself, hard-looking, distressing, annoying, wrongful, out of place on his mighty sister.

'Touch it,' she says, 'touch it, brother.'

Harcourt's form of address to him! Brother. Sister, sister, sister.

'No need,' he says softly. 'Is it a bad thing?'

'It's a rotten thing, says the doctor,' says Teasy. 'It's a thing to do a woman in. What can you do?'

'I don't know,' he says truthfully.

'No one can save me – I mean, Eneas, there's no help for it. But, sure you have to be – courageous, you know. There's no fear for the likes of me. Bride of Christ. Arra, you know. Useless.'

Back comes the sun and dresses his sister in warm, rich yellow. If there's a ditch of years between, no matter, he thinks. In his foolish suit he gets up, and she gets up, like a couple about to dance. And indeed their status is rigorously single.

'The best mendicant nun in all of Bexhill,' he says, and tenderly tenderly gets his arms about her and holds the long sack of bones against his breast and holds her there.

Dry as a tree tortured by drought she cries in there in the cave of her brother.

'Rescue, rescue,' she whispers, and he doesn't know what she means and doesn't dare ask.

19

LONGITUDE AND LATITUDE are written in his bones, he's a globe in a classroom, you could spin him and find your path to Antarctica with a childish finger. As a traveller of stature and a sorrowing man he decides to have a try out of an aeroplane. He has a yen now for the high clouds he's heard about, where the sunlight is perpetual and nothing can live but the big silver cigar of the aeroplane. People in armchairs as high as kites like a crazy sitting-room. Oh, he fancies being unmoored from sea and land, and visiting God's own quarters.

He sits in the soothing seat with his own number written on a card, in his magnificent suit. The book of life, the book of life ... The air rushes past like molten sparrows and the propellers boiling the flat air tear the aeroplane from the earthly runway. London lies below him in a bountiful arrangement of shining districts, Parliament, Palace and Cathedral, he is pierced back in his seat by its singing beauty. The song of London is deep, orchestral, like the sea herself. Immaculate women bring him a drink of tea, all is starch and pinned smiles. He's the emperor of the plastic ashtray, the extraordinary cone of air that blows at him from above. Well, he might be on a speeding bicycle, taking the highest hill known to mankind, with a savage whoop.

As the round window shows him a new Ireland, her

coveted fields, the heavy stone of Ireland's Eye, the casual arm of Dollymount strand lying in the sea as easy as a lover's, he weeps mightily. He sits in his chains of memory and weeps mightily. He's surprised by this love, his country shown to him in a vision of pouring light and evident peace, childhood, childhood singing in him, but also other matters, dark matters, mysteries, the tiny rivers of his blood mirroring the streams and embered lakes below in very paradise. Away beneath his aeroplane he can see the familiar gulls, their whiteness struck by sunlight, careering and scattering like very souls. Pappy, Mam, sister, brother, brother, Viv, Harcourt, Roseanne ... He puts his hard palms to his hard face and weeps, for Teasy no doubt especially, for mere time passing, for the brief soft downturn of a wing that seems to be a life.

Collinstown airport is a little kingdom of white concrete, with a watchtower as fabled as a castle. Out on the edge of the runway are set neat and elegant tables, where fine dames sit with scarves blowing off their delicate shoulders, drinking little drinks in the heady lake of fumes and flashing aluminium. The curve of the airport building absorbs the wave of perfume and flight, like the Great South Wall itself he has marvelled at in the sea near Ringsend, with the bright poppy of Poolbeg Lighthouse at the end, whose old engineers knew the heavy gold in the waves, and made their wall in long curves and angles accordingly. Everything in Collinstown is just so, the little fingers stuck out from the brittle cocktail glasses, the wind funnels betraying the passage of the wind, the very starch and aplomb of the man guiding in the suddenly leaden aeroplane. Eneas's mind rackets with perfection and precision, angles, plastics, successful magic, confident science. The skirts of the women and the flounce of the building are secretly dancing. He's an old father of another time, of ships and dark houses, but this new time conquers him.

*

He stands looking out through the enormous windows of the airport, for a last view of the extravagant matrons, the little breezes of the planes, the perfected fields. He rests his nose and face against the glass, sighing like an old dog.

'Eneas,' says a voice behind him, 'Eneas McNulty, is that yourself?'

He turns about and looks into the face of a man he does not know. It is a thin long face with a buckle in it that time has fastened there, a sort of twisted, intentful mouth. The dome of the head is hairless and full of surprising bumps, and mottled like the bonnet of a car in autumn, as if small wet leaves have fallen there in the peace of a long night. Eneas shakes his own head at the voice, at least familiar in its Sligo music, the mucky tune of Sligo.

'Ah, boy, you don't know me, you divil, and I know you. There's friendship for you.'

The man is spick and span, edged like a spanner, a screw-turner of a creature. Eneas stares politely, waiting for a declaration.

'You've changed, boy, but you've not changed much. You're still recognizable. I was watching you on the flight, you know. Remembering, remembering.' The man holds out a hand. 'Jonno Lynch, boy, Jonno Lynch.'

It is Jonno Lynch, Eneas thinks, the person that removed him from the book of life. Irish life anyhow. It is Jonno Lynch, standing here, old, fit, friendly, destructive. A silk tie nestles in the lapels of the Crombie coat like a snake.

The chin is shaved as a stone. Jonno Lynch. His father's old garden and a thousand years.

'Will you not take my hand, Eneas?'

Eneas shakes the bony hand in silence. He doesn't smile or frown. All men are equal under God's stars. Worthy of greeting.

'You're surprised to see me. Of course you are. Aren't you dandy now in your modern suit. A suit like that is the latest thing, I know. London town. Fellas on scooters with wild girls wear such suits, boy. It suits you, that suit.'

Eneas has no clue as to what Jonno means.

'How are you getting on, Jonno?' he says, slowly.

'Mighty, mighty. Oh, mighty. Booming. I was years and years in the Land Commission, great work, great work, breaking up the lands, you know, for the farmers, for the farmers. And latterly, beef, boy, beef, the coming thing. Me and O'Dowd. We never touch a bullock, but we're in the beef business. Paperwork. Mighty.'

Well, if Eneas understood him, he would answer him to the point. But it's all dark. O'Dowd, beef, Jonno.

'You remember O'Dowd, surely?'

'Oh, yeh.'

'And what line are you in yourself, Eneas? It's not policework has you so – so mighty. We thought maybe you'd gone out to Hong Kong maybe, to join the force there, or some such. Far away and no bother to anybody.'

'Is that what you thought?'

'Well, boy, that was the theory anyhow. Sure how are you, Eneas? Are you well? My God, boy. Think of the times we had in the old days. The orchards we robbed, the foxes we boxed. Holy Jesus.'

'Aye.'

'And here you are in Collinstown, be the hokey. What do you know? Christ.'

'Tell us, Jonno . . .'

'What, Eneas, what?'

'Do you remember the time you came to see me, in my Pappy's garden, long ago?'

'Oh. I do, yeh. A terrible business. Terrible. Oh, dark days. Oh, yes, Eneas, I remember it perfectly. Written on my soul it is. In letters of fire.'

'Is that right?'

'Oh, yes, Eneas. Certainly.'

'And are things, Jonno, are they different in Sligo now, could that sort of thing happen now, do you think, could it happen now?'

'How so?'

'Are things long ago, I mean, are things left back in the long ago, would you say?'

'Yourself, do you mean, Eneas?'

'Well, you're coming up to me, and orchards you're talking about, and friendly of course, and indeed, in the long ago we were friends, a person could say, but equally Jonno, a person could say other things, remember other things . . .'

'Now, look, Eneas, let bygones be bygones, dark days, and troubled times, I'm only saying hello to you, for old times' sake.'

'But, Jonno, what are old times? What are old times if they contain not just dark days but dark words, words to break any friendship, words of death, words of whatever, poxy dark words of death-sentence and time to go, Jonno?'

Eneas allows himself to tap the chest of Jonno's coat ever

so softly with a finger. It's like touching outrage, a little tumble of outrage in a Crombie coat.

'You speak of my suit, you speak of watching me, Jonno. You say a lot of things except the last thing you said to me in my father's garden. Does that still stand, Jonno, does that still stand? And shouldn't I take you by the throat now, Jonno, here in this bright place, just for the sake of the years of my life, and for all the times, Jonno, that your name and the name of O'Dowd brought demons into my sleep? The earth is a long and scattered kingdom, with cities, towns and roads, and on many a spot of that earth I've found your name in my dreams.'

'Well, fuck me, Eneas, if I know what the fuck you're saying. Gobbledygook. But maybe I get the gist. Maybe I do. It's not my hand you want to shake, it's my throat. You want to kill me. You want to kill Jonno Lynch. Is that it?'

'I want not to see you, I want not to see you.' The strength goes out of his voice, out of his bones. 'Does it still stand, Jonno, does it still stand?'

'What, Eneas? Does what still stand?'

'Sentence of death.'

Jonno Lynch looks at him with an open face. You could give him that much. Fearless. Old, and fearless. The mortal passengers pass up the corridor raising no dust, because there is no dust, only the polish of the linoleum, as if a thousand nuns had waxed it on their knees, to make a blessed convent of it.

'Well, you're talking, boy, you're asking. And I'll tell you. It does, Eneas, it does still stand.' And then hasn't anything to say, but in good Jonno fashion says it anyway. 'But, good to see you, boy, good to see you.'

And off with him incongruously in his coat, magnificent as a bookie crying out his prices atop a racecourse barrel.

*

When he reaches the old bungalow in Sligo, the garden shrugging in the dark, the heat of the late spring day slugging about among the overgrown roses, he finds his Mam and Pappy have turned the tables, have disappeared on him. For they are not there, and the rags and papers of neglect blown in against the porch tell him they are gone a good while. He traipses around the house and peers in the back window as of old, as if Jack and his daughter might still be there, but all is glimmers and shadows.

For good measure he walks out to the old walled garden under Midleton's famished woods, along the heavy ruckus of the old river, and succeeding memories of school walls and dandy houses. But the gates of the garden are shut off with corrugated iron and even in the troubled light of the moon he can see, through the heavy lace of rusted cracks, that the place has sunk into brambles, nettles and seedy grass. It behoves him to go back into the river-damp town and ask questions in the public bars. But one bar and one question finds Old Tom McNulty's address. Apparently it's a house the far side of the granite bridge they're in. He has to pass the Gaiety cinema on his way down the hill and over the river. Well, some things never change – the ladies of Sligo, differently dressed, maybe the daughters of the daughters of his youth, come out after being at the picture into the ordinary street with the blaze of something in their eyes, whoever are the stars of these days, he doesn't know. They fasten their coats firmly, set their breasts firmly against the walk home, content, elevated, beautiful. He doesn't know them but he knows the frisk of romance and California and honey in their paces.

*

'There was no one going out any more to the old place in Strandhill,' says his mother, 'so we sold the bungalow for safety's sake and took ourselves here. It's just another iron shack by the sea now, that lovely dance-hall. To think of it. The salt air going through like a circus act of knives. There was no one going out there to dance and God knows it was far enough for Old Tom to travel for nothing. At eighty-odd years, I suppose he was no draw for the dancers of Sligo. And Young Tom has the place bought now in Bundoran, mighty nice place on the cliffs, with a hotel and a ballroom, and lights galore that spill down the grassy cliff and onto that famous beach. And who would blame him? Oh, Old Tom is full of talk, and bitter talk it is, but I'm tired telling him the brass tacks of things. He thinks if he can still ride his bicycle, he can still have his orchestra. But sure who'll listen to that old music they used to play with the daft music going now? Even Young Tom has his work cut out to keep up with the times. It's not polkas and foxtrots now but country ballads and your man with the twisty hips, Elvis Presley.' And sitting in her damask chair she seems to want to give him an idea of those hips, and swivels her own without rising, and laughs, as if the dog Tam was still alive. And she was dancing to burst on the ancient hearthstone.

'It's queer times, right enough,' says Eneas. His mother looks as hard as an old thorn tree stuck out in the middle of a field and left alone against wind and rain. She wears a little dress as enveloping and black as one of Queen Victoria's, when she was in eternal mourning for Albert. Beside her is a high pile of her scrapbooks, as she calls them, where for years and years it seems she has pasted all the loose and likely items of a life. He doesn't remember her keeping scrapbooks, but the earliest ones date back to the time of his boyhood. She shows him old school reports of his and Jack's and Tom's, and Teasy with her mighty marks for everything from the nuns. He is vaguely confused that he doesn't remember the scrapbooks. At any rate now it's just her, the chair, the dark room, and the pile of dead history. His mother's a dancer no more.

'I saw Teasy,' he says, 'on my way over.'

'She told you?' she says.

'Aye.'

'The pity of it. Aye.'

'And Tom's wife?' he says, quietly.

'She's with him in Bundoran of course.'

'With him in the hotel? Roseanne?'

'What? No. No, his wife, his real wife.'

'Oh.'

*

That night he sleeps deeper than dreams and in the morning his father makes a breakfast for him.

'Jaysus, that's a good rasher, Pappy.'

'And the bread's grand, hah?'

'First class.'

'And you should know, who has seen the whole world. What a mighty thing that is. To have seen the whole blessed stretch of the world. The blue countries, and the red ones, and the yella.'

'How's that? Ah, on the atlas, do you mean, Pappy?'

'Yes, I look up the countries in the atlas, down the library, to see where my sons are, exactly.'

'The writing hand is a rusty hand, that's true.'

'Ah, yes. Surely. And do you have money, Eneas, for a suit like that?' And feels the cloth between thumb and index finger. 'That's no charity cloth beyond redemption, that I had to deal with above in the asylum. This is – classy, classy stuff.'

'A bit of a windfall, Pappy. Pappy?'

'Yes, Eneas?'

'Do you remember – do you remember, Tom's first wife, that, you know, was got rid of, or, or, whatever it was happened her?'

'Yeh. Of course. Roseanne. I do.'

'Where is she, Pappy, now?'

'Arra, Leitrim.'

'Leitrim?'

'Yes.'

'And, Pappy, where like, in Leitrim, like?'

'Oh, the county home, where else? The poor girl, she lost her wits. We popped her in. I don't know. I suppose she's still there. Where else would she be? If she's still alive. It's a queer hard thing when a person loses their wits. I seen many a fine person reduced by the same malady, and put suits on some of them. You know, Eneas, that's a bright colour of a suit, now you stand there at the window. Blue, is it?'

'Yeh, sort of electric blue, I think they called it.'

'Electric? Like the plugs, like?'

'Yeh.'

'Very good.'

*

It's a cold hard day in Leitrim and maybe, he thinks, it often is. Stones and ditches have the rags of cold weather on them, mosses and frosty wet. Gripped in his right fist he has a twist of snowdrops.

The matron's old and lame, and she is surprised to see him and hear the name he asks for.

'She never has had a visitor.'

'Oh,' he says, 'well.'

'Great spirit she has, lionlike.'

They move through the yellow corridors.

And the matron makes a door scrape open. Eneas is thinking suddenly of the iron shack, and the roses, what did she call them, something of St Anne's? He must tell her about that rose called 'Peace' that Benson was growing in Africa. That will be something of interest to her, certainly.

There's only a bent person in the corner, as far unlike a lion as he could imagine. She has a heavy woollen skirt on and a black sort of a memory of a cardigan. He thinks despite all of her heated dark breasts lying on his own chest reddened by desire in the long ago. The face when it turns, under the cowpat of grey hair, is not familiar to him. He doesn't think there will be much use in mentioning roses to her now.

'Roseanne,' he says, 'is it you?'

'Did they not shoot you yet, then?'

'No, they haven't, truly.' And shows her the snowdrops. 'Flowers,' he says.

'Snowdrops, sure give them to me.'

He hands them over like an army dispatch.

'You're well treated, are you?' he says.

'Well, you give me flowers, like a lover.' Then, pleasantly enough, 'I wasn't waiting for you, you know.'

'I often thought of you, in Africa . . .'

'Is that where you were? Well, that's a long way, brother.'

She puts the snowdrops to her nose.

'No scent,' she says expertly. 'The sick and the mad,' she adds, more mysteriously.

'I just thought I'd come out and see you, since I was home anyway.'

'Well,' she says, looking at him. 'I wasn't waiting for you.'

He goes back away out the road to thumb a lift back into Sligo. Swinging his arms, swinging his arms, hawthorn, hawthorn.

Bread-and-butter bushes was the name for the hawthorn, on the way to school, up the nuns' field by the raggedy ditches, and you could eat the leaves with relish, under the rain.

Swinging his arms, hawthorn, hawthorn.

*

A bright suit's not enough.

Next time he walks down to the post office to get his official letter with the army pension in it, there's another letter waiting also, poste restante.

> Beasley's Hostel,
> Isle of Dogs,
> London,
> 3rd April, 1959

Dear Brother Eneas,

Now I've been wandering these last months and ever hoping to find you. I've been looking, brother, into every passing face, to see if you are there. I crossed to the Horn of Africa scared out of my blessed wits by recollections of Lagos, and also, the very fierce fellas of the wilderness that would gladly kill and cook a man. I was standing at the door of the freight car, crossing to Kenya, shouting out your name in case you were near. Standing like a fool and shouting out at the lost lions and the burning bushes and the straw villages. Eneas, Eneas, was my eternal shout. And no blessed answer in the wilderness of my homeland.

The Isle of Dogs was a place you mentioned as a haven for men like us and I have scoured the Isle from stem to stern, every poor dosshouse and house of lonesome girls, and find you nowhere. This is a letter to say I am alive and looking for you and hoping to see you. The world is wide but I have trust in God's instincts and the light of His kindness. I do. I am writing to the only other place I know that may be connected with your name, unless you are still in Lagos, a district now closed to me. I am afraid to write to Lagos and leave a clue for murdering men but all the same I did write to the company there but they send word they know nothing of your whereabouts. I am even afraid to write to you in Sligo lest I might stir up a hornet's nest to devour you. Forgive if you will the force of friendship but I am not willing to be parted so needlessly. I would explain all if I could only ascertain your location.

It behoved me to leave Nigeria in a violent and dark fashion, to wit, escaping the terrors of Lagos. I've a tale to tell of murder and misery pertaining to my late lamented father and your friend Harcourt bears the scars of a beating and imprisonment. But God allowed me freedom at last in the darks of the night because murdering men love to drink worse than us and my head was clear and I ran out into my Africa like a mighty rabbit and got loose from them. I burst forth and tasted freedom.

And hurried down to the stockyard but you were long gone, whither I did not know, safely I hoped and prayed. It was my hope that you'd jumped the expected train to Kenya. And I leapt on the next train myself in my misery of loss and fear. For if you were gone back into the dark town I could not follow you. Fear worse than a child's, brother Eneas, and darker than tar.

But I've sought you ever since, in Nairobi and secondly along the coast, with no reward. And I doubt in my heart you could be in Sligo, it being your dark Lagos after all, full of wretched killers. But Sligo's the only name I have after the Isle of Dogs, and God send this letter to you in the upshot. You see I sorely miss you, my brother. And hope this letter finds you and finds you well.

I remain,
yr obednt servnt,
Port Harcourt.

In any court in the land he would count it a remarkable letter. Not just because it has reached him but also the birds of friendship flying about among the words. Yes, sir, it is a mighty thing to enjoy the fact of a friend in the world. A mighty thing. He is affected to his boots by it. The old tone of Harcourt carried in a perilous letter. The living force of it.

*

So it's back to his old task of hail and farewell.

'Well, take care, son, as ever,' says the Mam, and takes a hold of him, and would kiss his face but she can't reach it. 'Will you bend down to me?' she says. 'And take your punishment like a man.'

And she kisses him quick, like he has it written on his hat

at the seaside. She's buoyant, weirdly so, excited. Everything a mystery!

*

His Pappy's more subdued, more puzzled. They go out into Father Moran's Park along the river. The old man is as lithe as a boy, right enough, stooping to pick up sticks and stones to fling into the salmon-coloured river, silver and black. On the other hand he himself, Eneas himself, is tired and his joints feel creaky. His father gambols about the riverbank.

'Here, Pappy,' he says, taking out a roll of notes in an elastic band. 'Something to keep the wolf from the door.'

'What is it?' says the old musician.

'Cash,' says his son.

'Good on you,' says Old Tom. The old man pockets the fold of notes and laughs. 'You're a bit of a wonder to me, Eneas. Always were. Quaint little lad, sitting up waiting for me.'

'Ah, well, yes.'

*

He contents himself with the night boat to England.

'Farewell,' his Mam said to him, and 'Bye-bye,' and isn't that right and on the button? Parcels speckled by rain . . .

The thought of Harcourt, the victory of Harcourt's letter, offers a balm.

Oh, he was going to be the great man in Sligo, but, all in all, when the few sums are totted up, you've to start off great to be a great man. He is a little smidgen of a fella, a shadow, a half-thought at the back of his brothers' minds maybe, a sort of warning to them, a kind of bogeyman to fright the children and put manners on to them.

It's one of the rare fine nights at sea on the Irish Sea with the dark blue heavens hammered by the hammers of God and the stars set in the cold enamel aching somehow there in their distances. He cannot help thinking of the sky as a realm of jewels but he supposes it is all fire and ruin just the same. All fire and ruin. He sits on a wooden bench like you'd find in a municipal park, up on the deck of the dark mail-packet, alone it seems of the passengers. The mysterious vents and round brasses shine in the friendly moonlight. Below him the fleeing emigrants are stilled in their flight by pints and smashed-up songs, preferring the stale air, disregarding the clean, clear night of honest stars. Somewhere in the first-class he imagines dark strangers sitting, noble, immaculate, aglow. And he leans his head back against the iron ship and opens his face to the quiet sky, and wonders how deep the sounding-lead would go here, let down by the eternal 'boy', and scratches at himself in his privacy, and if there is stardust then he is getting it now, it will be lying on his cheeks as cool as cups.

He would rather, yes he would, Roseanne by his side, and indeed he knows Harcourt would not grudge him Roseanne, no, sir. But she had not been waiting for him.

And it rushes at him now like a leopard, one of those mighty fellas in Dublin Zoo that walk about in their cage and look the men to do you mischief, should they ever escape and wander out into the city on a dark night. Like one of those leopards, something flows up the side of the mailboat and crosses the rust-speckled deck, and fastens its long white teeth into his throat. And the mouth tears at his throat, the heavy molars dragging on his voicebox, and a flood of blood comes up through his neck from his drowned chest, and pours out through the magnificent gashes. And his very voice is wedded to that leopard darkness, the one drowning and the other in a delight of rage and strength. Tears fall uselessly down to wash the murder from his throat. And he hugs himself with his long arms in the suit suddenly peculiar to him also, and the leopard departs and this notion, this cockamamie notion of blessed love he has about her, about Roseanne, is not manageable suddenly after all but stabs at him, on the lonesome deck of the mail-packet, and who's to see him, and what odds a man alone, and bugger the thing, and thank the good God there is no one to see him, shrunken into his tears, stabbed and stabbed by the sudden grief – eternally, entirely, and no, not uniquely, never so, in this wide creation of solo persons, alone. In the matter of a wife, alone. He thinks and thinks, like his brain was a metal plate and hammer, striking, striking, of the harbour of her sharp breasts, and is mur-dered, murdered.

Deep in his callused hands now, his starry face.

*

He goes from his mother's kiss to Harcourt's, because unexpectedly he is kissed by Harcourt, a rough kiss planted in at a wrong angle, but a kiss for all that. In fact Harcourt clasps him wordlessly and thrusts his face towards him but is so overwhelmed that he only manages to kiss Eneas's lapel. He misses the face entirely. And then he stands holding on to Eneas as if the storm of the world might carry him off again, the tornado of accidental things, and by God it's true that Harcourt's own face is screwed up queerly and lemonlike tears are chasing each other down his cheeks.

'Good old fella,' says Eneas, like you might to a frighted horse, and he almost pats the old bastard's shoulder. 'Jesus.'

'Jesus is right, brother, Jesus is right.'

'You had a buggering hard time of it there in Lagos.'

'You think so, my brother?'

'Yes, sir. I saw the house. I saw what they did to ... I saw what was his sad and regretful end ...'

'You saw all that. I'm sorry you saw that. Because only demons could do that to a man, a poor old man with his days behind him.'

'I know, Harcourt, man, I know.'

'Made me watch them, boy, made his poor son watch. Part of my sentence. Then they dragged me out into the dark of that district we knew so well, and thanks be to the Great Bugger himself, but they had plenty of cola-nut wine in them, and when I saw a gap I filled it with my flying heels, running I was thinking from my good father's death. Nor did I go back to bury him and have lost the reputation of a dutiful son, sacred to any man, and fecked myself on to that fire-breathing train ...'

They are facing each other in the lobby of Beasley's, one of a hundred lopsided dosshouses on the Isle of Dogs, refuge of sailors. There's an old man heeled up like a cart on a plastic seat that's redder than lipstick, like a big lump of storm debris. And Eneas knows that all over the salted streets of the Isle lie these beached sailors. And he laughs his half-forgotten laughter. Judas, ages since he laughed that saving laughter. A lifetime. And he feels for the first time in a stretch a peculiar peacefulness. Peace, like Benson's rose. And he thinks of Bull Mottram and the shortness of a person's days and he smiles. He thinks of a lot of things standing there without quite knowing exactly what they are, vague, rushing things, scenes from his goings about and general things. He couldn't say for ten bob how his heart is fixed in the matter of Harcourt. But never, never in all his living days has he taken delight, such delight, in the mere sighting of another human being. The mere sight of Harcourt there, with his lemony tears and his gabbing, the little bobbing iceberg of his deep sorrow, well, to tell the truth it's a tonic. He feels like a fella of twenty. A hero at his ease. A lucky creature. A man blessed and enraptured. Oh, a king.

*

Nothing for it now but the inspired purchase of an old house at the southern edge of the Isle. He liberates his money to the vendor and in addition gives a couple of hundred to a builder to feck in a toilet and such and put locks on the rooms. To every inmate a lock. It is like a marriage house, though there is no bride, unless Harcourt is the bride. And the builder paints for Eneas a mighty sign, at cost price, for glory's sake, which shows to the choppy waves of the channel and the Thames, Northern Lights Hotel. And into this hotel they receive the battered wanderers, the weary sailors, the refugees from ferocious lives, the distressed alcoholics, the repentant murderers if Harcourt's suspicions are ever accurate – and the general flotsam of the great port river of life.

And nightly Eneas blesses the Northern Lights Hotel like a small farmer includes his holding in his night prayers. Each week the War Office dispatches with astonishing faithfulness the sum owed to him for his wartime gallantry. And if an angel were to descend and inform him that paradise was at hand, he thinks he might linger nonetheless in this fortunate isle instead. It is the tin-tacks of days and the slumbers deep as wells of the nights that gild the dark terrain behind his eyes. Away goes care on long-famished legs and in lopes the great figure of sufficiency. The medicine of nondescript and toiling years restores him. Restores Harcourt also – not a trace of his epilepsy disturbs, in his own grateful phrase, his 'social standing'.

In the dawns a pale wrung light slightly evil falls from the small window of Eneas's own room, where a simple chair is set, for looking out. There's a black sea-trunk against the wall, and some old pictorial magazines – oh, a hard nest maybe for a single man. On a single hook on the door is a ragged dressing-gown, and a yellowed pair of pyjamas leaks out from under the ancient bolster. A few jam-jars, in the grip of dust, have wandered in from the world of shops and preserves, to catch the wasps that plague his kingdom in the summer. The river moils past. At their unknown appointed times ships slide by unseen.

And yet it is a pleasant station. It is a station fashioned after the hankering of his heart. Ordinary heart of no fabulous requirement. The gaining of this place all the same to him is a high achievement. The arena of friendship with Harcourt and the general usefulness of their haven in the sea-weary hearts of sailors – both are palaces and jewels to him. He has been brought at last to the preferred spot. And as a journeying man it is fitting to him that it is an ancient port, as old as England herself. And as he watches the fleeting tide swell the river and deflate it, by turn and turn, he thinks of this district before the first wanderers, a riverbank wild as America's West, and the rage of birds tearing worms out of the printless mud. And the queer silence of that ancient noise and the pristine absence of men and women, loving and shouting. And he wonders did God Himself stand there before mankind, stand there with his ample creation, feeling the wind of His winds against His face, the water of His waters against His feet? And did He paddle in the river He had made?

*

When he thinks of Sligo now it is as a place eternally the same. Certainly no news of death or even life reaches him. Perhaps it hurts him that no characteristic letter arrives to him from his mother but equally his old habit of not writing to her persists, and in his easy moments he assumes that she is as happy to think of him as write to him. He is not so great an illusioned fool as to forget that indeed in the course of his bockety life he hasn't received more than a handful of letters. The documents of his existence are scant and few. Nor indeed, by the lights of his old concern of safety and concealment, has he actually communicated his whereabouts to her. He is content to leave the matter year and year, and the years accommodate him. So Sligo slips behind him, fixed, at anchor. And as for his notorious sentence of death covered now in the rheum of time and the lichens of the decades, it is emptied of its terrors. He cannot feel it any longer beat against his living heart.

Far away there is freedom for Nigeria and so Harcourt is ever to be an Englishman. There is freedom for Nigeria but Harcourt must abide in the Northern Lights Hotel. It is strange that though many years separate the freedoms of their homelands, Eneas and Harcourt are scraps of people both, blown off the road of life by history's hungry breezes. Therefore their hotel must be both homeland and home, though homeland and home have but two citizens. The craziness of it doesn't drive them crazy. Side by side they are citizenry enough and their constitution provides for

284

their concealment and abandonment. Abandonment is the proudest principle of their order.

By these vague beliefs Eneas lives and in the ordered motions of each day he rests his faith. As the years go on the hotel neither prospers nor struggles. The saga of grease and grime has no more impediment than the occasional death of an inmate, a finished man carried down into the lobby and out into the bare hearse of Carnew and Son, Grocers and Undertakers. Carnew needs no shining brasses. These deaths are not violent but the easy epic deaths of the lonesome. The proprietors of the Northern Lights Hotel don't fail to observe the proper obsequies of their inmates, whether Methodist, Jewish, Baptist or renegade. The rabbi is called for to gather his man to the breast of Yahweh, the never-written name, or the minister for a strayed sheep of the Presbyterians, scratched though he be by briars. Father Connolly is fetched for to honour the end of the odd stray Irishman. Therefore the Northern Lights is a kind of lean-to or hedge-school of the religions of the world and all are united at last in the long peace of decay.

20

LONESOME DAYS are nothing to Eneas McNulty. Here he is in his seventieth year, as hale as a nut, as fast-bottomed as a new bucket. His every gesture as easy-natural as a dancing man's. His mind goes back betimes to the dance-hall of his father and his brother. Where all the souls of the district were dancing – dancing souls as fierce as foxes. Where the queer starlight infected the very hairdos of the beauties of Sligo. And every girl of twenty was a beauty, for youth alone he sees now was loveliness, glamour and charm. Out of the great trees were charmed the black-coated birds, every man a willing dupe to the starlight in the tresses tortured into perms in the Friday Mecca of the hairdresser's.

But the time that has begun to stand in front of the time of Viv – that old vision which for so long took first place, took centre-stage like his father's band and dancing orchestra of yore, planting its eight sets of polished boots and hitting out the Yankee tunes – the thing he sees now betimes when his mind wanders back to those haunted lanes and strands, those still-glimmering lamps, the November rain eating into the car-lights, is Sam Dickins dancing with his girlfriend of twenty-three years, Mary Deegan. And Sam Dickins has a club foot covered in that mighty shoe made for him by the cobbler – Blennerhasset, the planter's whelp – but he knows the weight of that shoe and swings it through the steps. Where other men are doing three steps, he's swivelling on his normal boot, and swinging that club foot. You can see him count the beats, you can see Mary Deegan laughing for the joy of it, the prettiness of it. Oh, Jesus, and all night he's dancing with Mary Deegan, too busy dancing for marrying he says, and there's many, many a girl would take her place. He's a dixie dancer! Lord God, Protector of the Meek, he swings that foot. You can say to him, as he goes out sweaty and radiant into the frosted night, Mary on his arm, 'Good dancing,' and by that same Lord he'll say, 'Not so bad!' Eneas is ever thinking of that. Because in his heart he believes he understands the weight of the thing that was given amiss to him, whatever limb it is, soul or otherwise. But with Harcourt in the high times of the Northern Lights, he has discovered the weight of it, unearthed the number and is dancing now, swivelling one foot where other men would take three steps, swivelling his good foot, and throwing the other.

*

One night, coming in from the blackness of the wharf, the Isle of Dogs smeared over with a crust of filthy rain, his coat heavy with it, and three fat loaves of bread under an arm for the breakfast, he finds Harcourt jumpy and flushed behind the counter of the lobby. On a usual night Harcourt is trawling his way through Iceland, Berlin and such with the well-worn knob of the radio. But all is silence in the old house, as if the inmates themselves were aware of Harcourt's queer excitement. Harcourt gives him a fierce stare as he comes in as if expecting – God knows what apparition. The lobby is ill served by a bulb of poor wattage and the foul weather further blackens the lair of cobwebs and darkly marked linoleum. Harcourt tears out from behind the counter and drags his friend in over the threshold and bangs the door and even puts the old iron bar down across it, a thing he never bothers to do.

'Hey, hey, what is it, Harcourt? Don't pull an old man about so.'

'See anyone out there?'

'Not a soul . . .'

'Got to get a lock on the place . . .'

'Why so, Harcourt? Be plenty of old fellas trying to get in later.'

'They'll have to tell their names through the keyhole. Where you been wandering, brother? Expected you hours ago.'

'No, you didn't, Harcourt. I always go out for an hour and bring back the old bread at this time. Baker wouldn't know what to do with himself if I didn't fetch the unbought loaves . . . Seven years I've done that . . .'

'Brother, man, never mind the feckin loaves now. We've had visitors, untrustworthy-looking visitors, not pleasant, not as kosher as you'd like, men in dark coats. What do you call them, bowsies!'

'Eh, what bowsies you mean, Harcourt?'

'Your kind of bowsies – Sligo bowsies.'

'Looking for rooms, like?'

'Looking for you, you mad bollocks.'

And he pushes Eneas further back from the door and beckons him into the safer realm of the three brown plastic armchairs and the spider-thin table with a grimy magazine on it dating from nineteen sixty-two. *Illustrated London Weekly*.

'Why looking for me? Done nothing, Harcourt.'

'You done something, something – they know you. Oh, they're polite, polite bowsies, but I can tell, there's a sort of angle on everything, questions ordinary, but too many of them, too friendly, and they're all excited, like me now, like they were creeping up on something, a deer or a fish in the river – creeping, creeping. Oh!'

'I don't think they can be anything serious. Look it, they'll be friends from the boozer, looking for a loan of a ten-bob note . . .'

'That's right, Eneas, be stupid. All right. Now, first thing, after you go out, for your hour as you call it, your evening in the public house . . .'

'Three pints of ale, Harcourt, nothing to keel a man over . . .'

'Feck that,' says Harcourt. 'First man in is this cleaned-up fella, you know, mighty-looking fella as a matter of fact, big tremendous head of white hair, straight-backed, maybe not a Sligo man I would of said, but says he's from Sligo, says he's Jack McNulty, Eneas . . .'

'Ah, sure, look, that's just my brother, Harcourt. Well, Jesus, can't say I'm too pleased he's found me, but, well, no, I am, I am chuffed, I'd like to see him, is he coming back? You'll have told him to come back?'

'Of course I told him.'

'Could of stayed here the night, eh? Didn't think of that?'

'Oh, yes, bugger turns up, never seen him in my life, certain resemblance to yourself maybe, well-to-do sort of a character, not so bad, but do I ask him to stay the feckin night – no, sir, not with your history.'

'Ah, well. No matter. So when will we see him?'

'Well, I told him to come back in the morning. You know, and if you didn't think he was who he said he was, you could thump him with a hammer, you could get a look at him coming up the street or something . . .'

'It's only Jack . . .'

'All right.' And Harcourt crosses his arms with a measure of meaning and grandeur.

'So?'

'So, half an hour later, I'm in here, doodling with the radio, got Moscow for a few seconds as a matter of fact, in comes these two lads, big black coats on them, you know, you'd be kind of laughing in your head at them, you know, feckin old tribesmen I would of said, to borrow a phrase of yours . . .'

'Gobshites . . .'

'Yes, gobshites. Came slithering up to me, smiling, I don't care for strangers smiling at me, and I didn't think they were men looking for lodgings, though I hoped they were. But they had no kit, they had no weary look to them, they had no – they weren't sorted in themselves, they weren't shipshape, they weren't the kind of men we like here.'

'Who were they then?'

'Well now, my brother, they were asking for you too.'

'For me?'

'Oh, yeh. That black lingo, you know, couldn't barely catch it, the young one had, but he didn't talk much, it was the other one, the old one, that talked – smarmy as a knicker salesman. Feck, Eneas, smarmy.'

'Any name?'

Now Eneas's voice is more clipped. This is business of a kind. The business of other days. Expected business maybe, maybe not this long while since. Dark coats.

'Maybe this is nothing to worry about,' says Harcourt. 'They had no weapons or nothing like that. I mean, I get all excited when I hear rats in the wainscoting, I do. Oh, Jesus, I'll have to sit down. I'm not up to this, my brother.'

'Any names?' says Eneas. But he knows the names already. Well, he thinks he knows one of the names.

'Then, these two are here talking to me, and another man comes in, Christ Jesus, it could be Euston station on the Easter holiday, and he says, something like, "What's the story, Lynch, what's the story?" – an ancient sort of bowsie this time, older than the old man, I mean, quite tender in his shoes, shaky, not right for going about and visiting flop houses on the Isle of Dogs.'

'Right.'

'Should of been at home in bed in Sligo or wherever he comes from.'

'Sligo.'

'You think?'

'They say Sligo?'

'This other fella, Lynch, he says, "Just after asking, Mr O'Dowd." "And what he say?" says, I suppose, the same Mr O'Dowd. "Said nothing yet of worth," says Lynch. "Well, is he here or not, Lynch?" says the tottery man. So Lynch he turns to me, and he looks into my green eyes, and he says, "You heard the question, now, what we want to know, is Eneas McNulty here?" "No, no," I say, "haven't I just told the other man was here, no, Eneas McNulty is not here." "So, do you know his present whereabouts?" says this man Lynch. "I do not," I say, and I'm trying to look him in the eye too, you know, like an innocent man would, but I'm not so innocent. "What do you want him for?" I say, pleasant as a barmaid. "What for, indeed," says Lynch. "Murder, and other things..." "Murder?" I say. Then Mr O'Dowd seems to think better of his friend's remark, and tells them to come away, and doesn't even look at me again, and only the young man looks back before they go out, looks back with a dark filthy look worse than winter . . .'

'Jonno never could hold his tongue,' says Eneas. 'They should of only sent the young fella in, and made a decent enquiry, something normal, nothing to get the wind up you. But of course in they all troop like the brave soldiers of Ireland they are, each one surer than the last they know how to deal with it. Jesus, feck, I can tell you, Harcourt, I feel like a hundred and ninety years old at this minute. A hundred and ninety.'

And he slumps back in a plastic armchair. It's as greedy as a mouth, sucks his back into itself, like he might vanish into the weary brown plastic. The two friends say nothing for a little, Harcourt glancing, glancing at the gloomy figure in the chair. And indeed, you might think a hundred and twenty years had been heaped on Eneas's head, he's melded with the shadows from head to toe.

'Sweet buggering Jesus,' Eneas says.

'What'll we do, brother? Is this the kibosh? Are you action stations?'

'And I didn't even want to see my brother Jack. Not so much. They must have followed him. How did he find me? War Office I expect. Him being a major and all. "I'm looking for the whereabouts of my brother, Sergeant McNulty. My name is Major John McNulty, Retired." The whole feckin drill of it. Doing for me.'

Then there's a terrific banging on the barred door, and Harcourt leaps up like a shot rabbit, and flings himself, seventy years and all, across the grubby lobby, and grips the iron bar like he'd hold it in place against the hordes of Attila himself, and would be glad to take any Sligo bullet that might tear through the old wood – but no, it's only Moses Seligman, the Yankee Jew, that sailed around the Horn seven times and never saw a storm.

'Moses, Christ, get yourself in,' says Harcourt, 'come on, brother.'

'Where's your hurry, Mr H., and why the locked door?'

'Don't talk to me now, Mo,' says Harcourt. 'I can't stand it. I can't hear another word.'

'This is not like you, Mr H. You have an ache? My uncle travelled in powders, Mr H. I can help you.'

'You're kind, Mo, kind. Be going up to your bed now. I'm just going to close up now.'

'You never closed up in your life.'

'I'm closing up tonight.'

'There's Mr Masterson still in the Crown, and I saw some of the men across the way in Jackson's little place, the whiskey place . . .'

'I'm shutting the feckin door!' says Harcourt, and wildly. 'I'm shutting the feckin door.'

'Men will have to come in,' says Eneas from the shadows, his shadows and the general shadows.

'Oh, hello, Mr M., I didn't see you . . .' says Moses Seligman.

Now Harcourt is standing powerless at the door, wanting to let the bar down, but powerless, stymied.

'How come I can't shut our own door! How come I got to stand here, brothers, and keep the door open against the enemies of Eneas McNulty? Why in Jesus' name do I have to do that!'

Moses Seligman in his discretion nods at Eneas and goes

away up the stairs – he can be heard making every creak creak the four flights to his valueless eyrie. Four bob a month. No extras. No glass in the window!

'It doesn't matter, Harcourt,' says Eneas. 'If they come, they come. I'll tell you, most of my born days I waited for them to come. They said a few times they'd come and they never did. But lately, these last years, I haven't cared about that. I don't care about it now. We can talk to them. See what they want. They can shoot me if they wish. What odds?'

'I . . .' But Harcourt has no words readymade for that.

'Did anything ever happen in your life you could avoid? I don't think so. They ran you out of Lagos but you were meant to get out of there. God's will. You were a young man still, sort of. We were meant to run this bloody old place together. It's no matter, just death, death in one of his less appealing faces.'

'Well, you sit there, old man, and spout philosophy. But I'm saying no one's going to be shooting you. They wouldn't dare shoot you. This is England, brother.'

'Isle of Dogs.'

'No one's shooting you. I'll see to it.'

'How, Harcourt?'

'I'll feckin – we'll leave here now, like we always did, we'll leave this kip to rot, it's not worth a fart anyway.'

'Ah, thank you, thank you. But it wouldn't do. They'll be flying after us if the mood's on them now. Even if they go home, I'll *think* they're flying after me. Ah, no, Harcourt, better have it out with them now, I'm too old for that old life of fear at the back of the head and nowhere to call home.'

Harcourt walks back across the lobby and sits himself in front of Eneas.

'OK, brother, we'll wait so.'

'You think?' And Eneas laughs, a big braying laughter.

'We're too old for wives and too old for politics.'

'We are!'

*

They sit in the chairs all night, half dreaming and dozing, but no one comes through the portal of the Northern Lights Hotel except the stragglers from the pubs and drinking dens. And when those men bump their way through the dark lobby even Harcourt isn't alarmed at the possibility it might be the avengers of Sligo. Yes, yes, they're too old for jumping at shadows.

About four – and Harcourt would rise and try and find the time on his useless radio, but he's too stiff – they both perk up again, as if they were monks, and always rose at four, to go out into the broken light to start hoeing and digging and praying . . . Harcourt thaws out in a few minutes and finally rises and fetches himself into the back scullery to brew some saving tea and brings out the victorious cups and tin pot to his smiling friend.

'See, they never did come, and maybe they won't come now,' says Eneas, listening to the solid rain beyond the confines of the hotel, glad of his hotel, his shelter, glad even of his life, precarious as it might be. It's not a district of birds, but nonetheless he senses the birds of England beginning ubiquitously, down by the shattered mines of Cornwall, up on the sacred glens of the Lake District, wherever the birds of England made their nests. Imaginary birdsong fills his dark head. He smiles and smiles at Harcourt, drinking the excellent tea. In the midst of dust and dirt and ancientness, the excellent tea of Port Harcourt...

'See, they never did come,' he says, but this even as Jonno and another man troop in through the night-laden door. He knows it is Jonno because Jonno is imprinted on his brain like a potato stamp they used to make at school together, a potato stamp. Star or circle or such, dipped in the paint and pressed damp and raw on the paper – Jonno Lynch himself. The other man is a mere boy, probably born when him and Jonno were already ould fellas, nearly. Eighteen or so, who could tell?

'Well, Jesus, Jonno,' Eneas says, getting up, 'you've given us a right old night of alarm and panic,' he says, without panic.

'Sit down, you fuckin traitorous bollocks,' says the young fella.

'Oh – that's no Sligoman, Harcourt,' says Eneas, 'that there's a Dubliner, yeh, a gentleman of Dublin city.'

But he sits down. And Harcourt sits down. They could neither of them say why. Practice in their dreams maybe.

'Fuckin five fuckin o'clock,' says the boy. 'Fuckin dawn, it is.'

'That's right,' says Eneas.

Jonno Lynch approaches nearer. The good ten years have told against him. He's not the chipper man in the airport anyway, the sleek man, the mighty man. But no matter. Confident as ever in his footless way.

'How are ye, Jonno?' says Eneas, like they were in a pub, a pub in Sligo and many years behind them of drinking and companionship. The way it should have been in a real feckin country.

'You know the score,' says Jonno.

'What?' says Eneas.

'Fuck you, Eneas, you know the score, shut your mouth.'

'Shut the fuck up, you cunt,' says the boy. And he brings out a gun into the bleak shadows, only a shard of a shadow itself. 'And you, you fuckin nigger with your fuckin bad answers, you fuckin sit where you are, like a good boy, the whole fuckin time . . .'

'Funny time to be doing this, Jonno, after all these years,' says Eneas conversationally. 'Hah?'

'All comes round, Eneas. All comes round. Nothing going on for forty, fifty years, then, bang-bang-a-doodle, we're back in business. Have to show the young the ropes. Fight's on again, boy. Oh, we'll have the great days now. Freedom for the poor lost Catholic Irish of the North. That's the new story. Marching and giving out against that old pagan queen Elizabeth. Well, we fought her father in our day, hah? Maybe her grandfather, was it? Hah? The North, Eneas. Haven't you been reading the news?'

'The North of what?'

'Hah, you're the wide-boy. Always was the wide-boy. North going to go up like a bloody ould November bonfire. Liberty. Love of country. Things you don't understand, Eneas. Things that make great men. Great notions. Powerful classes of feelings. Patriots! Belfast, Derry, Portadown. Lisburn – haven't you been decking the news, boyo?'

'It's old news, Jonno. Doesn't make good reading when you're old neither. I prefer the comic strips. Eh, Dagwood, and the like, Mandrake, you know.'

'Day's come, Eneas. It's nighty-night. Got to clean up the old black-lists. Work outstanding. Debts to be paid in full. No more interest on your loan of life, son. Because, jaysus, there'll be fresh black-lists now. You got me now?'

And Jonno seems to bellow into himself, like a bull inside out, to fetch the decency and friendship out of his bowels, to make a lion of himself maybe. Eneas recognizes it. The fierceness of fighting men, men in the bleakest terror of killing. He suffers suddenly an iota, a handful even, of pity for this Jonno. And Jonno bellows deep into himself without a sound, a terrible sight indeed. And he nods at the Dubliner and the Dubliner lifts the old gun but before he fires Harcourt stands up abruptly and shouts at him. It isn't a shout with a word in it, but a life packed into it, certainly, those weeks running across Africa in terror and grief, and all their gimcrack happiness betimes. It's such a magnificent shout that the young man is stilled for a moment. Anyway it's difficult to kill a man with a heavy old gun and Eneas knows he'll have to step up to him close. All in all he doesn't mind having a go for freedom.

He half rises and half lunges and grabs onto Jonno's legs and Jonno goes over very sweetly. Then in the moment he lies there with Jonno he wonders why he has jumped at the man without a gun. He has a fierce sense of having trumped himself mightily and he closes his eyes fast against the shot that must surely be coming at his ear.

But instead Harcourt has launched himself at the Dubliner and the two fall back over one of the brown plastic chairs and the gun fires louder than a mine-blast you'd think and the lobby lights for the fraction of terrific power and then the dark is worse by that measure again after the shot.

'Fuck, you bastards,' says the youngster again, and Eneas can tell by his voice that he's floundering the back of the chair and maybe Harcourt has that Nigerian grip on his windpipe, because the voice is flattened and tinny.

'He's dropped the bloody gun!' shouts Harcourt. 'Can you kill that other fella?'

But that other fella isn't moving at all, as if the gunshot has shocked him into quiet. Jonno Lynch is queer but he isn't this queer. And now here comes Moses Seligman down the stairs with his mariner's lamp, the only thing he has never pawned. The Dubliner tears himself away from Harcourt the fiend from Lagos, the seventy-year-old fiend of a strangler, and kicks Harcourt expertly in the bollocks, and Harcourt roars again.

'Get up, Mr Lynch,' says the boy with some politeness, 'the rats are coming out of the woodwork! Let's fuckin go!'

But Jonno won't get up. Eneas holds his legs fiercely and raises his own face to get a dekko at Jonno. Jonno Lynch, bright pal of youth and demon of his old man's dreams.

'Let him up, let him up, or I'll shoot you, you cunt,' says the boy.

'He hasn't got the gun,' says Harcourt, by the chairs, with the gun.

'Get up, Mr Lynch, or I'll kill you too!'

'He can't get up, son,' says Eneas. 'Jonno Lynch is dead. You've killed him already.'

'Oh fuckin hell,' says the man, 'oh fuckin mammy,' and out on to the brightening wharf with him, and everyone half deaf after the calamity, and Moses Seligman astonished with the storm lamp raised aloft.

21

It is a lonesome and a difficult thing to have your childhood friend dead beside you, certainly. It is a bad dark deep thing.

With the silence and the appearance of grave-robbers they carry Jonno Lynch up the two flights of stairs to Eneas's room and there they lay him out. The seven current inmates crowd at the door. The old soldiers among them know the sight of a man killed by a bullet and even the sailors are not distressed as such by the picture of death.

'Brothers,' says Eneas. 'This is no good situation we have here. This is a man I knew once at home killed by a young fella from the same sad place. Trouble is, no one saw that shooting except the killer and he's legged it to God knows where. He'll be like a cockroach in the cracks of life from here on, God help him. For it's a long world of grief and trouble for such as him. But, brothers, fact is maybe we could explain it all to the police and maybe not. But Harcourt and me and maybe some of you don't like to do that if we can avoid it. If they can't find the true killer here they may prefer to think one of us did it. Who can say about that? They like to put someone in jail. For the look of the thing. I have the gun in my britches pocket and others have touched it besides the killer. What I have to say to you, gents, is I'm closing the Northern Lights Hotel. It is no more. If it is agreeable I'd ask you to pack your bits and bobs and go. But I tell you, the management regrets this, it does, gents.'

The faces of the men are still in the frame of the door. It's like a church meeting, the overflow of a church meeting. Dawn light touches onto them all in its different devious ways. Making gold the tawdry hair, sneaking glosses on to sleep-encrusted moustaches. Harcourt's face shows a tremendous confidence he does not feel. Indeed and his knees are secretly banging about in his ample trousers. It's to be expected. The sky has fallen on their heads in the upshot.

'It'll be hard for us,' says Moses Seligman. 'A person gets used to this old place.'

'Bless me, I know,' says Eneas. 'Well, I know it.'

'If we can accommodate you, we surely will,' says Jeff Masterson, first mate those many years in the little traders of the South China Seas, with all the noble politeness of a man with pennies to his name. Police don't suit them, no.

'OK, Mr McNulty,' says Moses Seligman.

Away they drift like moths to their various niches, their various knapsacks and handy bags.

'What's the plan?' says Harcourt. He's looking down at Jonno Lynch. His voice is dry and sharp.

'I don't know. Can't leave him like this. We're going to have to do something mighty.'

'What?' says Harcourt, reasonably.

'I'm thinking now, we're going to have to burn the place. Burn the old place with Jonno in it, and let them make of it what they will. We'll put my old blue suit on him and maybe they'll say it's me. And me and you will go off quiet and natural and see what's what elsewhere. We done it before and we're old now but we done it before and this is a catastrophe.'

'Jesus, Eneas.'

'It's not a good thing. Rats like that young fella are never found. This is a murdered man, a murdered man. We could dump him in the river but sooner or later they'll find him, yes they will, and even if they never did, he'll rise up one day from his moorings like a blessed angel, see if he doesn't. We'll have to burn the place and hope they'll think it's me. Then Jonno Lynch never existed, at least on the Isle of Dogs. O'Dowd will never talk. The whereabouts of Jonno Lynch will be a mystery, one of the many mysteries of Sligo. Well, to tell the truth I don't know what to do, unless it is what I say. I'm thinking too, my brother Jack will be here this morning, and any minute.'

'We could tell him maybe. He'd help us. Your brother.'

'Jack McNulty is a respectable man. He won't want to hear about this. No, he'll just have to make what he can of it. Poor Jonno must have followed him from Sligo, lurking on boat and train, trailing him like a blessed killer. He'll find the hotel burned when he gets here, and no trace of his brother, except a ruined body in his brother's old room. I suppose it will be grief for the Mam. They'll put Jonno Lynch in the ground maybe and have my name over him. There'll be grand prayers said. Hell, yes, we'll throw that old blue suit of mine on him for good measure. Everyone knows that old blue suit. Give us a hand.'

And the two roll Jonno about a bit and put on the worn blue suit once so fine and bright and then stand back regarding for all the world a sleeping man, a fella taking a nap in the morning in his worn blue suit. Eneas McNulty himself.

'I tell you,' says Eneas. 'He was a decent boyo once. He was a sweet boyo once. What a to-do. What an ending. God bless the poor man.'

'If you're dead, Eneas, you can't get your pension.'

'We lived pretty fine in Lagos without it. We'll live without it again. Happiness has its term, my Mam used to say.'

*

So down they go then and they'll have to work fast because the world is waking outside. The inmates leave one by one, setting their faces against the future. Hands are shaken briefly. But mostly it's dousing Eneas's room with paraffin and the old stairs and the rim of the lobby. It won't need much help to burn, Harcourt judges, the old hotel is a sort of tinderbox in itself, wood and plastic and rubbish. And as Eneas and Harcourt work, they sense more and more the good in Eneas's plan, the elegant simplicity of it. Despite the terror of the night, their hearts are bettered by the work.

'It'll be a clean sheet all over again, Eneas. We'll have to think on our feet again.'

'We will.'

'And we've great experience of the world, and we can turn our hands to a hundred jobs, in spite of age. We'll work our way somewhere warm and be old dogs in the sunlight.'

'Why not?'

At the same time Eneas is thinking of Jonno, going along the wall to rob the apples of the Presbyterian minister. You can't be too sad about a man that came to kill you, he supposes. All the same he is very sad. And not least to lose the ark of the hotel. But sorrow needs time and he has none of it now.

It's not long in the doing and now they stand in their coats in the lobby with matches. They can take nothing with them but truly they have little to leave behind. They go up the stairs again to Jonno to strike a match so the fire will be fiercest there. Eneas flicks the buzzing match and lets the flame build to a bud and drops it on a pile of old papers drenched in paraffin.

'Jesus Christ,' he says.

Then back down to the lobby with them. The whole place stinks of paraffin and they know that soon a noisome smoke will be pumping out the windows of the hotel so their flight must be rapid. And indeed they are just at the door, just about to pass through onto the quays, when a little sound is heard. Or Eneas hears and Harcourt doesn't, and Eneas stops on the threshold.

'Hold on a sec,' he says.

'Come on, come on,' says Harcourt.

'Just a sec. I hear something.'

And indeed now Harcourt hears it too, a sort of little shouting noise almost like a dog barking away over the roofs. Maybe indeed a dog.

'It's just a dog,' says Harcourt. 'Barking to be let out for a piss.'

But Eneas listens intent as a watchmaker. The bark changes and is more like shouting again, human shouting, and he thinks he even knows the shout, he thinks it is his name, definitely his name, his lost name.

'Eneas, Eneas, Eneas!'

'That's Jonno shouting,' says Eneas quietly.

'Your Jonno is dead as doornails. We saw him.'

'We saw him, but maybe he isn't dead. Maybe just the semblance of death. Like in an old story.'

'And if it is? Why doesn't he shout for his pals that wanted to shoot you? Hah? Why does he shout for you?'

Eneas moves back towards the smoking stairs.

'You can't go up there now, my brother.'

'We have to get him,' says Eneas, 'we have to. You know.'

'Never turn back at the door. Don't you know nothing? He's burning,' says Harcourt, thumping the front door for emphasis, 'he's burning, he's burning. Come on with me.'

'I will come on with you, Harcourt, I will,' says Eneas, 'but I can't leave Jonno.'

The shouts of his friend behind him, the cries of Jonno before him. And he motors his seventy years back up the stairs as fast as exhaustion will let him. He has a terrific feeling of betraying Harcourt. Oh, he loves that Harcourt. His brother. But he'll have Jonno out in a trice. Buggering Jonno can't be left.

When he opens his door not only does the handle fuse to his palm but the whole door flies forward when he opens it, and out pours a huge demonic tide of roaring fire.

*

And Eneas McNulty's days on the earth are over and his queer requiem is the crazy music of the fire. He knows his days are over because he rises now through the flames as round as water, up and up, rising stiff as wood through the rainbow of the flames. He is eminently surprised but at the same time eminently informed. He rises in a fashion of immaculate peace and the fire does not harm him.

On the one hand he sees his brother Jack toiling along the wharf in his spick-and-span civvies, heading for the now impossible rendezvous, and on the other, Harcourt forced out of the Northern Lights by enormous blooms of smoke and veritable dragons of flame. Eneas rises, smooth as a fish. The brittle light of the sky crackles overhead.

He comes then easily to the limits of a familiar garden. The hollyhocks have bloomed rashlike against the granite walls and the pollen of a thousand oaks falls like a fragrant army out of Midleton's wood. The flowers burn in the damp grasses.

In the shade of his Pappy's three holly trees his sister Teasy waits for him, smiling and then laughing, hurrying out on to the cinderpath to greet him. Her habit looks like an upturned bucket on her. She spreads her arms in an embrace of childhood. She is the gold ambassador of that rubbed-out terrain. The cold desert in his mind's eye floods with the thousand small white flowers that are the afterlife of rainfall.

'Come in with yourself,' she says, and hugs his bones.

'Are you all right, girl?' he says.

'Best,' she says, 'best.'

'That ould thing's sorted?'

'It can't trouble me now, sure.'

And she brings him up the cinderpath to the old iron door that used to lead to Midleton's wood when the walled garden was still part of Midleton's estate. In his father's time it was always locked fast by keys and rust. But Teasy has the trick of it and pushes it open for him.

'Go on up, you,' she says, 'and never mind nothing.'

And he remembers again the regard he has for that Teasy, and the love he has for her, and through he goes. He's very touched he must admit by the care of her talk, though it was ever so, and the way she has helped him through the garden. Because he knows he needed someone to meet him.

Midleton's wood when he's through into it isn't troubled by much except the calls of the wood-pigeons, co-co-co-ricco, familiar and forgotten, and a mighty tumbling of fierce white light that as a matter of fact seizes on him a little and he rises again as if by way of favour of it.

He passes a number of bottles with thick blue glass and the faces of people he knows etched in them, calling to him or singing merely he does not know, as the bottles are quite silent. His own heart beats thickly as if his blood has come to butter, turned and turned in the churn of the world and come to butter. This rinsed buttery feeling generates in him a fire of concern and regard. Even as he rises he understands that the thread that binds the dark turns and mazes of a life is bright with that feeling, yellow with it, as important as any letter. Why even a prisoner wishes to breathe the chill air of each morning is explained by that bright thread. Now that he looks so intently at the people he has known, without the least distraction, caught in their bottles, they blaze for him, they bloom. They are treasure. A good answer. And he waves to them like a small boy leaving with excitement and sorrow his local station.

He rises, he rises. Fast as a hen pheasant breaking from cover he rises.

And in bidding farewell to the lonesome earth, he knows suddenly and clearly the hard sadness of leaving the beautiful stations, the soft havens and hammered streets. And he gives recognition, with a lonesome prayer, to the difficulties of all living persons, and wishes them good journey through the extreme shoals of the long lake of life – with a last fare-thee-well and a God bless. To Harcourt in particular, his living brother.

His whereabouts, his troubles, his sun-marked face, his songs and chattels are nothing now. And if there is a book of life – which there may be – he knows in the upshot no person's name is written there, and all are thrown at last without reprieve, king and commoner, into the lake of fire, and the great steam of stars. But the lake of fire into which all men are thrown is admirable, eternal, and clear. Once through the fire they are given their suits of stars. God the Tailor accepts the fabulous lunatics of the earth and stitches the immaculate seams. Sense invigorates the cloudy souls. With charity cloth beyond all redemption, they are redeemed.